'A book to gulp down in one sitting . . .
The sparkling writing and immediacy of the
characterization plus a gripping mystery raise this
well above the average detective novel'
Sunday Telegraph

'One of my top ten crime novels for 1992'
Scotland on Sunday

'Both gritty and poignant, with a heroine to match'
Kirkus Reviews

'Donald's young, street-smart female sleuth,
a rare breed in contemporary British crime fiction,
is an appealing protagonist'
Publishers Weekly

AN UNCOMMON MURDER

Anabel Donald has been writing fiction since 1982 when her first novel, *Hannah at Thirty-five*, was published to great critical acclaim. The Notting Hill series – her five crime novels about female sleuth Alex Tanner – met with equal success in the 1990s, and were followed by *Be Nice* – a female dystopian novel inspired both by William Golding's classic *Lord of the Flies* and thirty years of Donald's own experiences as a class teacher – in 2002.

Anabel Donald

AN UNCOMMON MURDER

PAN BOOKS

First published 1992 by Macmillan

This edition published 2018 by Pan Books
an imprint of Pan Macmillan
20 New Wharf Road, London N1 9RR
Associated companies throughout the world
www.panmacmillan.com

ISBN 978-1-5098-5855-2

1 3 5 7 9 8 6 4 2

A CIP catalogue record for this book is available from the British Library.

Typeset by Palimpsest Book Production Limited, Falkirk, Stirlingshire
Printed and bound by CPI Group (UK) Ltd, Croydon, CR0 4YY

Visit **www.panmacmillan.com** to read more about all our books
and to buy them. You will also find features, author interviews and
news of any author events, and you can sign up for e-newsletters
so that you're always first to hear about our new releases.

Chapter One

Early in life, I wanted to be a private eye. In California. Sunshine, adventure, independence, infallibility and hundreds of dollars a day plus expenses.

Each time Mary – our thin, myopic, greasy-haired social worker – moved me from foster-home to foster-home, my private eye paperbacks were the first thing I packed. I tried to build up a collection. I begged them off second-hand market stalls, when I was still small enough to be appealing. After that, I lifted them.

When I was youngish – around ten – Mary'd help me get my things together. 'Do you really want all these books? We must leave room for Edward,' she'd say, picking up the grimy teddy-bear I never had the heart to tell her wasn't mine. It belonged to my mother, who certainly needed it more than I did in the mental hospitals Mary took her to. What did she mean, *all these books* – I only had about a dozen, then.

The foster-homes were mostly in the pinched, half-respectable streets around the council estate in Fulham where my mother and I lived in a fifteenth-floor flat, when the doctors got her tablets right. Most of my foster-parents were kind enough, or meant to be. One of the men actually spent three weekends making me a bookcase. He had a heart attack and died before he finished it, though. By then I was eleven and knowing enough to suspect his motives.

When I was thirteen, my fantasy evolved. I still wanted to be a private eye, but I also wanted to marry Lew Archer. Failing Archer, I'd have settled for Travis McGee, but I didn't really want to leave California for Florida, especially since John D. MacDonald said development was ruining it. Realistically, even ruined it would be better than Fulham. Besides, Fulham was being ruined too. It was the affluent seventies. Yuppies and Sloanes were moving in. The streets were jammed with builders' skips, the air full of dust and 'listen-to-me' voices, and the second-hand paperback stalls at the market charged ridiculous prices which the Sloanes were too stupid not to pay. Yuppies, of course, bought nothing second-hand.

When I was fifteen the careers officer at my school told me that there were no such things as licensed private investigators in England. I knew that already, but I nodded appreciatively. That was my survival formula, an appreciative nod. When I was four and in my first foster-home, it had worked on what, looking back, was a very kind woman who managed not to look shocked when she said, 'In this house, Alex, we generally use a toilet. It helps keep the floor clean, you see?' Subsequently, it worked on doctors ('I'm afraid there's not much we can do for your mother'), on the Social Services ('Are you sure you can manage, Alex?'), on my head teacher ('You're university material, Alex'). If I used it enough, they left me alone. I nodded like a cuddly car accessory until the careers officer heaped me with pamphlets on the role of a clerical officer in the Civil Service. Then I went to college, trained as a secretary, and joined the BBC.

Now I'm twenty-eight. I'm a freelance television researcher. The mean streets I walk are usually in the Greater London area and I've never even handled a gun, but I am paid per day plus expenses, and last November, I investigated my first murder.

My involvement began, I suppose, when Miss Potter was mugged.

It was teatime on a surprisingly warm November afternoon and I was walking home from Notting Hill tube station. November 1990 was a good time for the news media. Several of my friends were with TV crews in the Gulf, waiting for the peace negotiations to fail. The lobby correspondents were creaming themselves with excitement: would Thatcher go? Would Heseltine make it? I wasn't thinking about the Gulf or the leadership crisis. I was worrying about the prospect of no work till after Christmas. I turned off my usual route home, Westbourne Park Road (smart, expensive, residential), into one of those big, wide garden squares (very smart, ridiculously expensive, stucco-fronted, residential), for reasons I'll explain later.

About fifty yards ahead of me two young blacks were trying to mug a neatly dressed old woman. They weren't succeeding because she evidently didn't understand the conventions and wasn't letting go of her handbag. One of them tugged at it, the other swore and aimed half-hearted blows at her face.

Don't be ridiculous

Fuckin cow

This is a criminal act. You should be at school

Fuckin old bitch

I shall press charges

I'll kick you in the fuckin head

HEEELLLLPPPP

When she started screaming, they ran, which solved my problem. I'd cheerfully have mixed in – they were only kids – but I couldn't chance it because I was carrying a laptop computer I'd borrowed from my friend Polly and couldn't afford to replace. That kind of thing doesn't happen to real private eyes. I skulked until the muggers had gone, then walked up to the old lady. She just lay on the pavement, too shocked to get up, not too shocked to pull her brown tweed skirt well down over her knees. When I reached her she was lying with her eyes closed. I guessed she was embarrassed by her scream: she looked as if she'd been brought up not to raise her voice in a public place. Her cheek was covered with blood from a cut over one eye and her shopping basket reeked of gin. She wasn't drunk, though. She'd fought the muggers too effectively for that, she was well turned out and she didn't have a drunk's face. She was about seventy.

She opened her eyes, saw me, and clutched her handbag. 'Kick away,' she said stubbornly, 'I will not relinquish it.'

'Want some help?' I said. I must have looked like another

mugger, to her. She didn't look as if many of her mates wore jeans and Doc Martens.

'I have not been drinking,' she said. 'I've had enough. The country's disintegrating. It's all gone too far. I blame the upper classes.'

'Let's get you home,' I said, grabbing her under the arms and pulling her up. She was very light: I had no problem lifting her, still holding the computer. 'Where do you live?'

'Here. I'm staying just here.'

'In this house?' I was surprised, and pleased, but the old woman didn't notice; she was still rabbiting on.

'Harrods is a circus, the buses are filthy, the streets are a disgrace, everything in the shops is shoddy and grossly overpriced and they've evicted me. I only wanted a day's shopping. That was all I wanted. It's not much to ask. You're very kind, my dear, here's the key. Thank you. Please do not accompany me inside. I must insist you do not accompany me inside. This is not my house, I am responsible for protecting the property.' She tried to close the door against me but was too shaken to stand by herself.

'Let me take you into the kitchen. You could do with a sit-down and a cup of tea.'

'I really must sit down, but I warn you, I can identify you and I am perfectly prepared to give evidence in a court of law. There is no valuable portable property here. Are you going to rob me? What's your name?'

'Alex Tanner. I'll make a cup of tea. Don't worry – tell you what, I'll give you my driver's licence and my wallet, OK? Put those in your bag till I go. Like a deposit. I'm not a mugger or a robber, I'm a very ordinary working girl. I earn plenty, I don't need to rob people.'

'How do you do, my dear. I am Sarah Potter,' she said shaking my hand, and I thought she was beginning to get a grip on herself, but then she was off again. 'I read *London Fields* but I didn't believe it. Artistic licence, I thought. It's not my house, I'm looking after it for an ex-pupil. They've evicted me. All my things are in storage. I like to read travel books, I like to be informed. I haven't been in London since 1958. I left it in good order. Harvey Nichols, Swan and Edgar's, the Chelsea Flower Show.'

'Not in November,' I said. 'The Chelsea Flower Show is in the summer.'

'The Royal Academy, theatres, women correctly dressed in hats and gloves. My head's bleeding. I only bought half a bottle of gin and it's broken, but they didn't take my bag. Oh dear, I think I'm in shock.' She took the mug of tea and sipped it.

I wiped the blood from her face with moistened kitchen paper. 'The cut isn't too bad. You don't need stitches. Is there anyone I can call?' While I was talking I'd looked round the immaculate, expensive, fitted kitchen, confirmed the owner's name in the notes on the bulletin board by the wall phone, and realized my luck. I cleaned her face with renewed enthusiasm. If she was the Sarah Potter I thought she was, I'd have washed her feet, because through blood, gin and the delicate lavender toilet water she wore, I smelt work.

'No. I've made up my mind. I don't owe them anything. They're supposed to be running the country. For hundreds of years, they've run the country, and they can't even police the streets of London. *Pax Britannica*! Fine words. Democracy! Education! A new examination which awards certificates for a study of history which does not concern itself with facts! Neglected children! Selling arms to Saddam Hussein! It's chaos, futile chaos. There's no loyalty, no sense of obligation, not even common courtesy.'

'I don't want to leave you alone,' I said, peering into her handbag which was lying open on the table. She snapped it shut.

'Leave me, my dear. You owe me nothing. I'm perfectly well. I have plans to make. I won't let Charlotte get away with any of this. I may be old but I am still – *still* – to be reckoned with.'

It wasn't just luck, my finding Miss Potter in the street, unless you define luck as preparation finding opportunity. I was there because, as always, I was looking for work. As a freelance I have to snap up a job before the other scavengers come sniffing round, so I keep my eyes and ears open all the time, particularly in producers' offices. In the past three years, I've done a lot for Barty

O'Neill. The last time I was in his office dropping off an invoice, he'd left me alone for a moment. I went through the papers on his desk. Most of them were irrelevant but there was a promising list of names and addresses, headed 'Sherwin Murder'. One of the addresses was quite close to where I live. The name written beside it was 'Penelope Lucas'. Of course I had no idea who Penelope was, but it was evidently work not play, so when he came back, I fished. 'Anything in the pipeline?' I said.

He looked down at his list and up at me. 'Not worth your while,' he said. 'I'm dragging my heels on a colour supplement piece.'

'Who for?'

'*Observer.*'

'Any chance for a doco?'

'Doesn't look like it.'

I couldn't pursue it without pushing, so I didn't, but I wasn't convinced. He didn't usually waste time on one-off pieces. He was an independent producer who specialized in high-minded exposés of the British government and Establishment. He exposed corruption if he could find it, bumbling bureaucracy if he couldn't. He made documentary films for television and when the doco was shown he'd plug it by writing a companion piece for a quality Sunday. If he was working on a doco without using me it was very bad news because he was my most regular employer. I didn't want to sound desperate so I let him put me off and changed the subject, but I'd memorized the names and addresses on his list and as soon as I could, I wrote them down.

Next day, I was in a library on a German TV company's time and I started running Barty's names through the computer. Bingo with the first one, Rollo Sherwin. There was a whole book about Rollo, Lord Sherwin, by H. Plowright Lemaire, published in the late sixties. It was on the shelves: it had last been checked out in June 1981. I hoped H. Plowright wasn't holding his breath for Public Lending Right income because I didn't have my reader's ticket with me so I lifted it.

Back at home, on the sofa under a duvet to keep out the chill,

I skimmed through what turned out to be an account of the unsolved murder of Rollo Sherwin at a hunt ball in Warwickshire in the late nineteen-fifties. I had never heard of the man, or the case. Of course it happened before I was born, but real-life murders have always been an interest of mine and I was surprised not to have come across rehashes of it. That probably meant it wasn't really unsolved, merely not brought to trial, with the obvious suspect still alive and in a position to sue. It looked tailor-made for a colour supplement piece: the book had plenty of photos of good-looking, glamorous people and with an aristocratic lot like that the chances were the contemporary snaps would still be knocking about.

According to H. Plowright Lemaire, Rollo Sherwin had been a bit of a goer and the ball where he met his death in a shotgun blast had been well attended by his ex-mistresses and their husbands. The police's main suspect was his delicately beautiful wife (see Plate 3) who was also possibly having a thing on the side with the local doctor (see Plate 4d), whom she subsequently married. At this point I reckoned the chances were the wife had recently died and that was why the *Observer* was interested in it: not only the police but also H. Plowright seemed to have no doubt, within the constraints of libel, that she had done it. Just another domestic murder. The up-market trimmings and the period charm might sell it, but I couldn't see Barty's interest. Lord Sherwin had apparently failed to distinguish himself from cradle to family tomb. Only sexual scandal, no political activity. If H. Plowright was anywhere near right in his estimate of Sherwin's sexual affairs, he wouldn't have had time.

I wasn't going to spend too long messing about until I could see my way to getting paid. I did check through H. Plowright's index to identify the names on Barty's list: most of them were there. Penelope, the one with the local address, was one of Rollo's four daughters. She'd be in her early forties and long married by now, and the surname on Barty's list must be her husband's.

I put the Sherwin murder behind my ear to pursue when I next saw Barty, and that was why I was walking past Penelope's house on my way home from Notting Hill tube, to suss it out. In November, darkness falls early, and plenty of people don't draw their curtains. I like looking in to watch households at play. No luck, however, with Penelope's household. I'd been past twice and each time the curtains had been firmly drawn, with very little light leaking out and no chinks to give clues to a working girl. The third time it'd been afternoon, and I picked up Miss Potter.

She really was a find. She was also on Barty's list and according to the Lemaire book she'd actually been living in Rollo's house at the time of the murder – the children's governess. I was delighted to have picked her up and after I'd made tea and soothed her a bit I stayed around, listening. She was very shaken and I calculated the odds: should I take advantage of the coincidence now?

I decided not to. I might have got something out of her, but then again when she recovered I might have lost her as a source. Even more important, I wasn't yet cut in on the deal. I was on my best behaviour, though, to keep her sweet. When she thanked me for helping I was all ready to refuse her offer of compensation for my time and trouble but she didn't even offer me a fiver. I kept smiling anyway, as an investment. If she thought of me as the only remaining selfless member of the younger generation, all the better. It would give me moral leverage.

Chapter Two

I rang Barty as soon as I got home. He said if I came over and joined him while he finished up, he'd take me out to dinner. It would be one of his friendly little Italian restaurant dinners, of course, not a posh place he'd take a girlfriend or an important client, but it would be free food and several hours that I wouldn't have to pay for the electric fire in my flat. Besides, I enjoy his company. He's quick-witted. My neighbour Polly says I fancy him, but that's not quite true. He's not very tasty: in his forties, tall, thin, bony, with an Irish jaw. It's more that he pretends he fancies me, which spices up our dealings.

It stands to reason my childhood scarred me, as everyone's does, in all kinds of ways I don't recognize, but I do recognize one – a seething lava of impatience. I dragged through most of my early years being forced to do, slowly, things which in my view need not have been done at all. With my mother, when the tablets weren't adjusted, listening to her account of instructions she received from her voices (Winston Churchill, the Pope, Clark Gable). With one set of foster-parents, scouring an already immaculate flat. With another set, playing board-games of nerve-grating tedium. Nearly always, being chatted to, advised and *understood*, by foster-parents, teachers and social workers who seemed to me hard-pushed to understand that they had nails at the end of their fingers.

As a child, I thought all this would stop when I grew up. Not long into my BBC training I discovered it went on everywhere, between apparently consenting adults, most of whom had the mental turn-around time of a giant oil tanker. Barty doesn't. I've had telephone conversations with him that lasted under thirty seconds. Naturally, I enjoy his company.

Another thing about him; he's good with film. Film is the only art-form I understand. If I'd been a man I reckon I'd have started as a trainee cameraman and become a director. Barty's camerawork is terrific, he's got a great eye for a shot and he's a really talented editor. He can cut mediocre footage and make it tell any story he wants.

He's a terrible romantic, though. He thinks he's streetwise and cynical but he's a conspiracy theorist with the common sense of a newt.

When I reached Barty's office the latest in his series of feather-brained, decorative Sloaney assistants was still there. This one, Annabel, is brighter than most. She understands VAT and remembers my name. 'Oh, hello, Alex,' she said. (Actually she said, 'Er herler Erlex,' but you'll have to imagine the rest of her dialect.) 'He's on the phone to Los Angeles. Go right in.'

I went in and sat on a pile of Samy camera boxes. Barty was leaning back in his swivel chair, feet propped on his littered desk. The Sloanes aren't allowed into his office to tidy. 'Hope Los Angeles is well,' I said, reading as much as I could see of the labels on the film cans beside me. 'Give it my love.' He wiggled his fingers in greeting, finished the call and sat up.

'I was talking to Bournemouth, actually. Annabel's still a touch enthusiastic.' He raised his voice. 'You can go home now, ducky. Take the letters to post.'

'OK,' she called back and went. I breathed out, feeling better. Barty doesn't appear to take the Sloanes seriously, but I distrust them. They are too tall and too blonde, their legs are too long, they have too many shiny well-disciplined teeth and they walk as if the earth is lucky to support them. Why shouldn't it be? I'm sure their daddies are. Barty's first wife was like that. It would be reassuring that he's already divorced one of them if men didn't so often marry the same thing twice, and though I've no ambitions to be his wife, he's much more useful for me unattached. He puts plenty of work my way and a wife might point out that he'd get a far better return on his money if he stopped dabbling in investigative documentaries and bunged it into commercial property or the safer end of the stock market.

'How's the colour supplement piece coming on?' I said.

'It's on hold. Why?'

'It wouldn't be on the Sherwin murder, by any chance?'

'Why would you think that?'

'Reasons.'

'You've been reading my notes again.'

'D'you want some help?'

'Why? What've you got?'

'I may have a source, but let's deal first. You've put the article on hold for at least a week. That means you don't really want to do it.'

'Don't understand me so fast. Maybe I have an interest in it, and a source of my own.'

'You'll have to get someone to do the picture research, anyhow. You couldn't lay your hands on a view of the Houses of Parliament without help. I can do all that stuff, and I was interested in the case as a child.' (I knew he knew I'd read his notes but I didn't want him to guess how much I'd done from scratch behind his back. He can be paranoid.) 'I read a book by a man with a poncy name.'

'H. Plowright Lemaire.'

'Could be.'

'Then you know who everyone thinks did the murder.'

'Sure. The wife.'

'Did you know she died three months ago?'

I'd got it spot on. I felt pleased. OK, it was obvious, but my line of work is mostly obvious, a form of painting by numbers, and it's reassuring to get the numbers right. 'I didn't know,' I said. 'That frees her up as a target, yeah?'

He frowned. 'That means I can print the truth.' *Truth* is a buzz-word for Barty.

'We can print the truth,' I repeated, like a mantra, stressing the *we*.

'I don't know that I can afford you, Alex. It's just a one-off, because the Sherwin murder caught my fancy when I was young. I followed it in the papers; it was my bloodthirsty phase, when I wanted to be a policeman. I didn't think Laura could have done it.'

'Laura was the wife? Why couldn't she have done it?'

'She was so beautiful.'

'Not much of a defence,' I said, marvelling afresh at the extent to which intelligent men will follow their dicks to Disneyland. 'There could be a heck of a lot of work in it. Over thirty years have passed, most of them'll be dead and the rest'll be lying through their teeth because they've had so long to edit their memories.'

'So why are you angling for it?'

'I told you, I have a possible source. And I need the work.'

'Who's your source?'

'Can we make a deal?'

'Not on a per diem,' he said, and I knew he meant it. Another reason I like him: he means what he says. 'It's not worth it to me.'

'I'll do the whole thing, pictures, piece and all, for seventy-five per cent of your fee plus expenses. I'll get the truth if I can, and if it wasn't the beautiful Laura I'll say so, and she can step radiantly exculpated into the Great Beyond, clutching her Miss Congeniality trophy.'

'Real expenses? Not one of your collected works?'

'Real expenses, excluding meals. I'll clear anything big with you first.'

'I'll probably rewrite your piece.'

Barty thinks he can write. He's nothing special, but then neither am I. 'Fine,' I said. 'And I get co-credit. My name first.'

'They're paying for mine.'

'Give me a *with*. Bartholomew O'Neill with Alex Tanner. Then you can translate it into Finnish for all I care, so long as I get seventy-five per cent.'

'It's due in the first of next month,' said Barty casually.

'That's bloody impossible. Specially if you want time for a rewrite.'

'So? I'll only need a couple of days.'

'Renegotiate the deadline.'

'I already have. Twice. If I don't come up with it this time it'll go to a staffer.'

'What's the fee?' He told me. It'd be worth my while, if I could get hold of the people – a big if. What the hell. Travis McGee worked on contingency. 'Deal,' I said.

'Deal,' said Barty.

'What about development? If it goes to a doco?'

'We'll discuss that if and when. Now, who's your source?'

'Who's yours?'

He cracked his knuckles impatiently. 'You and your bloody games.'

'It's my living, Barty.'

'We've just done a deal.'

'And I need to know your source because I'm doing the work.'

'My source is the governess, Sarah Potter,' said Barty. I said nothing. 'I used to know her. She was my sisters' governess. She came to us not long after the murder, but she never would talk about the Sherwins, then. I'm hoping it'll be different now Laura's dead. Miss Potter's still alive, or she was two months ago. She sent me a birthday card.'

'Would she be reliable?'

'Oh yes, she was a terrific old girl. High standards, integrity, self-discipline, dedication. She always told the truth.'

'Nobody *always* tells the truth, nobody. There isn't that much truth to tell. Will she co-operate?'

'I've no idea, but I should be the one to approach her, pave the way. Only problem is, she isn't answering her telephone. She must be away.'

'Where does she live?'

'In Warwickshire.'

'Then she is away. She's house-sitting for one of the Sherwin daughters in Lancaster Gardens, just round the corner from me.'

'How do you know?'

'Because she's my source too. I picked her up in the street today. She'd been mugged.'

'Is she OK?'

'Yeah. Bit shaken. She said she wanted to be alone. Babbling about the decline of loranorder. Blaming the upper classes. She might be ready to talk.'

Then he took me to supper, gave me lots of pasta and made me laugh. If it hadn't been Barty I'd have thought he was genuinely chatting me up, but he couldn't be. His track-record was against it. He liked women beautiful, brainless, tall, blonde and posh. Not like me.

Chapter Three

After Barty brought me home I spent the night at Polly's borrowed laptop, finishing my current project (the Black Death: masses of technical detail on *Rattus rattus* for a jaw-crackingly boring Euro-doco), trying not to worry about whether I could deliver Barty's piece in time. If I couldn't I'd have wasted two weeks without even free food to show for it. On the other hand, of course, if I could I'd have made one and a half times my usual rate plus a useful credit.

I went to bed at five.

Barty woke me at nine thirty with the news that Miss Potter had invited me to morning coffee at eleven, and she was prepared to help. He thought it sounded promising. That meant nothing: to Barty, most things do.

I'd have preferred to see Miss Potter later in the day, when I'd had time to make notes on Lemaire and get some questions sorted, but I couldn't afford to mess her about. I gulped as much of the book as I could with my breakfast, spent three quid on a taxi to drop off the Black Death piece complete with invoice, and rolled up to Penelope's house dead on time.

The non-mugged Miss Potter looked younger than the seventy at least Barty reckoned and the dishevelled old mutterer I'd rescued. She was actually well preserved and rather good-looking, with regular features and plenty of white hair, about my height (five-four) but with a much narrower build. I was disappointed by how well she had pulled herself together. She was in the worst of states, from my point of view: self-possessed and very alert. I accepted her offer of coffee and home-made shortbread (I prefer shop-bought) and tried not to let her prissy manner make me inspect the soles of my Doc Martens for dog-shit more than once every five minutes. The coffee was good but the china cup was much too small. Miss Potter's voice was self-consciously clear about the consonants and pure about the vowels, and she removed tiny crumbs from the corners of her mouth with zealous precision. 'I used to live in Warwickshire,' she said. 'Do you like the country?'

I hate the country. It's either twee or bleak, full of people too interested in each other's business and much too conscious of class distinctions. But she was the source. 'Very much, what I've been lucky enough to see of it, but I'm a city person, myself.'

'Yes,' Miss Potter said, her eyes commenting on my appearance. I could only guess what aspect of it she found offensive. It might have been my Levi's and heavy cotton sweatshirt; it might have been my boots; she may have thought young women should not crop their hair and dye it red. On the other hand, I may have been misinterpreting her assessment as condemnation, easy to do with women of her age and type. 'How marvellous that you're a friend of Barty's,' she said. 'I'm very fond of him. Such a bright boy, always so considerate, don't you think so, Alexandra?'

'My name is Alex, Miss Potter.'

'Surely you were christened Alexandra?'

I hate prying. When people pry, I improvise. I wasn't about to confide that my mother had meant to name me Alice but it wasn't one of her good days and the registrar couldn't understand her. 'I was baptized Mary, after my mother, but she always called me Alex, after an old film she liked, *Ice Cold in Alex*. I suppose my full name should be Alexandria, but Mum never knew what it stood for.'

'And the rest of your family?'

'There isn't any. I come from a long line of single parents.'

'You have done very well, then, to reach your present position. I gather from Barty that research positions are much sought-after, and that you are successfully self-employed.' I knew she would try to change the subject, tactfully. She managed the change but not the tact. 'How gratifying that we have a friend in common. One of the pleasures of life, don't you think? Like re-reading a much-loved book. Do you enjoy reading?'

My pastimes are my own business, I thought, and sod the upper-class guff about who you know. This complete stranger picked you up in the street and you were grateful enough then. I resisted the temptation to tell her the truth, that when I couldn't sleep, which was quite often, I read two or three books a night. 'Do you mind if I get to work?' I said. 'Has Barty explained to you about the article and the time pressure we're under?'

'Indeed. He was always disorganized. Surely it will be impossible for you to complete your research in time?'

'I hope not, otherwise I don't get paid. He said you might be prepared to help.'

'That depends what you need to know.'

There was a definite note of anxiety in her voice. Good. If I could knock her off balance, I might get somewhere. 'Have you read Lemaire's book?' I said.

'Naturally.'

'How much of it is accurate?'

She looked disapproving. 'The tone was deplorable.'

'But were the facts right?'

'Such facts as there were, yes, I suppose so. Tell me, Alex, what will you do if your inquiries find nothing new?'

'Add some local colour and thirty-years-on quotes, find some memory-lane snaps, stir Lemaire round a bit, garnish with cheap amateur sociological comment and here-they-are-now pix, and serve.'

'And that would be consistent with your professional code of conduct?'

I just gaped at her. 'My job isn't a profession.'

'There must be rules.'

'I try not to rip off my bosses, if that's what you mean. I don't invoice for many more hours than I work, and I keep expense-padding to an agreed level. I produce what I'm paid for. Colour supplement pieces of this kind are mostly just coat-hangers for the pix and the ads.'

'And confidentiality?'

'Yeah. If I agree to it. Usually I don't. What're you getting at?'

She hesitated. 'I suppose I am interested in your philosophy of life: your code of ethics. I realize it's unusual and possibly intrusive to ask such a question so early in our acquaintance, but I am in an unusual position.'

She folded her hands in her lap, and waited.

Odd price you sometimes pay for information. 'Right,' I said, and considered. It was a classic interview question, superficially ingenuous, tempting me into an open landscape mined with who knew what unexploded prejudices and preconceptions. I'd been caught once before, and resolved then that in future, I would tell the truth, as far as the questioner could understand it.

'My philosophy of life. Triage.'

'I'm not familiar with the word. How do you spell it? Is it a religious faith?'

'T-R-I-A-G-E, and it's a military term. It's how field medics sort out cases for treatment. That one's beyond help, leave him to die; that one's OK for the moment, leave him till later; that one will profit from our help now.'

'In your view, that is how the Supreme Being treats us? Is that what you're saying?'

'I don't believe in a Supreme Being. That's how I try to treat everything. People, tasks – everything.'

'A question of priorities.'

'Yes.'

'You only spend time, emotion, money, where you think it to be profitable?'

'Yes.' She was quick. I liked that.

'Profitable in financial terms?'

'Not only. Not even mainly. It's more to do with life. Effective, positive life. Fun. Building things. Not hurting people.' I was embarrassed, now. The more I said the sillier it sounded.

'This – philosophy. Is it your own?'

'I think philosophy is too grand a term for it. As far as I know it's my own.'

'Very well,' she said briskly, and it seemed that I'd passed her test. 'To return to your article. I'm uneasy about – the whole enterprise. Does it not seem to you that the family have suffered enough? Why should the children be reminded of such a dreadful tragedy?'

'The children are in their forties.'

'Candida is only thirty-nine.'

Oh God, a trivial pursuiter. 'Old enough to face facts, surely,' I said, suppressing my exasperation. Her anxiety had gone. She was evading me. 'Someone's going to write this article. Now Laura's dead, it's only a matter of time. There might be books, television programmes, maybe a film. If you help us now at least you can make sure we understand, that we get it right, to be as fair as possible to the children.'

'Barty made that point, and it has some merit. It was on that understanding that I agreed to co-operate.'

'Right,' I said. 'If the Lemaire book is more or less accurate, I can use it as a basis to work from and we don't need to go over the ground again.' I gave her Barty's list of names and addresses, and asked her if the addresses were current and if she could think of any names I should add. As she read, I watched. She tensed up. Her neck reddened. She was upset. Now was the time for the big question. 'Laura wasn't the murderer, was she?' I said casually.

'I'll make some more coffee,' she said, and bolted to the kitchen. I followed her, silent, bringing my question with me. I didn't necessarily expect her to answer truthfully: in an important sense, she already had. She had told me she knew something I didn't, something that upset her. Now, I should be kind. I'd get more out of her.

'Don't worry,' I said. 'I won't press you. It's often painful.'

'What is?'

I'd been hoping she'd tell me. 'Digging up the past,' I said.

She concentrated unusual attention on the coffee grinder. 'I was very – disturbed, yesterday.'

'Of course. Shock.'

'I gave serious attention to my position. Loyalty is most important.'

'Naturally.' Promising. People most often talk about loyalty just seconds before they haggle over the price of betrayal.

'But there are priorities. There are always priorities. That is why it is so important to me to know your views on confidentiality.'

'Because you might be prepared to tell me everything on condition I'd only use some of it?'

'Exactly.'

She wouldn't be easy to deceive, but I was going to try, because if there was any real money in this for me, bugger confidentiality. I made a massive effort and produced my most honest expression. 'I can't give you a blanket promise. I'll need to know, first.'

'Last night, I considered my position. Perhaps it would be best if you read this.' Her neck was blushing again as she thrust some pages of typescript at me. 'Please read it now. In the other room. While I prepare the coffee.'

I went back to the other room, looking pleased, feeling pissed off. Why couldn't she just tell me? At this rate we'd be shuffling round the dance floor together until she was carried off to the great schoolroom in the sky where a third of the globe is still marked in pink for the British Empire.

At least her manuscript wasn't handwritten.

By the time anyone reads this, I shall be dead, beyond minding about anything, which of course includes whether I begin my story with a cliché. In my other books, I was always very careful to reshape and rework clichés, turn them sides to middle so my readers got their money's worth. *Her other books? First I'd heard. Maybe she desk-top published her own homilies.* Very important, giving value for money. Part of the standards I strove to live by and to inculcate in the many young people it was my privilege to teach and guide. *Pompous old boot.*

I don't know, of course, how long I will live. As I write it is 1990 and I am seventy, in excellent health. *She had arthritic hands. The whole truth, Barty?* I don't smoke or drink to excess and I have never indulged in promiscuous, or indeed any, sexual intercourse. I walk three miles a day, rain or shine, which is in my view quite adequate exercise. At the moment I am house-sitting for an ex-pupil and I managed the two flights of stairs to my bedroom carrying my suitcase without pausing for breath. With the exception of my parents, sadly killed in an air-raid in 1941, my family are uniformly long-lived.

Does it matter, you may ask, when I die? It does to me, though less as I grow older. It matters to my story a great deal. For example, if I last another twenty years my books may well still be out of print and you will have no idea who I am. *Who are you?* It is also remotely possible that the public will have forgotten the Sherwin murder case. That I doubt, however: unsolved murders in high life are rarely forgotten by the British and even as I write, thirty-two years after the event, I have been approached by a Sunday newspaper for help with a colour supplement article. Delightfully, the approach came from an honorary ex-pupil (I was officially responsible only for his younger sisters), now involved in the world of journalism and television. It was my trust in Bartholomew O'Neill, above all, which persuaded me to consider breaking the silence of a lifetime.

I am the possessor of important information: I have light to cast on the circumstances of the murder. That is what my story is about and I shall tell it as straightforwardly as I can, and as fairly. It is important never to judge until you have heard all the evidence, as I used to tell my young people. I always heard them out before I reprimanded them for a misdemeanour. Occasionally they had more than excuses to offer and the young feel injustice keenly. At my age, experience has taught one to expect it, and it is justice which comes as a surprise, none the less gratifying for that.

Here, the typescript finished. When I looked up, there was a still-pink Miss Potter watching me. I'm used to writers; if you don't tell them you love their work, down to and including laundry-lists, you have to spend hours doing a body-bag job on the fragments of their personality. 'I like it. Very good. Catches the flavour of the period.'

'What period?'

Wrong thing to say. 'Very convincing, very exciting, very – powerful,' I rambled.

'My dear, I do not believe you are telling me the truth. You are merely attempting to flatter me.'

'That too. But it's well expressed.'

Placated, Miss Potter brought herself to the matter in hand. 'But do you understand?'

I understood that she wanted to write her own story, that she half-intended to publish posthumously, and that if I wasn't careful she'd keep the best bits for herself. 'You begin, *By the time anyone reads this, I shall be dead*. Do you mean that? Aren't you going to publish in your lifetime?'

'I haven't yet decided. That depends.'

'On what?' Her meticulous preposition-juggling was contagious. 'What on?' I rephrased, unwilling to be brainwashed.

'On what you discover in the course of your researches,' she said briskly. 'My proposal is this. I will give you practical assistance over such matters as names and addresses. I have already given you the valuable information that Mr Lemaire's book, deplorable as it is, can be substantially relied upon as far as the facts are concerned. In return for my help, you will do some research for me. I may then, in addition, supply you with further information that I am the only living person to possess.'

'Research for you?' I was gob-smacked. Surely she must have grasped that I'd already be working thirty-six hours a day to get Barty's piece to the starting-gate? If she thought that I'd also wade around looking up references for her on crab-apple bottling or the effect of the National Curriculum on Swan and Edgar's, she could stuff it.

'I'm concerned about a missing girl. Charlotte Sherwin's daughter Zara, always known as Toad. She's only eighteen.'

'Charlotte Sherwin's daughter – Rollo's granddaughter?'

'Quite so, Toad Mayfield. Charlotte's husband is Ludovic Mayfield.'

'The politician?'

'Quite.'

Ludovic Mayfield was a familiar name, but the face was more elusive, though I had seen pix in the papers. He was a Cabinet Minister with some thankless job: Northern Ireland? 'The police will fall over themselves to find a Cabinet Minister's daughter,' I said blankly. 'I'd be useless. They've got the resources.'

'You don't understand. Her parents do not accept that she is missing. Her mother claims she is in Nepal.'

'The Foreign Office—'

'I do not believe she ever went to Nepal.'

'Why?'

'Because she has not sent me a postcard. I particularly asked her to send me a postcard. Nepal has long held a fascination for me, as she well knows. She promised to send me postcards. She is not a girl who would lightly abandon such a promise.'

Her naïveté took my breath away. In my view, once any red-blooded eighteen-year-old, even one who still allowed herself to be known as Toad, had escaped from Miss Potter's clutches, Miss P. could whistle for her postcard.

'I expect the postal service isn't great,' I temporized.

'She has been away for three months.'

'Our postal service isn't great either.'

'She promised me several.' Her face was set. She was not to be distracted. And come to think of it, three months was a long time.

'Surely her family has heard from her?'

'I'm afraid I can't tell you. Unfortunately, I have had a – disagreement – with Charlotte, her mother. As you realize, she is the eldest daughter of Rollo, Lord Sherwin. She was already living in the family house, but she inherited it and the bulk of the estate when her mother died. That was immediately before Toad's supposed departure for the East.' I made a note of it as Miss Potter went on. 'We are no longer on speaking terms. If you would be so good as to set my mind at rest in this matter, I am prepared to co-operate with you over the article. I assure you, my information is worth having.'

I agreed, of course. I had no choice. My impulse was to grasp her by the throat and shake the self-important old trout until her secrets rattled, but I believed that she knew something about the Sherwin murder, though it probably wasn't as crucial as she made out. I expressed courteous rapture at her offer, scribbled down some facts about Toad, extracted a half-permission to use Miss Potter's photographs and took her through Barty's list at high speed.

'Dr Bloom?'

'Laura's husband. The family doctor. Sadly, now dead.'

'Charlotte, Helena, Penelope, Candida?'

'The daughters of Rollo, Lord Sherwin. I believe Charlotte is at present in London. The Warwickshire address on your list is correct: I will add the London address and telephone number. The other girls are on holiday in St Lucia. Penelope has a house there. They are due to return in December.' Too late for me, damn. Barty wouldn't stand the airfare, even if I'd had the time.

'Rosalind Sherwin? Who was she?'

'The niece of Lord and Lady Sherwin. Previously a pupil of mine, in Kenya, for several years. She was living in Ashtons Hall at the time.'

'How old was she in 1958?'

'Seventeen.'

'Good. What's her address?'

'I haven't kept in touch with Rosalind,' said Miss Potter, and alarm bells rang in my head. I had Miss Potter pegged as Queen Keep-in-Touch, a mistress of punctilio, a persistent, guilt-inducing sender of Christmas and birthday cards.

'Is she married?' I pressed.

'I'm afraid I have no idea. As I said, I haven't kept in touch.'

Rosalind was even more of a must. I smelt dissension and disapproval, a fertile ground for information.

'Mr and Mrs Crisp?'

'The butler and housekeeper. Unfortunately, both dead.'

Apart from Miss Potter herself, that was the list. I had additions of my own: the Scotland Yard man in charge of the case and H. Plowright, if either of them survived. 'Who else should I see? Who was about the house, before the murder? Who were Laura's friends?'

'Lady Sherwin had many acquaintances but few friends. Katrina, Lady Paxton, was perhaps closest to her, as her daughter Stephanie was to Rosalind. She lives in Warwickshire. *Debrett* will yield the address.'

'You don't think she'll have moved?'

'The Paxtons haven't moved for four hundred years.' Miss Potter sat, composed, her hands folded in her lap, smiling as if she drew justification and reassurance from an inner vision of the Paxtons swelling in Warwickshire soil like a prize-winning root vegetable.

'Anyone else? Rollo's friends?'

'I'm afraid I have no idea. Lord Sherwin was much away from home.'

'Anyone else at all, living on the estate?'

'The estate manager, now dead. Some farm workers, in tied cottages. The actor who rented my lodge at that time.'

'Who was that?'

'I believe his name was Revill.' She spelt it. 'A famous actor, then. Employed at the Shakespeare Memorial Theatre.'

'Still alive?'

'I have no idea, and I cannot imagine how he could help you. He had very few dealings with us.'

Chapter Four

So far, that was all I wanted from Miss Potter. I headed for home and the telephone as soon as I could without losing her goodwill. I was happy and excited, for two reasons.

The first is that I like being in my flat during working hours, when I'm not unemployed. That's partly why I'm a freelance. My flat is very important to me. It's the only place that's ever been absolutely and completely mine. The bank owns more than half of it, of course, but they're not about to move in, arrange washing-up rotas and suggest a nice game of Cluedo. When I close the door behind me, that's it. Everything the eye can see, so long as it doesn't look out of the window, is mine. Chosen by me and paid for by me from money I've earned.

It's on two floors, the top two floors of a double-fronted but shallow house shoddily built on what, in Victorian times, used to be the winning-post of the old racecourse. You approach it up crumbling steps, through the battle-scarred front door (crimes against property are endemic in Ladbroke Grove) and a narrow hall. On your right is the door to the other flat. You go straight through the hall, not far as the house is only one room deep, and turn left up one flight of stairs to a small landing. Then you're facing my door. Open the door and you're in my living-room, sixteen by twelve, not bad at all for London, with a small room beyond which the estate agent's particulars listed as a second bedroom. It's seven by twelve and I haven't furnished it yet, though it is carpeted: the whole flat has fitted carpet, the best quality I could afford. Not good enough; it's already felting in places. The kitchen is off the other end of the living-room, big enough for a sink, cooker, fridge, washing-machine, built-in cupboards, a small table and four stools.

Up another flight of stairs (lined with bookshelves I put up myself for all my Ross Macdonalds, John D. MacDonalds, Elmore Leonards, Robert B. Parkers, Loren Estlemans, Howard Engels, Mickey Spillanes, Raymond Chandlers) you'll find my bedroom (with windows north and south, thirteen by twelve) and my bathroom big enough to keep clean in. It has a window, too. When I have hot water I lie in the bath with the window open. There's no heating or hot water at the moment because I'm in an on-going confrontation situation with my useless plumber.

Once at home, I took off my jacket and boots and got to work. The prospect of the task ahead was the other reason I was so happy. Finding things out is my purest and most reliable pleasure. First you watch, listen, read; then you pierce, cajole, bully, whatever it takes; then, you peel back the artichoke leaves to find the heart. In the process, for a week or a month, you become a citizen of someone else's country.

I didn't yet care about Sherwin the man, or the rights and wrongs of it. For all I knew, Laura had been provoked beyond endurance. I'd lived in enough families in my time to know the tension and the hatred and the passion they generated. Nor did I care about bringing a murderer to justice. What I wanted was to find out what Miss Potter knew or thought she knew, to find out how and why Sherwin died, and to earn my fee with a decent piece.

My first telephone calls were dead ends. Neither Barty nor Annabel was in the office. The answering machine message said, 'We're in the cutting-room.' I was annoyed. I wanted Annabel to help me clear up the Toad question because I didn't believe the girl was missing. The sooner I could prove it to Miss Potter, the sooner she'd come across with her Very Important Information. It could save me a lot of time.

I swore a bit and flicked through my 1972 edition of the *Writers' and Artists' Year Book*. Several phone calls later, it turned out that H. Plowright Lemaire had P. Assed Over; his woolly-headed daughter had destroyed all his notes; she couldn't remember anything Daddy had said while he was working on the book. She wasn't much for books or murders, really. She'd just tried to make a happy home for him, and after he'd gone, it was a relief to be able to keep a clean and tidy house without all those messy papers everywhere. The Scotland Yard man had also died, without leaving memoirs. Neither of my two police contacts could be reached to be pumped about the Sherwin file.

The Paxtons next. I'd dropped in to the library on the way home and checked *Debrett:* Lord Paxton was dead, and Rosalind's friend Stephanie was now The Honourable Mrs David Forsythe. Better than Featherstonhaugh: at least I could pronounce it. I dialled old Lady Paxton's number at the family house in Warwickshire, the only one I had. A cleaning woman answered, and readily gave me Stephanie's addresses and telephone numbers. One in Warwickshire, one in London. The London one was Eaton Square, even smarter than Penelope's: Stephanie had done well for herself. I didn't pursue it. Barty would be a much better bet to fix up an appointment there.

Finally, Patrick Revill. According to Miss Potter, he'd been a famous actor. According to Equity, he was still alive. According to his agent, he wasn't working any more. After a bit of chit-chat the agent gave me his address, a flat in Kilburn, and a telephone number. I tried the number: the phone had been cut off. I'd go round there tomorrow. That gave me the evening free to squeeze the last pip from H. Plowright.

I put on an extra sweater and settled to work. Some time later (two hours? three?) Polly came up from her flat (the other one in the building: ground floor and basement, bigger than mine but not, I think, nearly as nice) to cadge some coffee and talk about her lover, Clive. She had nothing much to say but she's still at the stage where speaking his name is enough, even after a year, presumably because she hardly ever sees him. He's a backbench Labour MP, married and balding. He orders, from catalogues, objects that not only break immediately, sometimes in the post or even before they leave the factory, but which have no conceivable use in the first place, like a battery-powered egg-timer with a three-egg facility. I gave her coffee and screened out her conversation by putting on a Victoria Wood video.

Polly's my age but she's retired. She was a model, made a pile of money, never spent any of it, retired at twenty-five to live off her investments and train as an accountant. Her legs are longer than Hadrian's Wall, her eyes wide, brown and deep enough to drown in. I'd be jealous of her if she wasn't so gentle and kind. She's far too good for the pathetic Clive. She yattered at me for a while: I kept working.

Eventually, I made us more coffee and asked her about Ludovic Mayfield: she was the nearest thing I had to a contact in Westminster, because last year Clive had fixed her up with some work as a researcher in the House of Commons. She could be sticky, though: her niceness prevented her enjoying gossip like a normal person, and her own experiences with the media had taught her to keep everything so far off the record it wasn't even in the studio.

'Why do you want to know?'

'Not for scandal. Background research.'

'Promise?'

'Double promise, scout's honour.' I threw my appreciative nod in for good measure.

'He's got Trade and Industry, I expect you know that. Since last Saturday.'

'Last Saturday?'

'You remember, the Cabinet reshuffle! Because Howe resigned! You must remember!'

Politicians, their wives and mistresses, and lobby correspondents take politics seriously. You have to humour them. 'Of course,' I said. 'Sorry. I wasn't concentrating.'

'And he's a dark horse. Well, some people think he is.'

'A dark horse?'

'In the leadership race. If Thatcher goes. Clive says that's maybe why she gave him Trade and Industry, to sink his career, since Thatcher's policies are systematically destroying both. He's been out in the cold for a while, about three years. He used to be in the Cabinet. Resigned on a point of principle.'

'Can you remember the principle?'

'Basically, he didn't like Maggie trampling over his face in her sensible shoes.'

'So you've met him at parties and things.'

'Yes. He and Clive were on a committee together.'

'Did he fancy you?'

'No.'

'Not even a teentsy bit?'

'No.'

'Is he gay?'

'I don't think so. I didn't get the impression he thought about sex much. He talked about the Common Market and his son.'

'Anything else about him? Drink, drugs, whips, bribes?' She shook her head to each one.

'He's respectably married. With a beautiful wife. Rather cool, very ambitious. I met her once.'

'Know anything about his children?'

'Two, I think. A very photogenic boy at Eton, the one he talks about.'

'What did he say about the son?'

'How clever he was, and how charming. The other child's a girl. She was there when I met Charlotte Mayfield. They were waiting for Ludo to join them for tea on the terrace at the House. The girl was shy and not very attractive. Puppy-fat and spots. Aren't you going to tell me why you want to know?'

I shook my head, thinking. If Mayfield was in the running for Prime Minister, what difference did it make? None, as far as I could see. Toad had gone east months ago. She'd left long before the leadership crisis. Even if something had happened to her on her travels, that could make no difference to her father, surely?

'Polly, what would it mean to the family now Ludo has his new job?'

'How do you mean, what would it mean?'

'Humour me. Anything you can think of. What difference would it make?'

'More money, though not a lot. Higher profile. More work for Ludo, less time at home.'

'And if he is in the running for the leadership?'

'That's another matter altogether. If they do chuck Thatcher they'll be looking for a leader who'll win them the next election, but I don't think it'll come to that. None of them has the nerve to oust the Iron Lady. If by any remote chance they did look for a new leader I can't see it being Ludo, myself. The most you can say for him is there's nothing against him. But if they have a leadership election soon his supporters will be canvassing madly and he'll be giving lots of photo-calls with his family.'

'And his family has to be whiter than white?'

'Sure.'

I clocked her information, though for the moment I could find no use for it. Except, annoyingly, it sounded as if Charlotte née Sherwin would be too busy being photographed to talk to me about her father's murder.

'I must go downstairs,' Polly announced. 'Clive might ring.'

'It's half-past one.'

'That's the point. He can use the downstairs phone once his wife goes to bed. It's Tuesday and she watches the late-night movie on Tuesday. She's got very regular habits.' She made them sound like a disability.

'Polly, do you want Clive to leave his wife? Do you want to marry him?' I seldom ask intrusive questions – I hate people asking them of me – but I was fond of Polly and didn't want to believe love had rendered her completely brain-dead.

'Good Lord no,' she said, and restored my faith in her. 'I don't want to break up a marriage, and I certainly don't want him as the father of my children. I'm in love with him, that's all.'

'Clive Clive Clive Clive,' I said, to please her. It didn't, she left and I went to bed. I could have done with another hour or two organizing my notes and questions, but I was knackered.

Chapter Five

When I woke up next day there was frost on the inside of my bedroom window and I knew I'd have to apologize to the plumber. I'd been without central heating for a month, I'm out a lot so the fire hadn't been on much, and the flat was damp. So I rang him up and grovelled.

I hated to do that when I was right to shout at him in the first place, but it's impossible to find a competent plumber in London unless you inherit one with the family silver, and next to impossible to get anyone even to make house calls and sneer at your central heating installation. Damp is bad for the flat, my only capital asset, and I was sick of lengths of copper piping as a major design feature in my living-room. He came at half-past eight and rubbed my nose in it. I had to make him three cups of real coffee before he'd pretend to fix the heating and I could get over to Barty's and press his assistant into service.

What I needed was to locate the missing Toad's best friend. She'd be a much better bet than the girl's mother, as far as uncensored information was concerned. This was a job for Annabel. It went against the grain to ask her – she thought enough of herself as it was – but her accent and contacts would save me hours of work.

Barty wasn't in the office yet but Annabel was, and delighted to help. She listened to my explanation in silence (she was worryingly bright), then said, 'Shouldn't be a problem. What school was Toad at?'

I passed over the notes I'd taken from Miss Potter's briefing. She found the name of the school, gave a Sloane squeal of recognition, and got on the phone. Twenty squealing minutes later she replaced the receiver in triumph. 'Wonderful! That was Spanker Trott, my old housemistress! Terrific old thing!'

'Oh, good.'

'Really cool. Didn't mind at all when we raided her knicker drawer and draped her capacious M&S cotton numbers round the Founder's Statue on the last night of term. I didn't know she'd moved schools.'

'Perhaps she hoped for a quieter class of girl.'

'I doubt it. Frightfully rowdy lot she's with now. Anyhow, Lally Lambert's the girl you want. I've never met her but I'm sure I can drag in some mutual friends. She's in London at the moment, putting in her Gap Year at Christie's. She and Toad were friends from way back. Shared studies, went skiing together, the whole bit. Spanker says she's a decent sort. Want me to fix it up with Lally?'

I was an ace away from saying I'd do it myself, but she was right, it would come better from her. She fixed it up. Lally'd meet me after she left work at a wine bar just off Piccadilly. They knew her there: it was owned by a friend. It would be.

I thanked Annabel as graciously as I could and let her make me a cup of coffee. 'Anything else I can do?' she said, excited by her success. There was, though I hesitated to ask her. Tracing Toad was actually outside my brief, it was a favour to Miss Potter, so it was reasonable to involve Annabel. But if she did any of my work on the Sherwin murder then I really should renegotiate my seventy-five per cent deal with Barty, and I couldn't afford to do that.

She was watching me as I considered, her large, royal blue eyes fixed on my smaller, short-lashed green ones. 'I needn't mention it to the boss,' she said. 'I'm terribly underemployed as it is and I won't be staying here long. I met a nice chap at a party last week and he's trying to place me at London Weekend Television.'

'What as?'

'A researcher. I'm older than you think.' I had assumed that she was like the other Sloanes, nineteen or so and just out of school, but now I looked at her she could well be post-university.

'Did you go to Oxford?' I fished.

'Cambridge, actually. I read Maths. I understand about you and money.'

'What about me and money?'

'That you need it. Barty thinks it's a game you play. He's hopelessly out of date. It's not his fault, it's his generation. If I can help, you should let me.'

Her shrewd kindness got right up my nose and I nearly refused. Then I remembered the plumber's bill and the possible new roof, asked her to track down Rosalind Sherwin for me, passed over my notes and went for a walk round the block. It was raining, but at least I wouldn't have to listen to the gilded connections of her old girl network bypassing my ten years of graft.

When I got back she passed me a slip of paper with an address and telephone number. 'She's married to a painter – rather a good one, actually. Magnus Jennings. They live in Crete.'

I couldn't resist asking how she'd done it. I can't keep my tongue out of damaged fillings, either. It served me right. 'She and my mother came out together,' said Annabel. I didn't tell her what I thought: my motives would have been too transparent.

Instead, I dialled the number. The phone was answered by a Greek woman, presumably a cleaner, though her English was unusually good. No, sorry, Mrs Jennings couldn't be reached, not for some time. She was at the hospital with her husband. Yes, he was very sick. Yes, it was very sad. Yes, it was a bad time. Yes, it would be better if I waited a while before trying to contact the family.

I replaced the receiver, peeved. I was counting on Rosalind; nieces are usually a good bet. They're close enough to be informed, particularly if they've been living in the house, but detached enough to come across with information. She'd have been particularly detached since she'd only joined the household a few months before the murder.

My next step was Patrick Revill. I thanked Annabel again, as fulsomely as I could manage, and set off for the wrong end of the Edgware Road. It was two bus-rides, a chapter or two of

Lemaire and a small profit on my expenses away, if I claimed for a taxi.

I reached Patrick Revill's flat forty minutes later, with a firmer grip on the Sherwin background according to H. Plowright. Rollo was only the fourth Lord Sherwin: his great-grandfather, a maverick entrepreneur from a solidly respectable, professional Warwickshire family, had started his career as a doctor, then patented and marketed a tonic which the Victorians gulped in such quantities that he could afford to buy Ashtons Hall and its estate, live in high style and do enough in the way of good works to earn his barony. His son, Rollo's grandfather, lived on his father's money, married more money and produced Rollo's father. He married an impecunious Scotswoman, the only functioning descendant of an ancient and batty family. She produced two sons, Rollo and Michael.

They married two sisters, Laura and Sophie Farrell, not for their money because they didn't seem to have any (their father, Colonel Farrell, was living at Ashtons Hall as Rollo's pensioner at the time of the murder) but almost certainly, judging by the photographs, for their looks. If anything, Sophie was better-looking than Laura, but even more ill-fated. Whether Laura killed her husband or not, she at least lived to a comfortable and secure old age.

Michael and Sophie were not so lucky. Rollo, as elder son, inherited the house, the estate, the Sherwin title and, from his mother, the lairdship of a Scottish island. Michael, the younger son, was given enough money to buy land in Kenya, where during the Mau rising he, Sophie and their dog Joss were hacked to pieces in the living-room of their bungalow. Their child Rosalind survived only because of the prompt and sensible action of Miss Potter, then her governess, who grabbed a revolver and bundled herself and the child into a linen chest and remained there, silent, for several hours while the Mau wrecked the house.

I was glad of the information but heartily sick of Lemaire's censorious style. His favourite adjective was *unimaginable*. The death of Rosalind's parents, Rollo's sexual adventures, family relationships at

Ashtons Hall and the savagery of the murder were all unimaginable. An odd affectation in a writer and most unhelpful for readers who presumably hoped the book would enable them to imagine it.

I shut the book in relief and left the bus at the traffic lights. Revill's flat was above a Pakistani newsagent and post office. The paint on the door was peeling and there were two bells, both unmarked. I rang them and waited, back on familiar territory. Eventually a window opened above me and a head looked out. Old; grey; either a long-haired man or a coarse-featured woman.

'Mr Revill?'

'Who wants him?'

'I do. To interview.'

The head perked up, revealing itself to be male and possessed of a professional smile. 'Is there a fee?'

'Yes.' He didn't look as if he'd stand out for much: Barty would wear it. He threw down a key and was waiting for me at the top of the stairs, a tallish old man who would have been very tall once, grubbily dressed in flannels, a nearly white shirt and a tweed jacket. The smell of cat piss was almost excluded when he shut the flat door; we were standing close together in a tiny hall and I could see the bristles his shaving had missed. He met my eyes and smiled, and I could see that he had been – still thought he was – an attractive man, being kind to me. The look's unmistakable: flirtatious, arrogant. Early on in my teens, maybe because I don't have it, I started dividing people into those with or those without. One of my foster-grandmothers told me it used to be called 'it'. Very little to do with looks, usually, though the Revill man also had the relics of those.

His room was small; tidy, but ugly and not entirely clean. It looked as if his furniture was the discarded pieces of assorted households, perhaps several divorces in which he was, materially, the exploited party. The walls were covered with old playbills and film posters, some featuring photographs of a younger Patrick. He had been handsome in an obvious way, with a seductive, droopy-eyed smile.

I sat on the sofa's exhausted springs and smiled as responsively as I could. Attractive people need a response to function well, spe-

36

cially when they're past it. 'Will the photographer be joining you here, or do you want me to come down to the office?' he said eagerly.

'I don't know yet if we want a pic. It depends how much useful material you give me.' His smile slipped, and I caught it. 'Oh, Mr Revill, I must tell you how honoured I am to get this chance to meet you. I'm a fan, but I won't take up your time with that. Shall we discuss a fee?' We discussed a fee. He must have been very strapped because he accepted even less than I expected and he didn't ask what information we were talking about. When I told him, he wasn't keen.

'I know nothing about the Sherwin murder. Would you like a coffee?'

I followed him towards the cupboard he was using as a kitchen. His hands shook as he filled the kettle, but perhaps they always did.

'It's background I'm after. You were renting a lodge on the estate at the time, and for some months before? You must have got an impression of the people, and you did actually attend the hunt ball on the night of the murder, so you can tell me about that.' He gave me a mug of coffee. He had used the cheapest instant powder which he had decanted into a Gold Blend jar, one of the most small-time, incompetent pretensions I've ever encountered. Or perhaps it was to comfort himself, not deceive visitors.

'I did rather get to know Lord Sherwin. Charming chap.' His voice was basically flat London, with actorish consonants, but the last sentence had moved dramatically up-market, suggesting companionship on the grouse moors followed by a whisky in the library. I nodded encouragingly and returned to the sofa. He stood by the window, looking out. He had a good profile. 'Bit of a one for the ladies, alas. That's what did for him.'

'You mean, somebody's husband . . .' I trailed off expectantly.

'Not necessarily a husband. Female of the species is deadlier than the male. *Cherchez la femme*. Stands to reason. Oldest motive there is, jealousy. Look at Othello. Shakespeare knew the human heart. Lord Sherwin's lady had plenty to put up with. I expect she was driven to it.' So he was another supporter of the Laura theory.

'That's very interesting. I'll make a note of that.' I wrote *Laura scribble scribble keep him happy.* 'Did you see or hear anything to back up your idea?'

'Not exactly,' he said coyly. 'Just that – someone told me a bit of background.'

'Someone in the house?'

'Hang on a jiffy. Who did you say you were working for? Who wants to know this?'

'I'm researching for Barty O'Neill. He's doing a piece for the *Observer*.'

'Who else have you seen?'

'Miss Potter.' I wanted to see how much he remembered, and from whom, so I didn't give him any clues.

'Who?'

'The governess. Looking after the Sherwins' daughters.'

'The virtuous Miss Potter! I'd forgotten all about her. Don't think I ever saw her, actually.'

'What do you mean, virtuous?'

'Always prating on about duty and honour.'

'Who told you about Miss Potter?'

He began to speak, checked himself, sipped coffee. 'I read it. In one of the articles about the murder. I kept up with the case in the papers. Being there, so to speak, not because I knew anything about it. Fascinating. The chap had so much. Everything, really. Land, money, position, pretty wife, children. Never had to do a hand's turn. Then gets his head blown off. Terrible thing.' He didn't think it terrible; he was pleased. I understood why and disliked him, and myself for understanding so readily. 'I was in the middle of a messy divorce, at the time. My first. You never get rid of first wives, you know. Not ever. It's the only marriage that takes, in my experience. I still think about her. Don't love her, but think about her, remember what we did together. The children, being young, getting my first part, that kind of thing. Never goes. I couldn't even tell you my third wife's name, off-hand. Mind you that's partly because she kept changing it. What's your favourite film?'

I nearly said *Death in Venice*, then clicked. He meant one of his. I was supposed to be a fan. I named his most successful film. He was gratified. I hadn't seen it, but that didn't matter; by the time he stopped reminiscing I could have written a dissertation on it.

'Really?' I said. 'Goodness, tell me more.' He did, then felt much better and leant over trying to read my notes, which read *boring war film stiff upper lip vain old bugger*. I covered them. 'Shorthand,' I said. 'Did you meet any of the young people in Ashtons Hall? There were three small girls, I think.' (One of my basic techniques: I invite interviewees to spot the deliberate mistake. Most people love putting you right on small points of fact; then they go on to tell you more than they intended.)

'Four,' he said. 'There were four. You should do your home-work.'

'Four, sorry. Did you meet them?'

'I sometimes saw them out riding. The youngest one was still on a leading-rein.' We were back with the grouse moor voice.

'A leading-rein?'

'To keep the pony from running away. She couldn't control it yet. Her grandfather walked along beside her and broke into a run when the pony cantered. I often thought he'd have a heart attack. Dangerous to exert yourself at his age. Come to think of it, I'm probably coming up to his age now. I must take care of myself!'

He twinkled at me, and I stepped up my responsive admiration to a hundred-watt admiring glow. Revill was a good way older, now, I thought, and did the calculation. Farrell had been just seventy at the time of the murder: Revill forty-eight, which meant he was now pushing eighty.

He was going on. 'The youngest girl was a lovely little thing, like her mother. They all were.' He stopped talking and turned his head away from me, still looking out of the window. It seemed he had, briefly, forgotten his profile. 'Good weather, that summer I was playing Antony. Some of the best work I've ever done. Care to see the reviews?' I didn't, of course, though I would have, but he made no move to fetch them. 'It was the turning-point, the beginning of the end. You don't know it at the time, but you can feel it. A kind of chill in the air, this won't last, it's going.'

'What, particularly?'

'You don't want to be bothered with the meanderings of an old man.' Like most self-evident statements of the kind, it expected denial. I denied it. 'My career, I suppose. Not that I haven't done very good work since. My Lear. Did you see my Lear?' I shook my head. 'Not surprised. Bit out of the way, Nottingham Rep. Not exactly the RSC. More than my career, though. Things running through my fingers, running away, time running away. And my marriage, and the children. Haven't seen them all that much since. They never call or come to see me; they didn't like the other wives, and their mother put them against me. How often do you see your father?'

'Never,' I said.

'Killed by the Mau Mau, was he?'

I assumed I'd misheard. 'Beg your pardon?'

'Forget it. Funny how you remember things, just little things, that happened years ago.'

I sat looking at my notes. The Mau Mau. Rosalind: it had to be. She'd have told the story, probably, boasting of it, perhaps: Rosalind the sensationally orphaned, tragic heroine. 'So you knew Rosalind,' I said.

'Oh yes. I knew Rosalind, but I'm not going to talk about her.'

I shifted my weight on the springless sofa. I had to see Rosalind next, if I could track her down. I wondered if what Revill was giving me was memory or fantasy, and if it would turn out to be worth spending Barty's money and my time on taking him to the pub.

Chapter Six

I pursued Revill about Rosalind, of course: I changed the subject, looked at his cuttings, said how well thought of he had been, looked at some of his fan letters, oohed and aahed about how much he had been lusted after, and took him to a pub for lunch. He drank Scotch, I drank Perrier water, and by the end I was sure he'd been screwing Rosalind that summer. He didn't claim it directly but his nudges and winks were broad enough to reach the back row of the balcony. The more he drank the more sentimental he became about her youth and beauty, her eagerness, their magic summer together. As I listened, I began to feel for her. He said Laura disliked her and treated her badly. I thought she sounded lonely; it couldn't have been easy, joining the Ashtons Hall ménage. Revill hadn't been a well-chosen refuge. He made me feel sick, and not just because he was so clearly past his sell-by date.

If his gossip did come from Rosalind, it was promising and I got some good quotes. He confirmed Lemaire's description of the Sherwins' marriage as rocky, adding that for some weeks before the murder Rollo had been talking divorce. Annoyingly, I got the impression that he hadn't seen Rosalind after the murder, so his assumption that Laura had done it was based on his own deductions.

I shook him off when he started repeating himself for the third time, and headed home.

When I got back to the flat in mid-afternoon the plumber had gone leaving an awesome bill and the central heating rumbling at full blast. There was a message on the answering machine from

Miss Potter. She had found her scrapbook of photographs and newspaper cuttings about the case. She'd be in for the rest of the day. Would I be interested in calling round to pick it up? Was I ever. If I had good photographs, more than half the job was done. I rang back and arranged to go round after I'd seen Toad's friend, Lally.

Then I had a long bath in HOT WATER. Another simple, intense pleasure, though not cheap.

Lally surprised me. She wasn't blonde. She was black, a person of colour. Her head sprouted beaded, tiny plaits. Otherwise, she was exactly what I expected: tall, slender, long-legged, self-possessed and superficially friendly. The wine bar was crowded but she found us a table once we'd met at the bar and I'd got us drinks. 'So,' she said, 'Annabel Chancellor tells me you're looking for Toad. You know she's on her Gap Year, travelling in the East. How can I help?'

She disconcerted me. She spoke the upper-class dialect I disliked, the arrogant clenched-teeth drawl. If I shut my eyes, I could have been talking to any of Barty's assistants. If I opened them, there was an Afro-Caribbean wearing her impeccable street credentials with her skin. 'Have you heard from her since she went abroad?' I said.

'Two postcards so far. Both from India,' she drawled.

'And you're sure she's OK? Not worried about her at all?' I fished.

'Of course not. Why should I be?'

If I hadn't had my eyes shut, listening to her, I might not have picked it up; it was a noisy wine bar. As it was, I couldn't miss it, much as I wanted to. Her voice was tight. She was lying.

I nearly swore aloud. I had hoped for absolute confirmation that Toad was meandering through Asia, pouring Daddy's money into open sewers and gaining experience with yak-drivers. I had no time to waste looking for a Toad who might be a voluntary Lucanette, gone underground in the upper classes. Neither, on the other hand, could I resist a puzzle, however insignificant. I kept talking while I thought. 'When did the last one arrive?'

'Last week.'

'What did it say?'

'What did what say?'

'The postcard.'

'The usual. Having a lovely time, wish you were here, that sort of thing. Why are you so interested?'

I explained about Miss Potter and the postcards. She said she remembered Toad mentioning Miss Potter, the old governess who lived in the lodge. Nice old person, Toad had said. Always kind to her. The suggestion was that Toad needed it, that kindness to Toad was unusual. And this time Lally wasn't lying: she sounded, suddenly, worried.

'Tell you what,' I said, tearing a page out of my notebook and scribbling on it. 'Here's my name and telephone number. Miss Potter is really bothered about this. Anything I find out about Toad will be absolutely between me and Miss Potter – no parents included. So if you or any of your friends hear from her – another postcard, maybe – give me a ring, all right? Ask around a bit. I'll be in later tonight, and the answering machine will take a message if I'm not.'

'Tonight? I won't have had another postcard by tonight!' Lally was shaken by my urgency, as I had meant her to be.

'Some of your friends might. Or they might know something. In confidence, OK?' I left before she spoke again. I wanted to leave her to stew. She might look sophisticated but she was young, she'd probably been cottonwooled from birth, and according to Annabel's ex-housemistress, she was a decent sort. She'd ring. I only hoped she'd ring to confide that Toad was shacked up somewhere with an unsuitable boyfriend, preferably somewhere in London so I could winkle her out to parade for Miss Potter.

That is what I hoped. I think, even at that stage, it wasn't what I expected. I suppose it was partly out of guilt that I stopped off at a library on the way to see Miss Potter, and looked Ludovic May-field up in *Who's Who*.

I made notes on the entry. Father a judge. Famous prep school (unusual to name a prep school in a *Who's Who* entry); Eton; Christ Church, Oxford; Sandhurst; Life Guards (not the Bondi Beach kind, the smart regiment); barrister, Lincoln's Inn. Married Charlotte Sherwin, of late Rollo, Lord Sherwin. MP for West Warwickshire. Minor government posts. Long list of clubs. By this time I guessed his interests were snobbery, misogyny and bread-roll throwing – that's mostly what you learn in all those male institutions – but he gave them as 'reading' (John Buchan and Dornford Yates?) and 'walking' (around Euston station for the rent-boys?).

I didn't like him much but he seemed deeply conventional. A safe father, surely? A father who wouldn't mistreat his daughter because the club secretary wouldn't like it.

When I reached Penelope's house, Miss Potter was distrait. She kept leaping to her feet, asking about Toad and offering me dry sherry. I noticed she'd started on it already, but she held the glass so precisely I didn't think she'd got very far. Finally I managed to procure a minuscule cup of coffee and some of her attention. It wasn't worth worrying her with the details of my interview with Lally, so I told her I expected to have pin-pointed Toad's where-abouts by next day.

'Really, Alex?' she said suspiciously.

'Really,' I said firmly. I sort of believed it. She went wittering on about her concern and, to distract her, I recounted the interview with Patrick Revill at some length.

'So Mr Revill definitely knew Rosalind,' she said.

'Didn't Rosalind tell you he did?'

'No. At the time, Rosalind wasn't telling me anything. We were hardly talking.'

'Was there a fight?'

'No. It was my decision.'

'Why on earth?' I flicked through my notes, found the page. 'You saved her life from the Mau Mau.'

'Just say Mau Mau,' said Miss Potter. 'You should not use the definite article.'

'OK, OK. You saved her from a fairly definite Mau Mau machete through the head, and you were effectively a mother to her, surely, for the five years after her parents died, before you came to England.'

'My dear, I can't expect you to understand. When we left Kenya, everything changed. Everything.'

'How can I understand, if you won't tell me?'

'My position was entirely different. At home—'

'You mean in Kenya?'

'Yes. I still, then, thought of it as home. At home, I'd been in charge. Of the house, of the staff, of Rosalind.'

'Was there a large staff?'

'Not unduly, for the time and the place. We had a head boy, of course. He was a Somali. There were also two Luo houseboys, the cook and the shamba boys in the compound. It was a large bungalow. Rosalind inherited it after her parents were murdered, but she was then only twelve, far too young to manage a household. At first I feared that her uncle and aunt would wish her to return to England and make her home with them, but I felt her life had been disrupted enough, and Lord Sherwin accepted my offer to remain with her, supervise the household and continue her education.'

'Laura didn't want her back?'

'Lady Sherwin's indifference was evident. Rosalind's grandfather wrote several times, wanting to see her, but he was then, as always, powerless. He had no money, you see. He was Lord Sherwin's pensioner.'

'Bit strange of Laura not to want to take care of her niece?'

'Lady Sherwin's aim was, then and always, to ensure her own comfort and convenience. Besides, according to Mrs Sherwin, Rosalind's mother – you know that the sisters married brothers?' I nodded, and she went on, 'According to Mrs Sherwin, Lady Sherwin was not an affectionate sister to her. She was a jealous woman, and Mrs Sherwin was not only the more beautiful of the two but was also Lord Sherwin's first choice of wife.'

'So Sophie turned down Rollo for the younger son.' I made a note, accepted a glass of sherry to keep Miss Potter company, and nudged her on. 'And things were good for you and Rosalind in Kenya.'

'We were very happy. If it had been possible I would have stayed in Kenya for ever. I suppose I had become complacent, and forgotten my true position. Coming back to England was a shock. My domain immediately shrank to the schoolroom and two night nurseries, which I renamed bedrooms. I was a governess, not a nanny, and I always felt the job description "nursery governess" to be a contradiction in terms. For myself I chose a room next to what used to be known as the nursery wing, though the house, being a rectangle, has no wings. My immediate predecessor had, for what Mrs Crisp the cook, a deplorable gossip, described as "Reasons", elected to occupy a corner bedroom at the other end of the corridor, handy for Lord Sherwin's by way of the back stairs. I was no longer responsible for Rosalind.'

'Sounds grim,' I said. 'You'd actually lost your home, hadn't you, and your status.'

'I still had status,' she said, defensive and peeved. 'I was a governess, a very responsible position. The four little girls had been without a governess for months. Charlotte had become undisciplined and fallen behind in her work. She was a very able child, full of energy and force of character, often misdirected. She bullied the younger ones. I was entrusted with an important task.'

'But you were homesick.'

'More sherry?' She was already refilling her own glass.

I shook my head. I hate sherry and I hadn't managed to choke down my first.

'Yes, I was homesick. So much so that I chose Kenya as our first excursion into Geography.'

She seemed to expect a reaction.

'Really?' I said.

She saw I hadn't understood. 'Yes, really, Alex. With four pupils whose education had been deplorably neglected, and whose grasp of the geography of their own country was such that they would have found it a challenge correctly to name the capital of Scotland. I set them to filling in an outline map of Kenya, because I wanted to hear the names. Charlotte spotted it. She asked me why.'

'What did you say?'

'That is immaterial,' she said. As far as I could see, much of what she said was immaterial, but this was her party. I nodded appreciatively.

Chapter Seven

I let Miss Potter ramble for a while, hoping for something useful, but the more rope I gave her the further afield she strayed. She still hadn't satisfactorily answered my question about the rupture in her relationship with Rosalind. Eventually I waited till she drew breath after a description of her experiences as a pre-war undergraduate at University College, London – lots of cocoa and prayer meetings – and approached the question from another angle. 'Look, Miss Potter, obviously Patrick Revill did know Rosalind. He didn't admit it, but he must have known her well, because when I pinned him down the only person in the house he'd met before the night of the hunt ball was Rosalind, and she must have invited him, or got him a ticket, or whatever you do for hunt balls. He said good morning to Rollo once—'

'Lord Sherwin,' said Miss Potter reprovingly. I gaped: surely, having his head blown off thirty years ago, Rollo was beyond caring about his style and title? 'I allowed your first few references to pass, but I do find inaccuracy irritating.'

'Oh, right. Rollo, Lord Sherwin. Revill said good morning to Lord Sherwin once, but he just saw the others in the distance, so the chances are he was at the ball at Rosalind's invitation.'

'Who did he say had invited him?'

'Lord Sherwin, but I thought he was lying. He knew a lot of details about her, though he claimed he didn't. He couldn't resist putting me right. For instance, he knew about her parents and how they died in Kenya, and your part in it. By the way, I wanted to ask you about that.'

'Ask away.'

'Two things. One, why didn't any Mau Mau look in the linen chest? If they searched and wrecked the place?'

'Oh, they did,' she said, pleased and pink, presumably at her recollected resourcefulness. 'I had covered us with sheets and an eiderdown, and we kept very still. What is your second question?'

'What was the revolver for?'

'Us,' said Miss Potter. 'I intended to use it on Rosalind first, then myself.'

'And could you have done that?'

'Certainly. So could you, Alex, presented with my alternatives.'

'Wouldn't it have been better to fight?'

'Not against such odds, with the possibility of leaving Rosalind unprotected.'

I was impressed: it was clear she'd had terrific nerve. Looking at her now I couldn't imagine it, but that's often the way. Two years ago I'd worked on a doco about heroes and the main subject, a VC who'd spent his time undercover in Crete, had been a small, shrunken old man who kept saying, 'I was lucky, I had a good war,' in a deprecating voice. I couldn't imagine him ever doing anything more assertive than kicking the cat.

Miss Potter appeared equally reluctant to dwell on her courage. 'Mr Revill need not have heard the story from Rosalind. It was common gossip at the time,' she said briskly.

'Not behind the scenes at Stratford. Revill only knew other actors. Until the evening of the ball he says he never went inside the big house, not even to the kitchen—'

'The servants' hall.'

'To wherever the cook and the butler and the cleaning women had their teabreaks,' I said, as uncontentiously as I could. 'Revill made a big deal of not having been in the house so I didn't necessarily believe him, but even so he wouldn't have been on gossip terms with anyone except Rosalind. She must have told him, and my guess is the acquaintanceship was quite close.'

'Impossible.'

'Why?'

'Believe me.' She sounded upset and determined.

'Do you have any particular reason to think so?'

'She was only seventeen, strictly brought up.'

'Delicately nurtured,' I said. The expression had struck me when I found it in a Victorian novel: it seemed both apt and anachronistic now.

'Quite so. She was a delicately nurtured young girl, and he was—'

'He was a famous actor with lots of fans. She could have been one of them. She could have thrown her knickers onstage with all the ordinary lower-class girls, couldn't she? And he could have picked them up? Metaphorically speaking? He said she was pretty. He was, indirectly, boasting about her.'

Miss Potter blushed and gulped her sherry. 'Was he married, my dear?'

'Yes. But his wife was in London.'

'Her whereabouts are immaterial. He was a married man. We won't pursue this avenue of inquiry.'

She was very agitated, and scratching round for reasons not to believe me. We were getting close to something useful. 'You've made the right decision about all this,' I said, to distract her while I tried to formulate a killer question.

'My dear, do you think so? I'm not sure. I didn't sleep at all, last night.'

'Were you worrying about Toad?'

'Regrettably, I was not. I was thinking about the past. I remembered so much. Everything. I lay awake, hearing voices I haven't heard for thirty years. I'm not accustomed to break faith. I've always been loyal, always. I don't want you to think that I'm just acting in a fit of pique, because those boys attacked me. It was much more than that.'

'Tell me.'

She twisted her hands together and winced. 'I don't know that I can. It's to do with duty and the responsibility of privilege. I have always believed that the only justification for the inequity in birth, wealth and education which pervades our country is the corresponding responsibility which the privileged undertake.'

'Noblesse oblige,' I said. I meant it ironically but she took it straight and nodded eagerly.

'Exactly so. The duty of the strong to protect the weak, to look after their interests and run society for the benefit of all. I always strove to form my pupils' characters so that they should return, in full measure, all they were fortunate enough to gain from the social structure into which they were born.'

We were sitting in Penelope's large L-shaped drawing-room, on one of the two sofas, facing the concert grand piano. I don't know much about furniture but I know when it's antique and much too expensive for me. All Penelope's furniture fell into this category and there was plenty of it. There were original paintings on the walls, the kind you hang out of the sunlight with their own little lamps neatly adjusted to bring out the patina or avoid the patina or whatever. We were sitting, in fact, in congealed money. I could most likely have lived for a year on one of the ornaments displayed so openly. No wonder Penelope wanted a house-sitter, and needed the complicated burglar alarm system, the grilles covering the windows, the triple deadbolt locks. 'What exactly would you say Penelope and her husband did to repay society for this lot?' I said, with an inclusive wave of my arm. 'What do they do?'

'Penelope is a wife and mother. She has three soundly principled children. Hugh is fortunate enough to be able to live on his investments. He is also an underwriter at Lloyd's.'

'Terrific,' I said. 'That's really helpful.'

'He serves as a magistrate in the country.'

'Where he hands down exemplary sentences to trespassers and poachers, I expect.'

'We are losing sight of the point, Alex.' Very cool voice. Pupil Alex was being obstreperous. 'Where do you look for leadership, if the leaders . . .' she trailed off into silence.

'If the leaders are corrupt, venal or incompetent? Exactly. When did that strike you?'

'I suppose I have long felt that Charlotte was not discharging her parental responsibilities towards Toad. More generally, it struck me in the form of a robber's fist to the side of the head. He was a child,

Alex, no more than fifteen. He should have been at school, at a decent school learning a trade, learning moral principles, self-discipline and good manners. Instead he and his friend had chosen to rob an old woman whom they had every reason to believe was defenceless.'

She helped herself to more sherry, without offering me any: I could tell she was nerving herself for a confidence, and turned, hopefully, to a new page in my notebook, but she swerved off again. 'I believe the formative years are all-important, Alex, and impressions gained in youth are never eradicated.'

'Psychology.'

'My own experience. When you were a child, did you ever go abroad?'

'The furthest I went was Boulogne, on a day trip from school.'

'Which school was that?'

'A comprehensive in Fulham.'

'Ah. Kenya is a very beautiful country,' she said, sipping her sherry. 'It was there I fell in love, in 1938, when I was seventeen. Perhaps I would have been prepared to – throw my knickers on stage.' I was struck by the image. If I had to imagine Miss Potter in love, I would see her fully clothed down to gloves and hat. I smiled encouragingly. She didn't notice. 'He was an exceptional man. An exceptional man—'

'They are, when you're seventeen—'

'A gentleman, an aristocrat. He wore a kilt. It was love at first sight. We met at the Caledonian Ball in the Muthaiga Club. You will keep this absolutely confidential? He was dancing with someone else. I'd left my wrap in the cloakroom and stood by the dance-floor, looking for my party. My eyes were searching the room for a familiar face; I was shy. He saw me. I forced myself to look away. I could feel his eyes on me as he danced. Then he left his partner and came towards me. He had most impressive knees. I didn't look up, that is why I remember the knees. Before he reached me, I was joined by my friends. They introduced me, and it was then I realized who he was. It was Lord Erroll.'

She paused for me to exclaim. I exclaimed, trying to place the owner of the aristocratic knees, who did sound vaguely familiar.

'You may have seen the recent film about his tragic death,' she went on, and placed him for me. Joss Erroll was the white settler in Kenya who spent the twenties and thirties bounding about seducing people's wives until someone shot him in the head. '*White Mischief* was, as these things are, a complete distortion of the facts. But be that as it may, I danced several times with Lord Erroll. A Gay Gordons, an eightsome reel and a foxtrot.' She paused, and I exclaimed again. 'Do you believe in love at first sight?' she went on.

'Sometimes,' I said, remembering the lustful glances I'd exchanged with the sound recordist on the Black Death doco and the sweaty night that followed. He hadn't rung afterwards.

'He whispered in my ear. He said . . .' she paused. 'I've never talked about this to anyone. Ever.' People often say that to me. It may be true. Listening is part of my job. It isn't difficult, but it takes concentration, and when it's well done most people find it irresistible: even, occasionally, people of Miss Potter's generation and temperament, who have spent their lives silent, believing that self-doubt is vulgar and introspection distasteful, like picking your nose in public.

'He said . . .' I murmured.

'He said, "You feel it, don't you?"'

Pause. Miss Potter topped up her sherry with the air of one who had delivered a bombshell.

'And he was referring to . . .?'

She looked at me expectantly. 'My dear, you surprise me. I always imagine you young people to be so much more – aware – than I was. He was referring to—'

'Of course,' I said. 'I understand.' I know I was slow off the mark but I don't think of men in 1938 having erections, and still less did I expect Miss Potter to refer to them, however obliquely. 'This was during the foxtrot?'

'I hardly think the question would have arisen during the eightsome reel, as you would know if you had ever learnt Scottish dancing.'

'And you were shocked?'

'I was surprised by his aristocratic frankness, yes, but it was also – thrilling. Quite, quite thrilling. I was pretty in those days, several people said so, but I never dreamt Lord Erroll would find me attractive.'

'What did you say?'

'Nothing. What could I say? I drew away a little but he was very strong, he held me close. It was a delightful sensation to be handled so surely. The dance was coming to an end, and he whispered in my ear again. "Meet me in the billiard-room," he said. "The billiard-room. In half an hour."'

'And did you meet him?'

'No. No, we didn't meet. In the interim, I discovered that he was married.'

At ten, she was still trying to keep me there. Things had looked up about eight when she offered me what she described as a light supper. It consisted of one piece of toast sprinkled with my half share of three eggs, scrambled. I'd then watched, ravenous, as she toyed (I'd never before *seen* anyone toy, but she did) with her share and then scraped it into the rubbish bin.

I'd learnt plenty about the topography of Kenya, the mariners and customs of the post-war upper classes, Miss Potter's views on the decay of standards and principle in modern England and her awe-inspiring capacity for sherry, but I was no further on with the murder.

Then she really dropped a bombshell. She told me that the lodge in Warwickshire she'd lived in for twenty years had been provided, at a peppercorn rent, by Laura, and that Charlotte had thrown her out after Laura's death.

Listening to her blagging on, trying to disguise my stomach rumbles by shifting in the chair and clearing my throat, I'd been doing some toying of my own, with the fantasy that she was the murderer. Only someone devoid of basic human feeling would give a person one and a half scrambled eggs and then bore them to death. I hadn't believed it, though, and the news about the lodge was the end of that theory. If Laura had given her the lodge, it was to keep quiet. Therefore Miss P. wasn't the murderer, but she knew who was, or she knew enough to worry Laura.

I wanted to go home and think it through. When I got up to leave she fetched the clippings book. With it was a large brown envelope. 'You mentioned photographs,' she said. 'You might be interested in these. It goes without saying that I expect them to be returned in good condition.'

'Of course.'

'With one exception. I am not, in any case, at all sure that it can be used. I certainly do not wish its return.' She extracted a smaller envelope and handed it to me. Inside, a scene of crime photograph. A close-up of Rollo, what was left of him after, according to Lemaire's report of the pathologist's report, a shotgun had been discharged within eighteen inches of his head. I'm not squeamish, but I couldn't look at it for long. 'Rollo, Lord Sherwin,' she said, as if I hadn't seen for myself. 'I confiscated it from Charlotte. She purloined it from the murder room.'

'Why didn't you tell the police?'

'They had not noticed its absence.'

'Poor man,' I said. 'Poor Rollo.'

'Indeed.'

Chapter Eight

When I got back from Miss Potter's, there was a package from Barty on the table in the entrance hall. I carried it upstairs, tearing it open as I went. Two books, both by Miss Potter, and a message from Barty. Had I read Miss Potter's books? No, of course I hadn't, but if I spent much longer with her I could write them.

There was no message from Lally Lambert on my answering machine. I was surprised and annoyed. Maybe I'd miscalculated. I'd ring her at work in the morning. I wrote myself a reminder and pinned it up on the 'Action' section of the Sherwin project board on one wall of my kitchen, then Blu-Tacked up some of Miss Potter's photographs, including the death photograph still in its envelope. I now had an Ashtons Hall rogues' gallery.

They were a good-looking lot, all of them, even Oliver Farrell. The little girls were posed with Miss Potter and bicycles in the drive in front of the house. You could tell they would swan through adolescence without puppy-fat or pimples or lifting fantasies from market stalls, and that they would emerge at twenty-one with a suitable husband and a trust fund. They would probably marry a big, handsome stupid man like Daddy. If Rollo had been stupid. His face didn't look exactly that; more unreflective. Probably the most serious self-searching he ever did was when he had to decide whether to fag for the Captain of the First Eleven or the Keeper of Boats.

I made myself a late-night coffee, put the Eagles on the CD, flicked through my notes on Lemaire and thought.

According to the pathologist, Rollo had been shot between twelve and one in the morning, though his body wasn't found until after breakfast the following day. All the witnesses had heard several shotgun blasts, which wasn't surprising since some idiot with a shotgun in the boot of his car had taken it out during the course of the evening and blasted away at some rabbits on the lawn. There were no fingerprints on the murder weapon, one of Rollo's own: it had been wiped clean. None of the guests could remember seeing anyone going into or out of the gun-room all evening. Everyone was vague about when they'd last seen Rollo, but the last public sighting was before midnight. Most suggested he had surprised a tramp in the act of robbing the gun-room. None could recall with any accuracy who he might or might not have been involved with or had any reason to suppose why he might have been shot.

What could Miss Potter be hiding? She might have seen the murderer, Laura or not, leave the gun-room. She might have information about Laura's motive. I was nearly sure the killer was Laura, mostly because she'd allowed Miss Potter to live in her lodge, effectively free. Laura didn't seem the type to take unselfish care of dependants. If it was Laura who had an interest in keeping Miss Potter quiet, then either she'd done it herself or she'd been protecting someone.

Who does a woman protect? Her man, her children, just possibly her parents. Dr Bloom, a most unlikely lover for Laura judging from the photographs (and why on earth had she *married* him less than a year after the murder? An impoverished Jewish doctor was a come-down), also made an unlikely murderer. The character that H. Plowright described was tender, peace-loving and affectionate, a New Man born before his time. Besides, he hadn't been at the ball. Equally, I didn't for a moment believe that the four little girls were involved; only in the pages of Agatha Christie does a baby Sloane adjust her headscarf, say 'OK-yah' and blast Daddy to glory. Laura's father was an extreme outsider because I couldn't imagine a motive. Besides, he had died of a heart attack a few months after the murder and Laura didn't sound to me like a woman who would protect her father's memory.

Laura's motive? Could have been property and money, because she got the whole lot. Could have been sexual jealousy – I agreed with Revill that nothing causes more passionate ill-feeling. Or sexual desire. She might have killed her husband to marry the doctor, unlikely as he seemed as a violent object of desire. On the other hand, she might have shot her husband for almost any reason and then married the doctor to shut him up.

I was sure it wasn't an unidentified woman whom Rollo had seduced and abandoned, or a jealous husband. Miss Potter wouldn't have buttoned her lip for that, she'd have thought adultery was letting the aristocratic side down and they deserved all they got. Miss P. had been loyal: that was what she was reconsidering now: and only her employers or her charges would have evoked that in her. Rosalind would have particularly, of course, but I couldn't see a motive, nor did it seem likely that Laura would lift a finger to help her niece. According to Patrick Revill, Laura had treated Rosalind in a spectacularly bitchy manner. Even allowing for adolescent paranoia, Rosalind's evidence on her aunt's feelings for her was probably the best we'd get.

My original excitement at Miss Potter's revelation about the lodge had subsided. OK, so Laura had thought Miss P. knew enough to want to keep her quiet. So Laura probably did it. And anyone who knew anything about the case thought that already. Not much of an angle for my piece.

I had another bath to take advantage of the central heating while it still worked, then sat at the kitchen table to skip-read Miss Potter's books, hoping for some facts. She got a good degree in History at London University, intending to work in Education – I think she meant being a schoolmistress – but after two years teaching History at Cheltenham Ladies' College the war was over and she was given the Opportunity to return to Kenya as a governess and her career was diverted into Other Channels. The magic of Africa exerted a powerful pull and she rambled on about the beauty of the landscape and the captivating innocence of the natives. She didn't mention memories of Joss Erroll (what had the billiard-room incident to do with the Sherwins? was it true?) but he was dead, of course, by now so she couldn't have hoped for a reprise of the foxtrot.

A Governess Looks Back took us as far as 1965 when she gave up governessing for ever. Astoundingly, enough people must have bought it for the publishers (a small house, since, not surprisingly, bankrupted) to give her another go. *A Housemistress Looks Back* was decidedly less perky, however. Her first book had a strange, lavender charm, if you liked that kind of thing; it had some good descriptions of people and places, the anecdotes were mildly entertaining, and the persona of the author was compellingly gung-ho, anachronistic and full of moral fervour. I was interested by the accounts of Rosalind in Africa; Miss Potter had been enormously fond of her, clearly, and the girl sounded, for someone of her background, quite a promising human being. I often looked up at her photograph, as I read. She was in a beach group, wearing a swimsuit, grinning at the camera. She looked around seventeen. The two boys in the group were looking at her; she was emphatically not returning their interest, but hugging her bare legs to her swimsuited chest as if to say, 'This is my body, buster, keep off.'

There was an idyllic feel to the Rosalind and Kenya section of *A Governess Looks Back*, as if Miss Potter, already sensing herself to be a member of an endangered species, had briefly found an Arcadian game reserve. There was nothing about her time at Ashtons Hall, but I hadn't really expected there to be. I was also intrigued by the Monatrea Castle section, with its glimpses of the young Barty and his really awful parents. Miss Potter never actually said people were really awful but she had a nice line in subversion. Her accounts of Barty's father, in particular – *'at times, an overenthusiastic disciplinarian; Barty was attended by the family doctor twice, that week'* – went some way towards explaining why Barty had spent his life energetically thumbing his nose at authority figures.

I quite enjoyed the first book, as I say, but the second was uphill work, mostly because it was so depressing. She didn't mean it to be; the entertaining anecdotes still came thick and fast, but they were shriller, more self-deprecating. She referred to herself more often as 'out of date' and as a 'spinster'. By now she was in her mid-forties and found it difficult to get work teaching History, which was what she wanted. I suppose she'd been out of the game too long. She started out working as housemistress in a very small, ramshackle privately owned boarding school. After a year she was sacked – *the Headmaster urged me to offer my resignation* – for spoiling the atmosphere at Sports Day by taking up a collection to buy test tubes for the laboratory. *I could no longer ignore the disgraceful neglect of basic provision for the scholastic endeavours of the girls in my care.*

She went on putting the welfare of the girls first, moving from minor school to minor school. Reading not very far between the lines, it was clear that her high moral and ethical standards and sense of mission often brought her into conflict with her bosses and with parents. Her references, by now, must have characterized her as a troublemaker; she frequently applied for jobs at more established schools but her applications were always rejected. She certainly seemed to have been much readier to rock the boat as she grew older. As a governess she had had her own views on the behaviour of her employers but at the time she had kept them to herself. Not so as a housemistress, and I could quite see why her bosses found her a pain.

She was also, apparently, skint. Naturally she didn't mention money directly, but her infrequent holidays were always 'thanks to the kindness of an ex-pupil'. She wouldn't have had a personal pension; governesses didn't, and the schools she worked in didn't sound generous or fair employers. The only comparatively cheerful thing in the last chapters of that gloomy book was that the Sherwins offered her the lodge. *Kind friends, discovering that I lacked a place of my own for half-terms and school holidays, came to the rescue and I was soon established, at a peppercorn rent, in a delightful lodge just outside a quiet Warwickshire village, where I hope to finish my days when I grow too old to work.* And even this pale shaft of cheer, of course, was to be blacked out by landowner Charlotte.

I finished reading at three and felt so depressed by her miserable life that I made myself a three-decker cheese, ham, pickle and mayonnaise sandwich. She'd really cocked up. At seventy she had no man, no friends, very little money, an entirely unsuccessful career full of ideological battles lost before the first shot was fired and a rented lodge torn from her when she was too old to transplant.

It would be hardly surprising if she disintegrated altogether into fantasy; the fantasy that she knew a secret that would give her power and, perhaps, money. She was beginning to give me the creeps. I hate failure and suffering and I won't stand by to comfort people as they go down for the third time. I've had too much of it.

I went to bed, hoping to sleep, but I couldn't. I wouldn't have been surprised if I'd thought about Miss Potter, but it was long-ago Rosalind I couldn't get out of my mind. That surprised me. I held no brief for Rosalind, who was as far as I knew merely one of Barty's Sloanes with a fifties hairstyle, a nipped-in waist, a circle-stitched bra and high heels. But I knew all about relocation, being thrust into different households with different rules. I had got used to it, acquired survival techniques: it never got any easier, though, and you always trod on toes and got slapped down and pushed away for it and spent nights trying to cry in silence so that no one knew you were upset because the last thing foster-parents could bear was the failure of their kindness. If they thought you weren't happy, most of them took it out on you. The exceptions were even worse. Some foster-parents enjoyed it.

How had the Sherwins been? Would Laura, as Revill suggested, have delighted in a sobbing niece? Did handsome Rollo's unimaginably roving eye come to rest on toothsome Rosalind? No, that wasn't right. I worked on an incest doco once and I can still remember one page of my notes, which just read:

IMPOTENCE = INCEST

Simplistic, but fair enough for a rule of thumb. So, no interference from Rollo, but maybe no interest either. Miss P. ignored her, for whatever high-minded reasons she gave herself. So Rosalind ended up with slimy Patrick. That could only have made her unhappy, and surely, in the fifties and delicately nurtured by moralistic Miss P., guilty.

Eventually I slept, lulled by the familiar sounds of shattering glass and fists on flesh as the local disco let out.

Chapter Nine

I woke up more convinced than ever that Miss Potter was coming unglued at the seams. Yes, she probably did know something: no, she wouldn't tell me. She wanted me around to talk at. Even if I did produce Toad, she'd find a pretext for continuing to sort through the contents of the knitting-basket she called her head. Meanwhile, I'd have to get on as quickly as I could without her. Resigned to making the best of it, I checked the action board as I ate my breakfast toast.

> *Retry Rosalind*
>
> *Retry Met Police*
>
> *? get pic of Revill? ask Barty. Looks a wreck now, depends on slant of piece*
>
> *Pursue Lally*
>
> *? Paxtons*

The butter was rancid. It suited my mood when I was reminded that Lally hadn't got in touch. More coffee, then I rang her at Christie's. She'd called in sick but she'd left a message for me: she'd ring me soon. I didn't have her home number and the receptionist wouldn't divulge it.

I groaned and tried Rosalind's number in Crete. No answer.

My next call was more successful. I got through to Ready Eddy Barstow, one of my police contacts, and faced a meet for a drink that evening. He'd help me if he could. He's a great networker: I haven't yet found a branch of the police where someone doesn't owe him one, or two, or three, and all I wanted was for him to cast an eye over the Sherwin files and give me anything H. Plowright hadn't got.

Then I popped over to Barty's. He was on the phone again. I sat on the pile of Samy boxes and waited. Annabel fetched a coffee.

'Right, Alex,' he said finally, replacing the receiver. Annabel had remembered I take three sugars. She was looking very beautiful in the kind of skirt middle-aged women with bad legs call indecent, but Barty didn't look up when she came in, nor did his eyes follow her to the door. No sign of a foxtrot in the offing. 'Nice to see you, but why are you here?'

'Two things. First, I need you to fix an appointment for me with Stephanie Paxton Forsythe.' I gave him both numbers and reminded him who she was, and watched with a mixture of respect and irritation while he got her on the London number and went into his charm routine. After a few minutes of blag he covered the mouthpiece with his hand. 'Now?' he said. 'OK to go straight over now?'

'Great.' Some more blag, then he rang off.

'She sounds a good prospect. A natural talker. Off you go.'

'There's something else,' I said. 'I want advice about Miss Potter. I'm worried that she's not a reliable source. I spent last evening with her. She kept belting back sherry and talking about the Festival of Britain, the new Elizabethan age, the homeless on the South Bank, the betrayal of the aristocracy, the welfare state, and the plight of the unemployed. I've never known her type to say anything about the unemployed except that they should get on their bikes and stop spending their dole money on drink. I think she's cracking up. She's alone in that big house that isn't even hers, feeding someone else's cats, surrounded by someone else's furniture. She's upset and she's rambling and I'm not sure she isn't keeping me on a string just to have someone to ramble at. You know her better than I do. How likely is she to invent secrets to make herself important?'

'Very unlikely.'

'How likely is she to disintegrate?'

'Very unlikely.'

'She's old, homeless and lonely.'

'Still very unlikely. She's unimaginably honest, unimaginably tough.'

Perhaps Lemaire's adjective was contagious, I thought, irritated, then saw I was being unreasonable. I'm often annoyed by people I like when they behave predictably, and Barty had just been too Bartyish. He exaggerates and romanticizes, and his geese are always a flight of wild swans. Still, if you extract the square root of his assessments they're usually on target. 'OK. She can have her head for a bit. Can I borrow your car, after I've seen Stephanie?'

'Why?'

'Miss Potter wants to visit the house where she grew up.'

'What the hell for?'

'Maybe because she's jerking me about. Unimaginably.'

Stephanie's flat was enormous. Two whole floors of an Eaton Square house. The hall and drawing-room was all I saw. The drawing-room was L-shaped, interior-decorated in shades of peach and cream, with the kind of over-long curtains that follow me about the carpet and trip me up when I don't look where I'm putting my boots. There were two huge sofas, facing each other squarely as if shaping up for a shoot-out, in front of the most hideously ornate marble mantelpiece I had ever seen. It looked like a Borgia tomb. There were plenty of antique tables and chairs, and everywhere there were photographs in silver frames. Apparently the Forsythes had lots of children, both male and female.

A natural talker, Barty'd said. He wasn't wrong. Stephanie made Polly look like Eastwood's Man with No Name. 'How do you do, Miss Tanner?' she began. 'Coffee or tea? Magda'll make it for us – MAGDA! Coffee, please, and lots of it, I hate London in November, don't you? The damp soaks into the bone, what a smashing jacket though, let me hang it up, do you have a motorbike? I've always wanted a bike.' She was built for leathers, broad, squat, bony. They'd have suited her much better than the wool skirt and Liberty blouse she was wearing. She had short pepper-and-salt hair and a wide face that looked as if it had endured fifty years of sunbathing, hunting, shooting, and fishing. Out of it, dark currant eyes sparkled with curiosity. 'Lucky you caught me this morning. I'm just off to Scotland. I know, I know, Scotland in November, but there you are, my daughter's about to have a baby.'

'Congratulations,' I mumbled.

'Nothing to do with me. Right. I know nothing at all about the murder, I'm afraid, but if it's background you want, just ask. Oh good, coffee. Have a croissant or three. Is that a tape recorder? Are you going to tape me? Why not. You won't use my name, though, will you? A source close to the family, something like that?'

I nodded non-committally and started the tape. I was discon-certed by her readiness to co-operate, and confused by the discrepancy between the surroundings and the woman. She wasn't a peach and cream type. 'Charming room,' I said.

'Thank you. Nothing to do with me. I hate interior decorating, don't you? So tedious, choosing patterns and colour-schemes. I just tell the chap to get on with it.' And sign the cheque at the end, I thought. 'So,' she went on lighting a cigarette, 'where shall I start? I don't know how much you know.'

'I've read Lemaire's book, and I've spoken to some people. You just talk, and I'll say if you've lost me. How well do you remem-ber the summer and autumn of 1958?'

'Frightfully well. I remember most things frightfully well. It's probably because I don't have much brain. Nothing going on inside, d'you see? So I notice things.' I didn't believe her about the brain: she had accountant's eyes, shrewd and assessing.

'You were a friend of Rosalind's?'

'In a way. I was Laura's *effort*. You know who I mean by Laura?' I nodded. 'Even Laura knew she had to do *something* for Rosalind apart from lie on the sofa and weep, so I was it. A Young Person for Rosalind.'

'Was Lady Sherwin ill?'

'No. Spoilt, idle and vain. Nose put out of joint by Rollo, who was a bit much, I suppose. Affairs all over the place. Very attractive, of course, and rather kind, when he could be bothered. Rosalind said he Understood her. Mind you, we were at the age where one thinks people Understand one if they don't actually leave the room when one talks. But he was kind to her, I think. Especially latterly, when she was so depressed.'

'Why was she depressed?'

Stephanie lit another cigarette. 'This and that,' she said. 'Laura was rather a bitch to her. Jealous, of course. Rosalind was lovely, have you seen photographs?' I nodded. 'I wasn't,' she said. 'My nickname was Pudding, for obvious reasons.'

'Was Rosalind's depression anything to do with her affair with Patrick Revill?'

She took it in her stride. 'Have you spoken to Rosalind?'

'Not yet. I will be. I've seen Patrick Revill, though.'

'Ghastly man. I wouldn't know anything about an affair, you'll have to talk to Rosalind about that. Actually I think she was depressed by a combination of Laura, the weather and the defection of her governess. Odd woman. After Rosalind's parents were murdered by Mau Mau, she looked after her, and ran the Kenya house. They were very close. Then, back in England, the governess devoted herself to the children, the four little girls. Would hardly speak to Rosalind. Rosalind took it badly. She was very much Miss – Potter, was it? Miss Potter's product. Frightfully high-minded. Determined to get her A Levels, go to medical school and be part of the reconstruction of England. I said, why bother, she'd only get married, and she said, she actually said, *Noblesse oblige*. I thought that was a bit much, frankly, specially since she wasn't strictly speaking noblesse at all. Her father was a second son, to start with, and it was only a recent barony, bought with money from that disgusting tonic stuff all the Victorians drank. Her great-grandfather's invention. Imperial Tonic, solid alcohol I expect. They mostly were. Alcohol and iron. The Victorians belted it back by the gallon, it probably blurred their sorrows, and they needed that, poor things. But it was trade, there's no getting away from it, not noblesse at all.'

The point was evidently close to Stephanie's heart. I agreed, as fervently as I could manage, that indeed it was trade, wishing as I spoke that I had been born to it. Then I would have a trust fund and top quality beige Wilton throughout my flat.

'So I told her to abandon high-mindedness and marry a duke. She could have. She was pretty enough. But surely that's nothing to do with the murder?'

'I don't know,' I said. 'The better the background, the better the piece.'

'You know your business, I suppose. Have another croissant.'

I did. 'So she was rather unusual?'

'Who?'

'The governess, Miss Potter. She saved Rosalind's life in Kenya, didn't she?'

'Bundled her into a cupboard or something, while her parents were being chopped up. Mind you, that's what they were used to, governesses, poor things. Keeping themselves quiet in a restricted space.' Stephanie gave a snort that made me jump, then I realized she was laughing. 'And dissimulation, of course, and tightrope walking. Ghastly job. Neither one thing nor the other. Living in the rift between Us and Them.'

As one of Them, I was unmoved by this description of the governess's plight. Don't tell me it wouldn't have been a sight harder being a scullery-maid. 'Did Rosalind miss Kenya? You say she didn't like the weather in England?'

'She missed it dreadfully. She talked about it all the time. She called it "home", and she kept telling me about the rainy season and her dog and her friend Fiona. August that year, she and Laura and the little girls came to stay with us at the seaside in Wales, and Rosalind was particularly mizz. There were lots of young people, we'd known each other for years, and she felt left out. I think she'd been a bit of a star at home, popular, no party complete without her, you know the sort of thing. She had the wrong swimsuit.'

'How do you mean?'

'You know what it's like at that age, you have to have exactly the right clothes, what everyone else is wearing. Like a uniform.

She had the wrong swimsuit and she complained about the rain and the sand in the sandwiches. She talked about Kenya and the beach parties she'd been to at – is it Malindi? She kept saying all those names, like a nun with the rosary.'

'Names?'

'Places in Kenya. Naivasha and Muthaiga and the Aberdares. And she kept trailing off to the telephone—'

Stephanie checked herself too late. 'To ring Patrick Revill?' I said.

'You'll have to ask Rosalind about that,' she repeated. 'She could have been ringing her grandfather, she was fond of him, Laura bitched at her non-stop, I remember. The telephone kiosk was next to the ice-cream stall. Rosalind pretended she was buying ice-cream and Laura kept saying she'd get fat. "Poor Rosalind, you'll look like Moby Dick," and so on. Nonsense, of course. Rosalind had a beautiful figure.'

'Rollo didn't help?'

Another snort. 'He wasn't there. He never came to Wales. As that housekeeper would have said, he had Better Fish to Fry.'

'The housekeeper?'

'The Sherwins' housekeeper. Name like Crimp. Frightful woman, completely out of hand. Gossiped all the time. Laura made no attempt to keep her in order, or her husband, the smug and incompetent Mr Whatsit. Laura was too idle, she was terrified they'd leave, and she'd have to get off the sofa and run the house. Not that she could've, mind you. When Rollo finally put his foot down over the hunt ball, she could no more have organized it than fly in the air. Mummy had to do it.'

'So the hunt ball wasn't usually held at Ashtons Hall?'

'Never. Always at a hotel. But Rollo lost patience with Laura, finally. There was talk of a divorce.'

'This was when?'

'Autumn 1958.'

Stephanie lit another cigarette and looked at me expectantly.

'Did Rollo have another woman?' I asked.

'Must have. Rollo always had another woman. If you mean

was there someone he wanted to marry, I don't know. I never heard a name.'

I stayed another hour with Stephanie, recording all the time. Latterly I found it hard to concentrate. She was giving me too much, and I was tense in case I missed a vital question. I could listen to the tape again and again, of course, but what I didn't ask she couldn't tell me. In self-defence, I asked about everyone: the little girls; Rosalind's grandfather Colonel Farrell; Dr Bloom; Miss Potter, Rollo and Laura again. Finally, I took her through the night of the ball.

As I prepared to leave, I felt uneasy. I should have been pleased, I had scads of material, but I was suspicious of her helpfulness. She wasn't the sort of person who cared about seeing her words in print: she didn't have time to fill: she didn't seek attention. Did she have an axe to grind? If so, what was it?

I asked her and she answered my question with a question.

'You haven't talked to Charlotte Mayfield yet?'

'Not yet.'

'A treat in store,' she said, and gave her snorting laugh.

'Why is that?'

'You'll see,' she said. 'Frightful woman.'

'You did say she was an unpleasant child.'

'Frightful child. Pot-hunter. Always bought made ponies.' I wrote that down for later translation by Barty: I didn't want to remind her that we weren't soulmates. 'Not that I ever rode, myself. Hate horses, stupid animals, but it was the principle of the thing. Same as the tray.'

I wrote that down too, for later translation, then realized that she was waiting for me to ask. She was no longer, apparently, speaking in Pony Club code. 'The tray?' I said.

'Last year. Charity do, in the country. Warwickshire Dialysis Association. Raffle. First prize, a Georgian silver tray. Worth a bit. Charlotte won it, and kept it.'

I'd have kept it. What the hell else do you do? 'Instead of . . .' I fished, and pretended to cough.

'Exactly, giving it back, to be sold for the charity funds. All those dicky kidneys needing machines, and all Charlotte says is thank you very much. The local MP's wife.'

Put like that, I could see the point. 'Didn't Mr Mayfield . . . ?'

'He wasn't there. Seldom is. I wouldn't be.' Another snort. 'Can't stand the woman. No manners. She won't like an article like this. That answer your question?'

Chapter Ten

'What a charming car, my dear. What is it called? Is it yours?' inquired Miss Potter, hung-over but game. Barty's car is a top-of-the-range BMW. The day I can afford a BMW will probably also be the day I'm appointed Director-General of the BBC, but I don't suppose Miss P. knows how much cars cost. She was probably nervous being driven by a woman, too: that generation often are.

'It's a German car, a BMW,' I said. 'I'm a very safe driver: I've had a licence since 1979, and no accidents. I'll take care of you.'

She didn't comment on the fact that I'd arranged to see her at ten and it was now nearly one: perhaps she didn't notice it. I didn't mention I'd seen Stephanie. Until Miss Potter started talking sense I was operating on a need-to-know basis.

I explained I'd borrowed the car and asked for directions for her sentimental journey. She couldn't give them so I took the address and tracked it down with the help of my A-Z. On the way, I told her about Lally. I had to give her something to keep her quiet about Toad: even through her hangover she was determined to press me, and more worried than ever. 'Terrible things can happen to young girls,' she said, and 'we live in a decadent society', and 'I've heard Toad speak of Lally, of course. I understand her grandfather was a tribal chieftain in South Africa.' In a pig's eye, I thought, with a name like Lambert. He had to be a descendant of slaves. Not that it mattered.

Eventually I managed to reassure her. I said, as convincingly as I could manage, that I was absolutely sure Toad was safe. She believed me. I almost believed me. I couldn't afford not to.

Then we talked about cars, my not being able to afford one

and her conviction that in any case I would be better off on a bicycle.

'Healthy exercise, Alex. I have always urged my pupils to ride bicycles as much as possible. The Sherwin children were particularly keen. We used to ride our bicycles to church every Sunday, for instance. The elder ones and I. Candida was too young.' Since she was hung-over I did not tell her that riding a bicycle in London was a short-cut to death by accident or asphyxia.

Blenheim Road was tucked away off Putney Hill, quiet, tree-lined, improved, insured, neighbourhood-watched, semi-detached. The houses would cost over two hundred thousand, even now with the housing market so depressed that my flat is actually worth less than the mortgage I'm struggling to pay.

'What number?'

'We never used the number. My mother called it Simla. The house on the left, with the red door.' I parked as close as possible; curtains twitched. It was the kind of street where people reckoned they owned the pavement and the road. Pretty soon, someone would come out and ask, rudely in a polite tone, if they could help us. Miss Potter looked green; she had hardly spoken on the way over. I thought she might be sick.

'It's still called Simla,' I said to distract her. The sign looked new and too bright, like a Heritage version of a 1920s original.

'It's the same sign repainted,' said Miss Potter, trying ineffectually to open the window on her side. I pressed buttons at random – I don't borrow the BMW very often – and managed to find the right one. She gulped the cold, damp air with relief. 'My mother was very attached to it.'

'The house? I can see why.'

'No, my dear. The sign. Do you mind if we just sit here for a moment or two? I feel a little unwell.'

'Have a barley sugar.' She accepted it with delight, even from the crumpled bag I extracted from a pocket of my jeans.

'The familiar companion of many a long-ago journey,' she said. 'I always used to carry them. I suffer from motion sickness; barley sugar was my standby, even in the Bay of Biscay.' She breathed deeply and looked less green. 'My mother treasured the sign, as I said. She had it specially made at Mr Brown's hardware shop on the Hill. I noticed as we passed that it is now a takeaway restaurant called the Laughing Potato. She chose the name Simla; her father was in the Indian Civil Service and she had happy memories of her stay in the hill station. They used to go up to the hills in the summer, you see, because of the heat. Europeans, particularly women, found the heat most trying. My mother had several proposals of marriage in Simla.'

'Is that where she met your father?'

'I had a very happy childhood. My father was in the Navy, so he was often away, sometimes for years at a time, but my mother and I were happy alone. We could have a light supper on trays. I loved my father, but the household was happier when he was not there. He made things uncomfortable, somehow. My mother behaved differently, more stiffly, perhaps. I thought that that was because men were so important, and because he was such an important man. I had no idea that there were difficulties . . .'

'But there were?'

'So I was told. Much later. In the summer of 1958, my Aunt Anna, my mother's sister, invited me to stay in her house in Tunbridge Wells. By then my parents had been dead for nearly twenty years. It was a most difficult visit. She was a widow. She drank gin and smoked cigarettes incessantly, and she said my father had been – no good in bed, that he had been a snobbish, pretentious, paranoid tyrant, and my mother had been in love with the vicar.'

'Umm,' I said. 'Was she?'

'Perhaps infatuated. She always said he was wise and good. He had freckles, and damp hands, and he used to lead us in prayer after tea. Alex? Are you all right?'

'Barley sugar stuck in my throat, Miss Potter.'

She thumped me on the back and I nearly, really, choked.

'Aunt Anna also told me that my life's work in education had been a narrow, fruitless self-delusion bred of fear and that Rosalind was a spoiled brat who needed a good spanking. I found the bread-and-butter letter for that visit hard to write . . . It was a particularly hard time for me to discover that my childhood view of my parents had been entirely misconceived.'

I shifted in the driving seat. How much more rope should I allow her? I couldn't see the relevance of anything she said, but that might merely be because I didn't know enough yet, and at least I wasn't getting a polished, self-indulgent official version. She seemed genuinely upset, and her memories were jerking out like rusty water from a disused pump, as if for the first time. I'd go with it a little longer. 'Do you think your aunt was right?' I said.

'Have you read the writings of Freud and his disciples?'

'Not Freud himself. I've read about him.'

'Long experience with children has convinced me that there is much to be said for his views. Not, perhaps, in their entirety, but nevertheless . . . Children invent their own world. I was no exception.'

'Right,' I encouraged meaninglessly.

'Forgive me, my dear. It's too much, all at once. I can't . . . put my thoughts in order.'

'Don't try,' I said as reassuringly as I could. 'Have another barley sugar. There's plenty of time.'

She patted my knee with a gloved hand. I nearly jumped. She wasn't a natural toucher. 'You're a remarkably kind young woman,' she said. 'A remarkable young woman in many ways.'

'I'm very ordinary,' I said. Sometimes I'm startled into truth.

'But you'll allow me my own opinion.' She had beautiful, bright blue eyes which glinted when she smiled, I noticed for the first time. Perhaps it was the first time she had smiled. I smiled back. 'I have a confession to make,' she went on. 'I had drunk rather a lot of sherry last night. I expect you noticed. I'm not used to sherry. I talked a great deal of nonsense.'

'Not nonsense.'

'Bear with me. It must have sounded like nonsense. I am, at present, very confused, never a happy state. I can't remember exactly why I asked you to bring me here this morning; I can only suppose I thought I would find it comforting to see the house again.'

'And it isn't comforting?'

'It isn't – anything. I can remember living here, of course, but only as if – as if someone I knew well had grown up here and described it to me.'

'Has the house changed much?' It was tarted-up, with those swagged curtains that look like Shirley Temple's knickers, a polished brass door-knocker and a bright pillar-box door guarded by two bay-trees.

'Yes. And no. It looks much brighter, like a house in a television advertisement. It looks – smart. My mother wouldn't have liked it, I think. It stands out. My mother always said that no lady should draw attention to herself.' She sat in silence for a while.

'And that's partly what's worrying you?' I suggested finally. She looked blank. 'I know you're concerned about Toad, but the Sherwin murder upsets you as well, doesn't it? You may get plenty of attention when the piece is published. Does that worry you?'

'I haven't even considered that aspect of the matter.'

'Then tell me what you're really worried about. What is the worst thing you can think of that will happen? It won't seem so bad if you talk about it.'

'That is the modern theory. I have no reason to suppose it correct. Discussing something unpleasant can't change it but it can cause a great deal of unhappiness, to oneself and to others.'

'Most of the people concerned are dead,' I said. 'I expect the murderer's dead, isn't she? Or he? And it was all a terribly long time ago.'

'I am not concerned about the – murderer.' She found the word difficult to say. I gave her another barley sugar.

'Try to put me in the picture,' I said. 'Tell me what's upsetting you.'

'I failed in my duty,' she said. I kept quiet, willing her on. She was silent. A clumsy prompt would derail her: I shut my eyes and tried to transmit waves of uncritical sympathy. Nothing. Finally, I had to speak.

'Your duty to . . .'

Half her answer surprised me. 'To Rosalind. And to Colonel Farrell.'

And that was it. She wouldn't explain, expand, or do anything except make general conversation.

The visit to Simla got me bloody nowhere, which is what I'd expected. We were back at Penelope's by three. I parked and waited for her to get out. I was itching to get home, to see if there was a message from Lally and to try Rosalind in Crete again, and to get on with it, if Miss Potter wouldn't come through. 'Here we are,' I said heartily. 'Back home.'

'I can see that, my dear.' She sat on. 'I don't want to be alone.'

'I have a job to do, Miss Potter.'

'Your task is research, is it not? About the Sherwin tragedy?'

'Of course.'

'Then your place is with me. I have the information you seek.'

'So tell me,' I said. 'You're stringing me along.'

'No. Not deliberately, I assure you. It is not easy for me.' She was trembling. 'I have never spoken about that time. I have tried not even to think of it. I only met you the day before yesterday.'

'Would you prefer to talk to Barty?'

'Certainly not. He is a man.' I sighed. 'I can see you find me annoying, Alex. However, it has long been a principle of mine to take no action when I don't know what action to take. More importantly, I need to get to know you.'

'Don't you know me well enough yet?'

'Not quite.'

I sighed again. 'You'll have to excuse me now, Miss Potter. Why don't you come to supper tonight? Nothing fancy, I don't cook, but I might have some news for you about Toad by then.'

No message from Lally: no answer from Rosalind's number in Crete. I settled myself at the kitchen table with my notes, the Lemaire book and my tape of Stephanie. It was time I got a mental picture of Oliver Farrell. I could see why Miss Potter felt guilty about Rosalind, but couldn't see where Farrell came in.

Lemaire had liked him, which put me off at the start. He referred to him several times as a *simple, upstanding soldier*. Simplicity has never seemed to me an asset, except in animals and children. Adults should know better. And in my experience *upstanding* means too stupid or stubborn to see that now is the time for all sane men to press themselves to the earth while heavy artillery, literal or figurative, whistles overhead. Lemaire's description of Farrell's achievements in the army confirmed my intuition. He had gone in at Gallipoli leading 240 men and four officers and come out with eleven men, one officer, and a horse. Lemaire didn't say whether it was a liberated Turkish horse, or Farrell's own. His own, I decided, and he'd gone into action upsitting on it.

His incompetence extended into civilian life, judging from Stephanie's description, which I hunted through the tape to find. It was tucked away after Magda's arrival with further supplies of coffee and croissants and before Stephanie described the night of the ball. 'Rosalind adored him – when she first arrived he was her only ally in the house. Not much use, though, 'cos everyone bullied him, especially the Crimps. He had no money at all, I don't think, and he was frightfully anxious not to get in anyone's way and to earn his keep. He haunted the stables and looked after the children's ponies. But he doted on Rosalind. He organized a kind of reception committee for her, apparently. When Rollo fetched her from the station. He'd made a banner – something like WELCOME DARLING ROSALIND – but it was too big and he got tangled in it, and Laura fainted, or pretended to. She wasn't a welcoming person, she was probably bored. Rosalind never forgot it, though. She always took his side against Laura. He felt very ill at ease at Ashtons. Anyone could see that. Rosalind said he was constantly making financial calculations in a Woolworth's notebook, trying to work out how he could afford a place of his own, but he was completely skint. He'd had enough to live on after his wife died but he invested it all in some scheme organized by an 'absolutely reliable' old friend. The old friend skipped to Spain with Oliver's money, as they reliably do.'

'How did Rollo feel about him?'

'Quite liked him, I think. He was good with horses. But Laura sniped at him in her quiet, sweetly bitchy way.'

'So there'd be no motive for him to kill Rollo?'

'Good God, no. He wouldn't have killed anything.'

'But he was a soldier?'

'Not a soldier. An officer.' Snort. 'He was very sweet.'

There was silence, and then a slurping sound as I drank coffee. I hadn't then, and I couldn't now, think of anything else to ask about Farrell. Instead, I called Barty. 'Hi, it's Alex. What's a made pony?'

'Give me a context.'

'Charlotte Sherwin as a child.'

'A "made" pony is already schooled. You don't have to work with it, you just win prizes – at shows or gymkhanas, whatever – straight away. Considered rather bad form, because you're using money to avoid doing the work. Bypassing the sweaty effort. Frowned on by genuine pony devotees, and ambitious mothers who would buy made ponies for their offspring if they could.'

'And a pot-hunter?'

'One who wants to win prizes, in any way they can. Probably a bad loser, whipping the pony who fails, stamping of feet and swinging of pigtails.'

'Thanks. Bye.'

'Take care.'

Ready Eddy was early. He sat at the usual table at my local, sinking a pint of Newcastle Brown and ignoring the pharmaceutical transactions at the bar. I've known him nearly ten years, ever since I went for a spin round the block with his youngest son Peter. He gets shorter and fatter but not older, though he must be coming up for retirement soon, and he's a superintendent now. He wears hideous light grey synthetic suits. His face is round, red, genial, his hands and neck hairy, his eyes piggy and sharp. Right now, they were eyeing up a tarty middle-aged blonde. He has astonishing success with women, hence, I suppose, the nickname. I fetched a lager and joined him. 'Hi, Eddy. What is it with you and sex?'

'Simple,' he said. 'I like it.'

'But how do you get so much?'

'I put the question to every woman I meet over thirty and under sixty.'

'And if they say no?'

'I wait, a bit, then put the question again. And I always say thank you nicely.'

'Even if it's terrible?'

'No such thing as terrible sex. How about it, Alex?'

'No, thanks, Eddy. I'm not thirty yet.'

'I'll be back to you. What else can I do you for?'

I explained, fetched him another pint, explained some more. He kept watching the blonde. I could only tell he was listening to me from his questions. 'Right,' he said finally. 'I'll give you a bell, let you know. Now bugger off, I've important matters in hand. I hope.'

There was still no message from Lally and when Miss Potter arrived for supper she spent ten minutes fretting about Toad. Then she made a social effort, and said she liked my flat: she ate lasagne, praised it, refused yoghurt, accepted an apple which she dealt with precisely, the unbroken peel curling round her neat fingers. After supper she sat in her usual upright posture on my *Sunday Times* special offer sofa, legs crossed at the ankle and tucked away to one side, hands folded in her lap. She wore a good tweed skirt, thick woollen stockings, a blue sweater in what looked like cashmere and a darker blue silk scarf folded round her neck and fastened with a hammered silver brooch. Her thick grey hair, usually carefully scraped back and gathered into a high bun, was tonight in a looser bun at the nape of her neck. Seventy or not, I'd have bet Ready Eddy would've had a go. I wished I could see it.

I still didn't tell her I'd seen Stephanie Forsythe: I wanted to listen to the tape a few more times and work out some killer questions. I just kept topping her up with cheap wine and let her talk about the Sherwins. 'Charlotte was a thoroughly unpleasant child. Penelope, on the other hand, is delightful. Such a pity you haven't time to meet her. She may very well have important background information. She's much too sensitive: utterly ill-equipped for life in this, or any other, society. It is very fortunate that she was cushioned by circumstances. She married a bluff, kind man and worried over her children's schools. Now she reads books, and dreams.'

'Haven't you talked to her about the murder yourself?'

'Certainly not.'

'I expect Rosalind will be useful,' I said, fishing. As always, the name upset her. She went pink and her lips trembled. 'I've got her phone number but nobody's answered yet. She lives in Crete. I got the impression she'd been there for a while.'

'I had no idea,' she said, shocked. 'In Crete?'

'Why does it matter?'

'I don't suppose it does, now. It's rather ironic. After Lord Sherwin's death, I resolved never to see her or speak about her again. Accordingly, I avoided the places where she might reasonably have been found.'

'What places?'

'Kenya, of course. London, as you know.'

'And you never went back to Kenya either?' That must have been a real sacrifice. She had a crush on the place.

'Never,' she said. 'I was quite sure that a complete break between us was necessary.'

'For her sake?'

'Mainly.' Entirely for Rosalind's sake, I'd guess, if she could still upset Miss P. so completely. And she'd given up Kenya. I hoped it would turn out to have been worth it.

'What did Rollo's death have to do with her?'

'I'm not sure I can answer you directly.'

'Answer me indirectly then.'

'It started, I suppose, in Kenya. In 1958. When I received the

80

letter from Laura. I'd hoped that Rosalind would attend a local white school for her A levels, go to England for her medical training, then return to Kenya and make her home there. I would meanwhile seek employment in Kenya, as governess or teacher. There were possibilities. I was determined to remain accessible to Rosalind as long as she needed me. I was, effectively, the family she knew.'

'What did Laura say in her letter?'

'Perhaps I will show it to you, one day. I never look at it, myself. I don't need to. Several of the phrases burnt themselves into my memory at first reading.'

I poured more wine. 'Just give me the gist.'

'The gist was that Laura needed a governess for her own children and it was time that Rosalind returned to civilization and rid herself of me. It was a warning to me, not to presume on my position, not to cling to Rosalind, not to seek to preserve an inappropriate intimacy.'

'Was the intimacy inappropriate?'

'I did not believe so. Further acquaintance with Laura led me to the view that, to her, all intimacy was inappropriate and distasteful, including that between husband and wife or mother and child. But at the time her letter had a profound effect on me.'

'It cut you off from Rosalind.'

'It led me to undue caution. It led me to distrust my motives and my judgement. It led me to refuse confidences from Rosalind, with tragic results. But it would not be fair to place all the responsibility for my attitude to Rosalind on Laura's intervention. It went deeper than that. To a certain extent, I suppose it would be true to say that I lost my faith.'

'Your faith in God?'

'Not exactly,' said Miss Potter. 'My faith in maps.'

'Maps? I love maps. You can find out where you are and where everything else is in relation to you; then you can plan how to get there without hanging round, waiting for other people to give directions.

'I am speaking metaphorically, referring to the map you are

given by your parents during your upbringing. Their view of the world, how it is ordered and arranged, and how you should make your way through it. I'm sure it's necessary for you to understand, Alex. It is important to me that you do.'

'So you felt you'd wasted your time, looking after Rosalind? Or being a governess at all?'

'Not wasted my time, precisely. Perhaps I felt . . .'

'Unappreciated? By Laura?'

'Again, not precisely. I would not, in any case, have valued Laura's appreciation. No. I was disappointed in Rosalind.'

'Rosalind in England?'

'Yes.'

'Because of the affair she was having with Patrick Revill?'

'I have already told you, that's impossible.'

'What then? Why were you disappointed in her?'

She got up and began clearing supper away, stepping over and around me in the confined space, then moving into the kitchen. I heard a gasp and the sound of plates clattering on the table.

'Something wrong?' I said, joining her. She was gazing at the beach photograph of Rosalind on my project board.

'She looks so unhappy,' she said.

Now was the time to push. 'She must have been very lonely.'

'I fear she was. She found a friend in Stephanie Paxton, of course. And she became very fond of Penelope.'

'Penelope was a child.'

'Children can be comforting companions,' she said in a tone which, in a lesser woman, would have been wistful. Her gaze had shifted to Rollo, I noticed. 'I believed, at the time, I was acting in Rosalind's best interests. Looking back, I see how distressed she must have been.'

Stephanie had said Rosalind was especially miserable in Wales, I remembered. With Laura, and the little girls – but she hadn't mentioned Miss Potter. 'When was that photograph taken?' I asked.

'August 1958.'

'Where were you?'

'I was at Ashtons Hall. With Colonel Farrell. The Crisps were on holiday.'

'Where was Lord Sherwin?'

Miss Potter blushed, and I decided to go for it. 'Miss Potter, did you ever sleep with him?'

Chapter Eleven

I didn't think she'd lie, I expected her to evade, but she didn't.

'No,' she said.

'Nearly?'

'That is hard to answer.' She sat at the kitchen table and I fished out another bottle of wine from the cupboard under the sink. She'd have to drink this one at room temperature and like it. 'You are right, of course, that Lord Sherwin did not go to Wales with his wife and children. However, he was away in Scotland for much of the time.'

Silence. 'But he came back?' I prompted, and pushed a full glass towards her.

'Yes. Late one evening. Colonel Farrell had gone to bed. I was in the library, reading. While Lady Sherwin was away I had the freedom of the house.' Pause. I didn't know whether to prompt her again. When the pause lasted too long, I did.

'And Lord Sherwin came in?'

'Yes. I heard his voice, calling through the house for his wife. He never remembered arrangements. I answered, and explained that the family were still away. He was pleased. He offered me a drink. He had been drinking.'

'Much?'

'Not excessively, but enough to be expansive with me. He had forgotten my name, again. He always called me "Miss Um". That night, he also called me "Miss Mouse". I made an attempt to get away. Not a very serious one. I reminded him of my name and accepted a drink. We talked.'

'What about?'

'He complained about Lady Sherwin. He spoke of plans to divorce her, sell the estate and move to Kenya. He spoke of his children. He referred to them as "the rabbits". He asked if I had ever noticed that blonde-haired children have pink noses. Then he asked me questions. About my life, my ideals. He asked me to tell him the most exciting thing that had ever happened to me, and if I had ever been in love.'

'A chat-up line? He was making a pass at you?'

'I must suppose so. I thought so at the time.'

'But you didn't respond?'

'I had nothing to say that he would understand.'

'You could have told him about Joss Erroll,' I said, half-serious.

She disregarded me. 'He said being a governess must be a crashing bore. I said it was often very fulfilling, and he laughed.'

'Were you angry, when he laughed?'

'Not exactly. I felt diminished, perhaps. He asked me why I'd never married. I couldn't answer.'

'It was because of Rosalind, really, wasn't it?' I wanted to give her a face-saving out. It sounded as if Rollo's seduction method was to reduce the object of his attentions to chopped liver.

'Partly,' she said. 'Only partly. I did have offers . . . I was waiting for a real man.'

'What's your idea of a real man? Someone like Erroll?'

'Lord Erroll was far beyond my expectations. Someone like Rosalind's father, perhaps.'

'Did he make a pass at you, too?'

'No, no, you misunderstand me. Mr Sherwin was a devoted husband. Loving. Loyal.'

'And attractive, like his brother Rollo?'

'Physically, very like Lord Sherwin.'

'Did Lord Sherwin kiss you?'

'Gently. On the forehead.' Her voice was soft, as she remembered.

Cream to soothe the chopped liver, I thought. Women were hopeless. Seventy years of potential; looks, brains, courage; and one of her high points is a drunken pass from a cheap goat like Rollo.

'Did he move down from the forehead?'

'No. I retired to my room, at that point. I was left with the distinct impression that I had received an offer which I could have accepted at a later date. What the Americans, I believe, call a "raincheck".'

'And did you cash it in?'

'I have already told you. I did not sleep with Lord Sherwin.'

'So you have.'

'That is what happened,' she said, and adjusted her scarf. 'Thank you for a delightful supper, my dear. May I help you with the washing-up?'

'Don't worry, I'll do it.'

She ignored me. 'Much better to have a clean kitchen in the morning.'

'Better still to stop running away from your bogeymen. Get it over with. Give me the information you have about the murder. Nothing is as bad as you fear it'll be.'

'Come, my dear, even at your age you must have learnt that frequently things are even worse.'

'Not with the adrenalin rush.'

'I don't understand.'

'The excitement. The thrills. You know, when you're afraid. Like parachute-jumping. Fight or flight. It's adrenalin. I worked on a programme about it last year.'

'Ah,' said Miss Potter, through washing-up noises. 'But what happens when the rush subsides?'

'You pick up the pieces.'

She left me with a very clean kitchen and a little to look forward to. Maybe I was nearer to gaining her confidence, but judging from that evening's performance, her revelations would be only tangentially related to my article. Unless I was missing something. There'd probably been more genteel hanky-panky with Rollo, though I was inclined to believe her direct statement that he hadn't bedded her. She'd have been too much like hard work for him, probably. Psalms among the pillows. Not enough, anyway, to fuel a *crime passionnel*, which in any case she couldn't have committed because then she couldn't have had a hold over Laura.

But why had Laura's suggestions of unnatural intimacy with Rosalind upset Miss Potter so much? It wasn't as if they were true. Joss Erroll, Rollo, Michael Sherwin – even Miss Potter's fantasies were heterosexual. I could see that someone of her generation might find it appalling to be gay, or even to be considered so, but enough to separate herself from the child she'd effectively adopted? And why had Laura made the suggestions at all? Just out of random malice? An easy poisoned dart to aim at a spinster governess?

I added to my action/question list.

? who/why wanted Miss P. & Ros back from Kenya? why then?
? Rollo need to sell estate if divorce? who'd mind?
? why divorce, finally? – true love for Rollo? who?

Later, I lay in my own bed in my own flat under my own duvet, too light for winter because when I'd bought it new I hadn't been able to afford a high tog one, and counted my blessings, as Miss Potter would undoubtedly have put it. Everything in my flat except the books had been bought new, even if it was not solidly made – I preferred first-hand to good workmanship. Everything was my choice, paid for by my money. I needn't be grateful to anyone for their official or unofficial generosity, and I needn't waste time appreciating it, or repay them by listening to their opinions, or dressing as they liked, or behaving as they chose.

I comforted myself like this quite often anyway, but was probably doing it now because Miss Potter's company set my personality rocking. It was so hard not to feel sympathy for her, and I couldn't afford to. If you feel too much for the hopeless cases, eventually you become drained, a hopeless case yourself. I was sure her secret would be sad and small and wouldn't comfort her. In her position, homeless, penniless, what could?

Homeless people. Homesick people. On this assignment, I kept coming across them. Long ago before the war, Miss Potter's mother, dreaming of Simla and, I supposed, the chance to make another decision, choose a different life with a different man. Rosalind and Miss Potter at Ashtons that summer, longing for Kenya. Farrell, wanting a place of his own. Rollo, wanting to leave.

The children must have been different. A country house childhood with an unloving mother, a casual father, a succession of governesses falling like skittles for a little touch of Rollo in the night: that would lead, surely, to a devotion to the house itself, their bedrooms, their dogs and ponies, the old boxes of dressing-up clothes, the trees they climbed, the view they woke to, the security the house gave them.

I still couldn't sleep. I poked my feet into the cold air of my bedroom, waggled my toes and thought about Laura's treatment of Rosalind. First she left her only sister's child to be brought up, thousands of miles away, by a governess. Then, when the child finally came back to her family, presumably hoping for a normally affectionate welcome, Laura sniped at her until Rosalind, lonely, voluntarily took up with Revill.

A callous, selfish, idle woman, Laura. Perhaps even cruel.

Which reminded me of something my mother once said. You'll have gathered that she was not generally a source of words to guide your life by, but this particular observation had stuck with me. Our tower-block neighbour was a flinty-mouthed woman who beat her children to teach them discipline, and wouldn't let them associate with me because I was 'common'. I'd cried about that, once, when I was about four, and Mum said, 'You're not common, Alex. *She's* common. It's dead common to be cruel.'

Common or not, murderer or not, Laura Sherwin was dead and I still had no angle for my piece. Nor was I getting anywhere in my quest for Toad.

The window was open, and I could see my breath drift and dissipate in the acid glow of the street light outside. I wished I could plug in to Miss Potter's mind, now. She wouldn't be sleeping either. She'd be too upset. She'd be going over her memories and some of them would be useful to me.

Chapter Twelve

I'd set the alarm for six. Greek time was two hours later than GMT: not many people are up and out by eight, and I was determined to get Rosalind before she left her house, which I imagined as one of the dazzling white cliff-side villas featured in Cretan holiday brochures. I grabbed a double-strength mug of coffee and took the phone back to bed by street-lamp light. Her phone rang and rang, the continental single tone mocking me with missed opportunity. Probably her blasted husband had died and she was flying his body back to England for burial, too upset to talk. I was so convinced there'd be no answer that it took me a while to realize that an English woman's voice was saying, 'Hello? Hello? Hello?'

'Mrs Rosalind Jennings?'

'Yes. What time is it?'

'Eight o'clock.'

'Do I know you?'

Not a good start. 'I'm sorry if I've woken you. I'm Alex Tanner, I'm a journalist and I'm calling from England. How is your husband?'

'If you've got up at six in the morning to ask me about Magnus's piles, you must be deranged,' said the voice, amused. It was an attractive voice, light and clear, with the accent of its class and generation: not the contemporary drawl, but clipped, with neutral vowels. Like Barty's.

I was relieved. Few people died of piles, and Rosalind didn't sound unduly preoccupied by Magnus's condition. 'I haven't. I spoke to someone at this number the day before yesterday. She said your husband was in hospital. I got the impression it was serious.'

'I suppose it is, for Magnus. I'm sorry, Miss Tanner, I don't talk to journalists, though come to think of it you're the first journalist who's ever wanted to talk to me.'

I was encouraged. People who don't talk to journalists don't talk to journalists full stop. They certainly don't hang around explaining their principles and situation. Female members of the upper classes find it almost impossible to sever communication abruptly, anyway, having been trained from birth as conversational geisha. 'Miss Potter asked me to call you. I'm not exactly a journalist, I'm a television researcher, but at the moment I'm working on a piece for the *Observer* on the Sherwin murder. Miss Potter said you might be able to help with background.' I had to keep her on the line. She'd talk if I could interest her. 'Miss Potter feels it's very important that the truth be told, so the family isn't hurt, and I want my piece to be as accurate as possible, and naturally you'd be a good source.'

'I'm surprised Miss P. mentioned my name. We're not on speakers, or didn't she tell you?'

'Speakers?'

'Speaking terms. She hasn't said a word to me in thirty years.'

'I gathered there was a disagreement,' I said blandly.

'I expect you did . . . Are you going to print this?'

'Not unless it's to do with the murder.'

'Not as far as I know. Look, Miss Tanner—'

'Call me Alex—'

'I didn't kill my uncle, and I don't know who did.' She didn't sound defensive: merely uninterested.

'Would it be fair to say that as far as you know, Lord Sherwin was shot by his wife?' That's what Patrick had said she thought; a way of checking on his reliability as well as her reaction.

'I suppose so, but I don't want to be quoted. I don't know. I have no evidence: I didn't then and I don't now. Does it matter?'

It is very hard to lie over the telephone. Great liars can. I can. I didn't think Rosalind could, and I believed her, so I moved on. 'Why was it exactly that you and Miss Potter came back to England when you did? Whose idea was it?'

'Partly Rollo's, I think. So I could do the season and so on. But Laura really wanted a governess for the children – governesses never stayed, apparently.'

'Why was that?'

'Not sure. Partly my uncle's tendency to make passes, plus my aunt's malicious indifference. It can't have been any fun teaching Charlotte, either. She looked like a little blonde angel but she could needle at weak spots like nobody's business. She liked to be in charge.'

I wanted to check Stephanie's reliability, so I said at random, 'Stephanie Forsythe tells me you were very fond of your grandfather—'

'She's helping you, too?' she said, surprised.

'—and that when you arrived from Kenya, he'd arranged a welcoming committee.'

Silence. Then: 'Good Lord. I'd forgotten . . . yes, of course. He made a banner. It said WELCOME MY BABY DARLING. He always called me his "baby darling". He was – a nice, nice man. The welcome went all wrong, because of the rat. Things he organized had a way of going wrong . . .'

I decided to ignore the rat. It was intriguing, but this was long-distance and I could pursue it with Miss Potter.

Casually, I slipped in, 'Patrick Revill tells me you and he had an affair, that summer.'

She laughed. 'Good Lord. I haven't thought of him for years. How is he?'

'Old. Poor. Lonely.'

'Oh dear,' she said with impersonal sympathy. 'When I first saw him he was so attractive. Absolutely to die for . . . What does Patrick and me have to do with the murder? Does it matter?'

'It does to Miss Potter. She doesn't believe it.'

'Oh yes she—' began Rosalind, remembered who I was, stopped.

I pursued. 'You thought she knew? About you and Patrick?'

'She must have done,' said Rosalind, 'otherwise why . . .'

She stopped again and I ground my teeth with frustration. I had to fill the silence, stop her ringing off, but I mustn't derail her. Did Miss Potter think Rosalind had done the murder? Was that her secret? If so, what had Patrick to do with it? Oh shit. When in doubt, state the obvious. 'She would have disapproved,' I said.

'Of course. That's why.'

I was beginning to get the point. 'That's why she stopped speaking to you?'

She let out her breath in a long sigh. She had the habit of honesty, to be expected in a pupil of Miss P.'s. Lucky Rosalind, who had lived so protected that she could afford to retain it. 'That's what I thought,' she said. 'It doesn't make sense otherwise.'

I plugged on. She agreed that Rollo had been talking about divorce before the murder, and Laura resisting it, but said she knew of no special other woman, and that Laura wouldn't accept it. I asked about a motive. 'I've no idea,' she said. 'My aunt liked her own way.'

'Enough to kill for it?'

'I can't imagine wanting anything enough to kill for it,' she said.

I could but I didn't say so. I never argue with the "unimaginable" brigade. I was, foolishly, disappointed that Rosalind had joined it: I had thought better of her. Perhaps it was the smugness of marriage and middle age. I took the next question from my list. 'What was your uncle like?'

'He was kind to me. He was attractive. A bit thoughtless, but a nice man. The older I get, the nicer I think he was.'

'How did Lady Sherwin see him?'

'I really can't . . . Other people's marriages are a mystery, aren't they?'

'What can you remember of the night Rollo died?'

'Sorry. Nothing useful. He was cross with Laura at the beginning because she didn't come down early enough. She was sulking about the ball being held in her house. Later, he danced with me twice: he was exactly his usual self. Carelessly kind. Very charming. He had a lovely voice. That's it.'

I looked at my notes. 'Why do you think Lady Sherwin married Bloom?'

'He spoilt her. He adored her: she could do no wrong. Buckets of love, admiration and approval. She was nicer, with him. He didn't expect her to be anything but beautiful. My wife the delicate aristocrat, that sort of thing. She was very idle.'

'Right. By the way—' my conscience stirred, just a little. 'Have you kept up with Charlotte at all?'

'Not much.'

'But you know her daughter Toad?'

'Poor Toad, of course.'

'Any idea where she is now?'

Silence. She was thinking. 'Penelope said she was in India or somewhere. Gap Year. But she wasn't born when Rollo was shot – what . . .'

'Never mind.' I'd been absorbing her description of Laura while I made my guilt inquiry about Toad. Now with her attention distracted, I'd try again. 'Mrs Jennings, hand on heart, do you honestly think the Laura you knew would have done anything as energetic and decisive as shooting her husband?'

'Come to think of it . . . But there was no one else, surely? Who else? No, I really mustn't speculate.'

It was no use pressing her and I wanted to keep the option of ringing back, if anything specific came up. 'I'll be seeing Miss Potter later today. Do you have any message for her?'

Long silence. 'Do you think she'd want one?'

'Yes. Yesterday, she looked at a photograph of you and said you must have been very lonely, that summer before the murder. She feels sorry about letting you down.'

'Oh, she shouldn't do that . . . If she really didn't know about me and Patrick, I can't imagine why she hasn't spoken to me since, but she must have had a reason. She was terrific, really. She brought me up. I was very fond of her. If you think she'd like a message, send her my love.'

I thanked her and rang off. If I needed her again I could always use the pretext of a real or imagined response from Miss Potter. By then it was six twenty-five and we had been talking for twenty-three minutes. I worked out the British Telecom rate for twenty-eight minutes (never raise it to a round number), logged it in my expenses sheet, made more coffee and reflected.

She didn't, deep down, think that Laura had done it. Increasingly, neither did I. Insubstantial, beautiful, probably anti-Semitic Laura who had chosen to marry an unhandsome, undistinguished Jewish doctor because she wanted to be spoilt. A woman who lay on the sofa and wouldn't reach out her hand for a magazine if she could get someone else to do it for her.

I was pleased. Stephanie was a good witness. So, making allowances for his vanity, was Patrick, and moreover one who was ready to talk and easy to reach. If Rosalind hadn't been in Crete . . . Never mind; that was always the way with hurry-up jobs, and if it wasn't a hurry-up job I wouldn't have got it.

I also had some ammunition to use on Miss Potter. I could insist, once and for all, that she accept the fact of Patrick's relationship with Rosalind; then, with luck, I'd find out why it had been so important for her not to believe it.

I had time for a long bath before my next scheduled event: the two bus rides that took me to my mother.

It was her birthday so I'd brought her two bars of nut chocolate. She has advanced Alzheimer's disease. She doesn't recognize birthdays and she doesn't recognize me but she still likes chocolate. She ate a whole pound bar as I watched. She's been in that particular hospital three years now. It's off the North Circular Road, handy for undertakers and the crematorium. It's not easy to talk to her. I've settled for pretending she understands, and I keep talking until she walks away. I reckon when she walks away I've visited long enough.

This time she hung around to hear a summary of the Sherwin murder. She liked Rollo's name and kept repeating it, rollo rollo rollo rollo rollo rollo. Then she changed it, rolo rolo rolo rolo, like the chocolate. I took the hint and gave her the rest of her present, the other pound bar of Cadbury's Whole Nut and two Mars bars. She grabbed them and shuffled away.

She used to be a pretty woman, my mother, much prettier than me. I remember how she used to look, a little, but as the years and the admissions to hospital, sectioned under the Mental Health Act ('Do you understand, Alex? It's better for both of you' – appreciative nod) ticked past, how she looks now and how she looked then got muddled. The patients in this hospital (it's not bad, as they go) are allowed their own clothes and I do buy her some, to suit her taste as far as I can remember it. Trouble is, when the clothes go to the laundry they all seem to boil down to the same colour, geriatric mud. She was wearing a summer dress, once bright green, now mud, and a thick mud cardigan I couldn't identify. It may not have been hers. She's thin and the clothes hung on her. Her back view was old.

I had a word with the nurse and left a supply of Fun-size Chocolate Bites. The nurses never have anything new to say about my mother but the least I could do was listen. I was all right, I was going to leave the decaying building with its decaying, incontinent inhabitants, and I needn't come back for another month, or for ever. I was lucky and I knew it. I felt lucky on the bus on the way back to the flat. I felt lucky when I stuffed all my clothes into the washing machine. I felt lucky in the bath as I washed away the smell.

Chapter Thirteen

I even felt lucky when I picked up my phone to try Lally at work, found she'd gone sick for a second day on the trot, and headed over to Barty's office to press Annabel into service. She'd certainly be able to get Lally's home number from someone. The door was unlocked so I went straight in. Barty was sitting at his desk firing pellets from a rubber band. He seemed to be aiming at the waste-paper basket: there was a circle of screwed-up pieces of paper round it. He looked tired, but he smiled when he saw me.

He was wearing a dark suit and a significant tie, one of those ties that other dark-suited tie-wearers greet with 'pass, friend, all's well'. That meant he was going to court, possibly as part of a pro-tracted fight to screen a documentary we'd made two years ago, about the bullying of black recruits in the Army. It didn't matter to me, I hadn't worked on a percentage.

'Suit?' I said.

'Court.'

'Want to talk about it?'

'No. Tedious.'

'OK. Annabel not in yet?'

'Do you want her?'

'Doesn't matter, it'll keep.'

'Have a chair. There's coffee in the pot.'

I took some. 'I've just been to visit my mother,' I said, surprising myself.

'Didn't know you had one.'

'She's in a mental hospital. Alzheimer's.'

'Does she know you?'

'No. It's her birthday. I took her nut chocolate.'

'Is that her favourite?'

'It always was. She scoffs it OK.'

He swivelled his chair round and aimed another pellet at the wastepaper basket. 'Are you free for dinner tonight?'

'If you want an update on the Sherwins you don't have to buy me dinner.'

'I do want an update, and you can tell me now. You don't have to be so defensive. Try for some charm of manner, girl. How about "Barty, I'd love to dine with you. What shall I wear?"'

'Barty, I'd love to dine with you. What shall I wear?'

'I've always liked you in jeans and those amusing Doc Martens.'

'Just as well.'

'But tonight, we'll go somewhere posh, and you can surprise me.'

He had certainly surprised *me*. Why Barty asked me to dinner I wasn't sure, but I wasn't going to speculate. I wasn't going to plan what to wear, because I didn't have much to choose from, and it doesn't really matter anyway what I wear, it makes so little difference. Polly always says that half the fun of going out with a man is looking forward to it and fantasizing, but I disagree. The warm fantasies make the cold reality worse. I'm not going to sit around telling stories about how passionately I'm loved and how my man can't wait to see me, while I keep one ear wagging at the silent phone.

Meanwhile I briefed Barty. He listened as impassively as my mother and he didn't even say rollo rollo rollo. When I finished, he grunted. 'I like the Miss Potter/Rosalind misunderstanding,' he said. 'If you clear it up, Miss Potter might talk. You know I never believed Laura was the killer.'

'For a really solid reason. Because you fancied her.' He ignored me. 'And now we've got evidence. Miss Potter's covering for someone, and it wouldn't be Laura. Miss P.'s a firm believer in law and order and every citizen's duty to co-operate with the police. I can see her protecting a child, just.'

'Would Rosalind count as a child? She was seventeen.'

'She'd always count as a child to Miss Potter. *I* still count as a child to Miss Potter.'

'Do you think Rosalind did it?'

'I think any adolescent can do anything. They're all barking mad. Don't you remember being that age?'

'No reason for her to shoot Rollo.'

'We don't know. If she really was having an affair with Patrick Revill she must have been a remarkable girl.'

'Why?'

'At her age, in that time, that place, that social set, I'd say it was very enterprising, particularly if she managed to keep it under wraps. Lemaire doesn't mention it, does he? I'd like to meet her.'

'I'll make sure to tell her next time we talk,' I said sniffily. 'She's nearly fifty by now, of course.'

'Where's she living, exactly?'

'In Crete, near Chania, with her husband.'

'What's his name?'

'Magnus Jennings.'

'He's a painter. Quite a good one.'

'I suppose you know him?'

'Met him once or twice. You've got to stop this, Alex.'

'Stop what?'

'Pokering up when I know people. Nobody works in television for over twenty years in a place as small as London without getting some contacts. You've plenty of your own. What about Ready Eddy? I'd trade Jennings for him any day. Get on with it, stop feeling sorry for yourself and pay another visit to Patrick.'

'Not yet. I'll drop in on Miss Potter, get her up to date on my call to Rosalind. Plus I want you to fix up something for me.' I wrote down two telephone numbers, tore the page out of my notebook, gave it to him. 'I want an interview with Charlotte Mayfield. If you set it up I'll call her and confirm a time. I need her for our piece anyway, and I might be able to get something out of her about Toad. I'd rather see her when I've heard from Lally, but I can't hang around for ever, and I have high hopes of Miss Potter this morning. Charlotte's next on my list.'

'Will do. Is she in London?'

'Dunno. I've given you both numbers, London and country.'

'Good morning, my dear.' Miss Potter looked deathly. Her face was pinched, her cheeks sunken, her skin tone greyish green. She spilt my coffee, pouring it. I pushed her gently on to a kitchen stool and wiped up the coffee.

'Did you hit the sherry again?' I asked.

'Certainly not.'

'But you didn't sleep.'

'Not a great deal. I – I'm not sure I'm – able to help you, at present. I think I shall go to bed.'

Whether her illness was psychosomatic or not, I couldn't tell, but it was real. 'Do you have a pain anywhere?'

'No. I am merely feeling unwell.'

I supposed she meant she felt nauseated. 'Will you be all right by yourself? Should I get a doctor?' I'd just as soon leave her alone to stew for a bit: it would short-circuit her attention-seeking game. She was just at the stage where a sudden withdrawal of attention on my part would irritate her into forcing her revelations on me when I reappeared, and I certainly wasn't going to tell her I'd spoken to Rosalind until she was well enough to concentrate. Her colour was worrying, though.

'I would prefer to be alone. Thank you for your consideration.'

'In that case I'll get on.'

'You are pursuing Toad?'

'Yes, I'm hoping to talk to Lally Lambert at twelve,' I half-lied.

'And where are you going now?'

'To see my policeman,' I wholly lied. I was actually heading straight back to Barty's.

He'd left for court. Annabel handed me a note.

Charlotte not keen, but will see you. She's in the country for

99

today, back here tomorrow. ? wrong way round. Ring her. Pick you up at 8. Barty

'So he's finally got up the nerve to ask you out,' said Annabel.

She was smiling, I didn't know why. It didn't seem gloating or smug, but how can you tell?

I mumbled. 'Yeah. Can you get on Lally's case for me?' I gave her the info. She smiled even more brightly at the prospect of something to do. She was underemployed. 'What does Barty mean. *? wrong way round?*' I went on.

'It's Saturday tomorrow. Odd that Charlotte Mayfield comes up to London for the weekend. Why doesn't her husband join her in the country for the weekend instead?'

'Maybe he needs to be in London for his leadership manoeuvres.'

'No one else is. Most people go to the country at weekends.'

Our social spheres were widely different, Annabel's and mine. Then I rang Charlotte Mayfield in Warwickshire and persuaded her to see me as soon as I could get there. She'd have preferred London, but I didn't want to wait, plus I'd have to see Ashtons Hall some time for atmosphere and if our interview didn't go well I might not get another chance.

She tried to block me until I said, 'Is there any particular problem in me coming to Ashtons Hall?' Then she backtracked.

'Not at all. Just that the house is closed, at present. We have builders in—'

'I don't mind at all.'

Something was spooking her. Good. Instead of slapping me down, pointing out (as I was sure was the case) that my convenience was the least of her considerations, she gave way. I looked forward to pinning down the source of her discomfort.

If Barty'd been there I'd have borrowed his BMW but I wasn't (perversely) going to accept Annabel's offered Golf GTi. I hung on for fifteen minutes on the off-chance she managed to locate Lally quickly; no luck. I left her to it.

Chapter Fourteen

On the train to Stratford, I sorted out my questions. Background and hunt ball, of course, then Miss Potter, Laura and the lodge. Whenever I could, slip in Toad. There were bound to be family pictures dotted about; courteous inquiries would be in order. She had something to hide, I knew it, otherwise she wouldn't have let me bully her about the venue for our meeting.

I felt good, every mile that choked past taking me further away from Miss Potter's irritating combination of pathos and self-righteousness and raising my spirits a notch. I was getting on with something sensible, a task with a beginning, a middle and an end.

I bought an individual pork pie and a not-at-all-Cornish pasty and gnawed my way systematically through them, washing them down with gulps of Diet Coke. I'd get to Ashtons Hall about lunchtime. If I was offered free food I'd eat it but I'd got the impression from Charlotte that I'd be lucky to be offered a drink of water.

When I'd asked for directions to Ashtons Hall Charlotte had said, 'Just give my name to the driver. Everyone knows it.' The taxi-driver didn't, of course. He was a Geordie come south to work in the building trade who had lingered in Stratford because, he said, most of the taxi-users there were over-tipping Americans or Japanese. His was the only taxi at the station. He really wanted to take me to Anne Hathaway's cottage, or, failing that, Shake-speare's birthplace. By the time I'd established the full extent of his ignorance the station was empty of passengers and the one station attendant had gone to lunch.

I called Charlotte Mayfield and got detailed directions

interspersed with impatient exclamations. 'This is ridiculous! Unheard of! Where did you say this man comes from?'

The countryside looked very unappealing in the steady rain. Ashtons Hall's village had ancient cottages with tiny windows and climbing things (shrubs? plants?) all over them, clustered round a small patch of green with a pond in the middle. To one side was a rickety wooden village hall, a shop-cum-post office, and a pub, called rather unfortunately Lord Sherwin's Head. The inn sign, however, showed an intact cranium, so I supposed the pub had been named before the murder. The other side of the green was a church, certainly too large for its present congregation. I'd have bet that Miss Potter was a stalwart attender though, and probably headed the flower rota.

The village could have been used without too much trouble to film Second World War period scenes; even the aerials were discreetly positioned. If I'd been given a lodge near there I'd have sold it immediately and buggered off to London but I could see it as Miss Potter's spiritual home. Half a mile away were the hall's gates and the lodge itself, small, grey stone, narrow-windowed. It looked cramped, damp and outdated. Also unoccupied.

The drive up to Ashtons Hall could also have been used without much trouble, this time as the opening of a sixties horror film. As far as a possible doco was concerned, visually so far so good. The drive was lined with huge, ponderous trees (oaks?) which cut out most of the already dim light, and it went on and on. Perhaps status in drives was measured by the mile. It was also full of potholes; not enough money was being spent on it. That made me feel even more cheerful. When the taxi's engine died by the front door the only sound was water overflowing from a gutter, the ominous creaking of trees and the frustrated howling of a distant dog.

It was a very big house: not in the Blenheim Palace class, but a long way up from Miss Potter's Simla. Window upon window faced me: three rows up, eight rows along. The right-hand end of the house was girdled with scaffolding. It looked grimmer, bleaker, than in the photographs on the pin-board in my kitchen.

I paid the Geordie, entered the fare and tip in my expenses book, and looked for a doorbell. There wasn't one. I looked for a knocker. There wasn't one. I pushed one of the double doors; it wasn't locked. I stepped into a porch. Beyond it were glass doors. These weren't locked either. Beyond them was a freezing hall, mostly wooden-floored. A normal-sized carpet, worn thin and beige, was reduced to hearthrug proportions by the scale of the room. Log baskets flanked the massive, empty fireplace; a circular table, about five feet in diameter, notably failed to fill the echoing bareness.

'Hello?' I called. 'Hello?' The dog's whining was getting closer, then a door opened and an elderly golden cocker spaniel waddled into the hall followed by a middle-aged woman in a baggy skirt and sweater. 'Mrs Mayfield?'

'What name is it?'

'Alex Tanner, Ms.'

She crossed to another door, opened it. 'Miss Alex Tanner to see you,' she said.

'Oh, so you found us?' This time it was Charlotte Mayfield, unmistakably. She looked just like a fair version of her mother back in the fifties, dressed in the current uniform of her class; good navy skirt, frill-necked striped shirt, sweater, navy tights, navy low-heeled shoes. Her shoulder-length hair was held off her face with a velvet Alice band. She looked younger than her age – early forties – but she also looked mummified. Her skin was deeply tanned and her light blue eyes empty of all expression. 'Come in.' She beckoned me towards her and led me into a very large, conventional drawing-room. It had a wood fire burning in a marble fireplace and was marginally warmer than the hall. 'Extraordinary thing about the taxi-driver,' she went on. 'I expect you had lunch on the train. Would you like some coffee?'

'Yes, please.'

'Could you bring us some coffee, Kate? Do sit down, Miss Tanner. No, not there – you won't be comfortable too near the fire.'

I hate being bullied; I wanted to sit in that chair. 'This'll be fine,' I said blandly, settling back into it and propping my damp boots on the fender.

'You'll find yourself unpleasantly near the fire,' she said, perching on a chintz-covered, sagging armchair opposite me. Her shallow eyes skipped like stones over my boots up my legs to my face. 'It was lucky you caught me,' she said. 'I'm just about to leave for London, to join my husband.'

'So you said on the phone.'

'My husband is very busy at the moment. He's a Cabinet Minister, you know.'

'Poor chap,' I said with synthetic sympathy.

'I'm sorry?' She was startled. She couldn't believe I meant it.

'I expect you are.' I pretended to take her literally. 'Never mind, he'll probably be out at the next election. There's bound to be a swing to Labour.'

She cleared her throat with a dismissive, dry cough. 'Yours must be interesting work,' she said perfunctorily. 'A researcher, you say? Working for Bartholomew O'Neill?'

'I'm a freelance. I work for Barty at the moment.'

'Charming family. We've had his nephews to stay. They're at school with my son. Do you know his older brother at all?'

'No,' I said, unbeguiled. Was it likely I'd know an earl? Would I want to? 'I rather got the impression Barty was a thorn in the family flesh. With all his exposés of the upper classes.'

'I suppose someone will do them, and we're safer with him.'

'I do hope not,' I said. It wasn't worth being polite. She'd already decided what she wanted to tell me, and I might irritate her into indiscretion. I could certainly never charm her.

'The wretched murder,' she said without any visible emotion. 'I can't imagine why people won't let it go. What business is it of theirs? But as it's Bartholomew O'Neill . . . Why did he decide to do this now? Do you know?'

'I believe he has new information.'

'Who from?'

'I've no idea.'

'More invention, I expect. What is this information?'

'I only work for him. He doesn't tell me everything,' I replied. It was what she expected; she accepted it.

'*I'll* give him a ring,' she said. 'But for the moment, how can I help you? Ah – thank you, Kate. Just leave the tray here.' Behind Kate, the spaniel hovered, expectant. It was evidently rather blind but it sniffed, eagerly, in my direction. 'If you must bring that wretched dog here at least keep it in the kitchen, please, Kate,' said Charlotte sharply. 'Have you been lumbered with it permanently?'

I'd assumed the dog belonged to the house. Charlotte's hostility immediately endeared it to me, and I stretched out my hand. 'Here, good dog.' It waggled towards me, tail and rear twitching together in ecstatic greeting, then licked my hand and arm.

Kate grasped it firmly by the collar and hauled it away. 'Joss stays with me until Miss Potter can make other arrangements,' she said, and left, stooping to drag the spaniel with her.

Chapter Fifteen

It was *my* Miss Potter's dog. She hadn't mentioned it. I could feel ideas rearranging themselves in my head and clicking in like tumblers in a lock. I had underestimated Miss Potter, or badly misunderstood her, or both. I had assumed that she was a typical, slightly garrulous, slightly pathetic, very lonely old woman, who told the chance-caught listener everything there was to know about herself that didn't relate to the Sherwin murder. The Miss Potter I thought I knew was close to breakdown, too distraught to make decisions and much too distraught to be anything but fully communicative about herself and her feelings. *That* Miss Potter would *certainly* have told me all about her dog, how heart-breaking it was to be parted from him, how loyal and loving he was, how kind the friend or ex-cleaning woman who was looking after him now.

But now wasn't the time to think about Miss Potter. Charlotte was pouring coffee from a delicate, probably Georgian silver pot which Kate had brought on a silver tray, perhaps the tray from the dialysis raffle. 'Do you take milk and sugar?'

'Please. Three sugars.'

'Are you sure? It's a very small cup.'

I hate petty interference. 'Better make it four,' I said, smiling.

She didn't smile and she gave me heaped spoonfuls with exaggerated flourishes of the wrist. 'How exactly can I help you, Miss Tacker?'

'Background material, really, Mrs Meyerfeld.' (I could play the 'Who on earth *are* you' game, too.)

'Mrs *Mayfield*,' she corrected me, and lost the rally, I thought.

'Mrs Mayfield, of course. How much do you remember about that time?'

'How do you mean?'

'For example, what was the atmosphere like in the house that summer?'

'What summer?'

'Before your father died.'

'My father died in November. Thirty-two years ago today.'

Anniversary. I paused, to feel the ghost. No ghost; plenty of draughts. Silver-framed photographs on the grand piano. From where I sat, gently roasting by the fire, I could see Rollo twelve inches by eight, absurdly but attractively dressed in full Highland kit. He was looking the camera in the eye, which became my eyes. He didn't seem interested in me. He wouldn't have been.

I checked my notes. 'It's background I'm after, from before the murder. Starting – say – in June.'

'Why June?'

'That was what Barty told me to do,' I said, draining my cup.

'Ah.' She understood, and respected, 'just following orders'. 'The atmosphere in the house. Perfectly normal.'

'And what was that?'

'What was what?'

'The normal atmosphere. Who was living here, for instance?'

'My mother and father, of course. Myself and my three sisters. My grandfather. My cousin Rosalind, from Kenya.'

'Anyone else?'

'I don't think so. My mother didn't entertain much. She wasn't well.'

'What was wrong with her?'

'She was delicate. Some more coffee?'

'Please. Was there no one else living in the house?'

'You mean the servants? There was a governess, a butler and his wife, the housekeeper/cook.'

'And the atmosphere? Was it happy?'

'Perfectly happy.'

'Were you a close family?'

'Not particularly. We didn't have to be. It's quite a big house. We didn't live on top of each other.'

She appeared unmoved; I didn't think she was concealing anything deliberately. I decided to needle her and see. 'Would you agree that your mother was having an affair with the doctor?'

'I don't think so. She married him later, of course, and he was a comfort to her in her illness. But an affair is very unlikely. She hardly ever went out.'

'But he visited here.'

'Very public visits. Mrs Crisp would have known.'

'Mrs Crisp being the housekeeper?'

'Yes. She was a terrific gossip. If she'd known, I'd have heard.'

She was still unmoved. 'So presumably you knew all about your father's affairs,' I pressed on.

'In broad outline, yes. From Mrs Crisp. I'm afraid the coffee may be a little cold. Shall I order some more?'

'No, thank you.' She pressed the bell anyway, and I thought of the poor woman who had to come all the way, surely a considerable distance, from the kitchen to fetch more coffee I wasn't going to give Charlotte the satisfaction of seeing me drink. 'And it didn't upset you?' I plugged on.

'It wasn't my business.'

'Some children might find a father's affairs very upsetting, whether it was any of their business or not.'

'That's possible,' she said. 'I wasn't that sort of child.'

'What sort of child were you?'

She showed the first sign of emotion since my arrival, and it was, predictably, impatience. 'I really can't see what that has to do with your researches.'

'Just trying to get the picture,' I said. 'I suppose your governess was very important to you?'

'Why should you suppose that?'

'If your mother was ill and your father was otherwise engaged, you must have been lonely.'

'I wouldn't put it quite in those terms. She was one of many governesses we had. Rather old-fashioned. More competent than most.'

'Is that why you rented her the lodge?'

'That was much later, and that was my mother's doing. She was inclined to be over-generous to dependants.'

'How many other cottages did she rent to ex-governesses?' Charlotte glared at me. I smiled back, feeling better now I'd needled her. 'And you repossessed the lodge, shortly after your mother's death?'

'Naturally. It is a valuable property.'

'What about the governess?'

'She must make her own arrangements.'

'Do you think she'll find it easy?'

She arched her eyebrows. 'I really have no idea.'

Silence. Nothing more for me to say, here and now. I shifted ground. 'Tell me about your cousin. How did she fit into the household?'

'Perfectly normally.'

'The governess came from Kenya with her, didn't she?'

'Yes.'

'Did you like your cousin?'

'I really can't see . . .'

'What that has to do with my researches,' I finished the sentence for her. 'Perhaps, Mrs Mayfield, that is why I am a researcher and you are not.'

She gave me an extremely chilly look. I stared straight back. She was disconcerted, as if she was unused to challenge. Her look changed to one of dislike and contempt. With great self-control, I didn't mirror it. She looked away first. 'My cousin was five years older than I was. At that age, five years is a considerable difference. She was another person living in the house, that's all.'

'And have you seen much of her since?'

'Very little. She married a painter. Quite well known, I believe. They live abroad.'

'Where?'

'Somewhere in Crete.'

'Could you give me her address?'

'I'm afraid not. We haven't kept up. I have no idea how you could find her.'

Her icy manner equipped her to be an excellent liar. Of course she knew Rosalind's address; or if she didn't, she certainly knew where I could get it. 'What a pity,' I said. 'What can you remember about the night of the ball?'

She thinned her lips. 'Must we?'

'If you would.'

'All the children went to bed after supper, of course. Everything was absolutely normal. That's all I have to say.'

'When did you last see your father?'

'He was dancing with my cousin Rosalind.'

'How did he look?'

'As he always looked. He was a very handsome man.'

'Did he strike you as upset?'

She shook her head.

'Mrs Mayfield, what were your feelings for your father? And before you answer, could I ask you not to say "absolutely normal"?'

'Why?'

'Because I have no idea what that is. Take my father, for instance. He was, according to my mother, a taxi-driver she met in a pub. She never could remember the name of the man or the pub. Before I was thirteen I lived in five foster-families with five sets of children who all had different relationships with their very different fathers. After that, back with my mother, I've lived with four different "uncles". I've never lived in a house with servants, never been to a hunt ball, never had a nanny or a governess or a grand piano emasculated by a few kilos of silver frames and a vase of dying chrysanthemums. I'd be grateful for a clue. What do you call a normal family and a normal father?'

'Why do you say the piano is emasculated?' she said coolly.

'Because you can't lift the lid, so you've turned it from a beautiful musical instrument into a monstrously unwieldy item of furniture.'

'Oh, do you play? I'm afraid it's rather out of tune. Perhaps another time. To answer your earlier question, I was fond of my father. He was kind to me. I seldom saw him; he wasn't specially interested in children. Perhaps, of the four of us, he was fondest of

Candida. He brought us chocolates when he'd been away. When I was quite small he gave me rides on his shoulders in summer. I was the only one of us who wasn't frightened, riding on his shoulders. He called us "rabbits", which may or may not have been an affectionate nickname.'

'You must have been very sad when he died.'

'Yes, indeed.'

'Who did you think had killed him?'

'I had no idea. Mrs Crisp said the police believed my mother had killed him, as you will have gathered from Lemaire's offensive book. That was quite impossible, of course.'

'Why impossible?'

'It was a passionate crime, or a clumsy one. My mother was neither.'

'Couldn't she have done it by accident? During a quarrel?'

'That is remotely conceivable, but it did not happen. I was with my mother in the aftermath of the tragedy. I understood her. We were similar, in many ways. I assure you, she did not kill my father.'

'If you had to take a guess at how it happened?'

'I suppose, a drunken quarrel with a mistress. Impossible to establish now.'

I had to admire her. The ice wasn't surface; she was frozen clear through, or had pretended to be for so long that it was a distinction without a difference. By comparison, Miss Potter was passionate and human, for all her entrenchment on the moral high ground. 'Anything else you think I should know, Mrs Mayfield?'

'I would be grateful if Bartholomew could let me see the article before it is printed, but I'll speak to him about that myself.' Fat chance, I thought, nodding.

If Barty ever made a doco, and if Charlotte was still co-operating, we'd want to use the murder room. So I asked to see it before I left, and Charlotte got up. I got up too, and walked over to the piano: it was Toad-time. Charlotte would be dropping her guard, thinking the interview was over.

Many of the photographs were of familiar faces in dated studio poses. Rollo, Laura, the Sherwin girls. No Rosalind. Adult Charlotte, impressive Ludovic Mayfield in penguin suit. More modern, though still formal shots of a boy and a girl, from early childhood to teens. That must be Toad and the brother Polly had mentioned. He had his parents' looks: she was dumpy and puddingy, with sad, anxious eyes. Guilt stirred in me. Get on with it, Lally, I thought. 'Your children?' I asked.

'Yes. Shall we go?'

I stood my ground. 'How old are they now?'

'Does it matter?'

That was openly rude, which she hadn't been till then. 'Not at all,' I said. 'Just general interest. They look mid-teens.'

'That was some years ago.'

'And what do they do?'

'They're both going to Oxford.'

'So they're up at Oxford now?'

'Not exactly. Do you want to see the gun-room, Miss Tanner?'

'Having a year off before they go?' I persisted. 'Having fun abroad? Isn't that what you do, before going up to Oxford? A Gap Year, they call it, don't they?'

She stood in the doorway, willing me to follow her, as edgy as she'd been since I arrived. She wasn't going to give me a proud, maternal update. She looked as if she wanted to put my head in the heavy door and shut it. 'Something like that,' she said, and walked away. I followed. She crossed the hall at a good pace and seemed to relax when we reached a corridor at the other side. I looked back at the hall but could see nothing remarkable, nothing that she'd want to hide.

She was proud of the house. As we went, she talked about plans for redecoration, about improvements she had made. I nodded and smiled. It just seemed to me cold, pretentious and impossibly big. As with most privately owned big houses I had seen, it had many corners of dirt and shabbiness, things that couldn't be overlooked in a small suburban house or my little London flat but were accepted in the grander environment of the country house. Grubby curtains, pockets of dust, carpets worn as thin as tablecloths and loose floorboards. Above all, it was cold. The central heating wasn't on; the log fire in the drawing-room was the only source of heat I'd seen. Odd. Even if she was about to leave for London, the house must be kept reasonably warm some of the time, surely, otherwise damp would spoil the furniture. She was proud of the furniture, too.

Then I stopped thinking about that; we'd reached the gun-room. It was a surprise because it hadn't changed. It looked, thirty years on, exactly the same as it had in H. Plowright's blurred pho-tographs of the murder scene. It was about twelve feet square; two of the walls were covered with glass-fronted cupboards, one still containing guns; the other walls displayed decaying trophy heads, stuffed and mounted fish, photographs. An ancient, cracked leather sofa and two assorted armchairs took up the floor-space that wasn't occupied by baskets and piles of sporting equipment. I didn't bother with an inventory but a glance took in tennis and badminton rackets, cricket bats, croquet mallets and hoops.

I knew from photographs and plans that Rollo's body had fallen on to the sofa and that the sofa had caught most of the remains of his head. I tried to feel myself into the atmosphere of the room; I sat on the sofa while Charlotte stood aloofly by the door, shut my eyes and tried to go back, but it was useless. The room was just a room, smelling of damp and leather, wellington boots and gun oil.

Chapter Sixteen

On the train back to London I burnt my tongue on British Rail coffee while I rearranged my thoughts about Miss Potter. She was, of course, still homeless, impoverished and seventy; but not lonely. Not according to Kate, who did turn out to be her ex-cleaning woman. She gave me a lift to the station. Kate's Miss Potter was an important figure in the village, columnist in the local paper, chairwoman of the Women's Institute, member of the Parish Council, centre of a social vortex of bridge parties, coffee mornings and teas with the vicar. 'She's very popular hereabouts. There was a lot of ill-feeling when Mrs Mayfield put her out of the cottage, and talk of a petition. The ladies who clean at the hall were all for giving in their notice, but Miss Potter wouldn't have it. She said she'd look after herself and I'll be bound she will. I'm just taking care of Joss till she comes back. Plenty of people hereabouts would've taken him, but we understand each other. He's getting on and needs a bit of fussing and minced chicken.'

I sat on an orange plastic seat in the grubby buffet car on the train, nodded occasionally at the Irish drunk opposite who was telling me the story of his life, watched the sodden countryside swish greyly past, and tried to work out the motives for Miss Potter's behaviour. If she had plenty of resources, if she didn't *need* to fabricate information about the Sherwin murder to keep my attention or my company, she had been deliberately misleading me.

Why? I boiled it down to two possibilities; one, she actually had information which she felt to be so significant, or so damaging to someone she cared about, that she was genuinely hesitant about revealing it; two, she had no information at all but was stringing me along until I sorted out the Toad question.

Of course, I hoped it was the first, but I feared it was the second, partly because I believed she had reason to worry about Toad. Charlotte had certainly been evasive about her – about both her children, come to that.

In either case, I felt decidedly better about Miss P. If she was playing with a full deck, then I'd enjoy the game. She'd manipulated me for the last time. Next time we met, I'd go in with my boots on.

That decided, I fetched another coffee, logged the expense and readjusted the drunk, who had passed out with his face in my notebook. Where had I got with Charlotte? She hadn't minded talking about the Sherwin murder. She didn't think her mother had murdered her father – I believed her about that – but, more significantly, she didn't appear to mind one way or another. Like Rosalind, she wasn't jumpy about it. Was that odd? It had been a long time ago, granted. She'd had plenty of time to get used to it. At the same time, surely a little curiosity would have been in order. Unless she already thought she knew the identity of the murderer, or unless she was really as cold as she appeared.

She was, however, jumpy about Toad. Or her son; she wouldn't talk about him either. She also hadn't wanted me in the house to start with, and in the hall particularly. I could make no sense of that anxiety but I didn't like it.

When I was standing at the bus stop at Euston I realized my neck muscles were knotted. I was nervous about the dinner with Barty. I tried deep relaxation breathing; consequently I stood like a nerd while people trampled each other to squeeze themselves on the bus. I missed two. The third smelt of warm wet clothes. I hadn't listened to the early morning news on the radio – I usually did – so I tried to make up for it by reading newspapers over people's shoulders. Iraq was simmering along: Tony Benn, a peace-rallying Labour politician, had been advised not to pay a visit to Saddam Hussein. I could see why. First because Benn was such small potatoes it was inappropriate for him to muscle in, secondly because his mad staring eyes would alienate a listener immediately. Except, come to think of it, Hussein also had mad staring eyes. Heseltine was stepping up his anti-Thatcher campaign, but there was no mention of Mayfield as a possible successor.

Back at my flat about five, I turned on the answering machine and listened to Annabel's message while I wrestled off my sodden boots.

Hello, Alex. I've got Lally's home number but she's been out all day. Her flatmate says she's rushing round seeing people. Something to do with Toad, she says, so I'm sure Lally will be back to you soon. She ended by giving me the number. I dialled it, on the off-chance. No answer. Not even a flatmate. At five on Friday, probably the flatmates had gone to the country. They were welcome to it.

I made myself a cup of coffee but I couldn't settle. I didn't want to see Miss Potter until I had plenty of time to spend on her, so I put on a dry pair of boots, went out and grabbed a taxi. Patrick Revill would do to fill in the time.

He still kept powdered coffee in a Gold Blend jar and his combined need for a further fee and an audience easily outweighed his distrust. 'I'm rather glad you've come back,' he said. 'Always a treat to see a fan.' I'd forgotten I was a fan. 'Plus I've been thinking about that time. What do you want to know?'

'Several things. We could start with the details of your affair with Rosalind.'

'No gentleman gives details of that kind of thing,' he said, pleased with himself.

He was gloating again. Whatever a gentleman is, if anybody still cares, Patrick Revill didn't measure up. Poor Rosalind. When I was seventeen I'd just started at the Beeb and I was going out with Eddy's son Peter. I'd thought I was really in love, partly with Peter and partly with his leather jacket and Harley Electra Glide. We had some good laughs and I learnt a bit about boys, sex and motorbikes. He was always nice to my mum. He fixed the mixer taps in the kitchen which hadn't worked right for years. I went on liking him even after he ditched me for a blonde graduate trainee who fancied a bit of rough. I still see him off and on; he's a free-lance cameraman now, doing well.

I suppressed my dislike and smiled encouragingly. Patrick would talk if I let him. He was lonely and he was vain.

'She ran after me. She arranged for me to rent the lodge, she threw herself at me. I – had reservations, of course, strong reservations.' You were scared shitless, I paraphrased. 'But what can a man do? She was young and beautiful. I was flattered. I felt sorry for her. She was very unhappy, and very – highly sexed. Her stepmother didn't like her, the governess wouldn't talk to her, the Sherwins' marriage was very rocky. There was a bad atmosphere in the house.'

'You got the impression the marriage was actually breaking up?'

'Oh yes. In early November, Rosalind told me her uncle definitely wanted a divorce. She overheard them fighting. Her room was above Lady Sherwin's, at the back of the house overlooking the terrace gardens.' I wondered why he remembered that so well. From what Rosalind had said? Or from personal experience? The night of the ball, or before? I tucked the thought behind my ear. He was still talking. 'She guessed it from things her uncle let drop, as well. She liked her uncle. They went riding together.'

'Surely somebody must have known about your relationship with Rosalind? What about Mrs Crisp?'

'I think we got away with it, though I had a few bad moments after the murder, I can tell you. She was usually very discreet and we didn't meet all that often. I tried to soft-pedal the whole thing.'

'When wasn't she discreet?'

'How do you mean?'

'You said *usually*, she was *usually* discreet.'

'Slip of the tongue.' He tried to catch my eye with a roguish twinkle. I did my best to twinkle back.

'I got the idea you'd been in Ashtons Hall before the night of the hunt ball,' I said, at random.

'You did, eh?' He looked uncomfortable. 'Now where can you have got that idea from?'

'It could have been from something Rosalind said.'

'You've spoken to Rosalind?'

'This morning. She was most communicative.'

'It was very – difficult. She was a very young girl, with a young girl's ideas.' And a young girl's body, I thought, which you didn't complain about when her legs were wrapped around your vain old ears.

'She was reticent about that particular episode,' I went on. She'd had to have been since I knew sod-all about it. 'But she told me one or two – rather unusual things.'

He looked even more uncomfortable. 'It was a flight of fancy. On her part. I made sure there was no one in the house, of course.'

'That must have been difficult.'

'They were all at church.'

'Even the Crisps?'

'Sunday was the Crisps' day off, that week. They'd gone over to relations at Oxford, leaving a cold collation for the family lunch.'

I peered at my notes, pretending not to be able to read my writing. 'When was this? It says here, October, I think.'

'No, no, no. Later. November. Not long before the ball. I only did it for Rosalind. She was stage-struck, you know, she wanted to – er, visit me, in my dressing-room. I couldn't have that, of course, there was her reputation to think of. She was a determined little thing, though, and a bit unpredictable, by then. You know what young girls are like, you can't trust them to be sensible. She wanted – a bit of fun, something different.'

What could that have been? I raked through my memories of Peter, trying to imagine myself seventeen again. The sex itself had been enough, I remembered, any time, any place, anywhere. It was great on the back of his bike, though I'd got bruised to pieces once when the Harley fell over. 'It's like that, when you're seventeen,' I plugged on. 'Taking a bit of a risk, playing games really, odd places, odd circumstances.'

'I felt very uncomfortable. Abusing Lord Sherwin's hospitality.'

'Where were you exactly?' I pretended to peer at my notes again. 'I made sure to put her towel over the sheet, and the kilt was entirely undamaged,' he said urgently. 'I've always been very careful with costumes. I replaced it in his dressing-room wardrobe, punctiliously, and remade the bed.'

'You must have been successful. He didn't notice anything, did he?'

'It wasn't him I was worried about, it was Lady Sherwin. Women are much more observant about these matters. There was a pile of satin scatter-cushions in pastel shades; one of them was her nightdress-case. I made a point of replacing them exactly. I only did it for Rosalind's sake. She was a very appealing little thing.'

An appealing little thing with the determination to get this limp dick to dress up in her uncle's gear and bang her on her aunt's bed. She'd probably blackmailed him into it by threatening to tell. I tried not to smile. The remembered fear was making him sweat. She couldn't have done it for fun; she must have known how frightened he was. I'm surprised he could make it at all, under those circumstances. Perhaps he hadn't. Perhaps she'd known he couldn't. Any way you looked at it, revenge was what she was after, to punish him, to humiliate him. It looked to me like pique. I suppose, remotely, it could have been a sexual charge; maybe she was funny for her uncle.

'While you were in the house, that time, did you notice anything? Apart from the scatter-cushions?'

'What kind of thing?'

'I've no idea, I'm just fishing.'

'I didn't notice much, frankly. I was listening for cars and footsteps. Have you any idea how long it takes to put on full Scottish dress? I noticed that first when I played Macduff. All those fiddly daggers and brooches and stocking-flashes.' He was still sweating.

'And this was just before the ball?'

'The weekend before, as I recall. It was – by way of a farewell. I'd already decided that after the ball, I was going to make a clean break with Rosalind and move out of the lodge.'

'Did you tell her?'

'Certainly not. She'd have been – very upset.'

She'd have played merry hell, and you were afraid of her. 'Did you give notice for the lodge?'

'Naturally. Some weeks before. Otherwise, I'd have been liable for the rent.'

And there was my answer. Rosalind knew Patrick was leaving, and that he hadn't told her, so she got her own back. Another piece for the jigsaw. Might be useful, except that increasingly I had more pieces and less picture.

Chapter Seventeen

I was back at my flat by twenty past seven. Time to get ready for Barty. I was poking through my wardrobe when Polly banged on my door.

'They're clamping in the street again, Alex, they did next door's Mercedes and he was livid. Have you heard on the news the IRA have blown up another MP, isn't it dreadful? I've never met him, though, he was a backbench Conservative. You look busy, shall I get you a coffee?'

I went back to the wardrobe. 'Fine,' I said.

'Are you going out? Who with? Is it business or pleasure? Don't tell me, I can guess from your grin.'

'Am I grinning?'

'Eat your heart out, Cheshire Cat. Is it Barty?'

'Yup.'

'I told you he fancies you.'

'You said I fancied him.'

'Both. Trust me, about this I am never wrong. About everything else, yes. You haven't really looked at another man since you met him.'

'I've done a great deal more than look.'

She shrugged her shoulders. 'Isolated lust. Doesn't count. Here, let me help.' She burrowed into the heap of clean clothes on my shelves. 'Why don't you ever hang things up?'

'Because I never wear them. I just keep them for when I have to tart up for work, and then I iron them before I put them on.'

'I've never seen these before.' She hauled out an Italian outfit I bought in a mad moment in Venice, egged on by the costume designer for a feature film I worked on about the Doges in the sixteenth century. I'd blown all my ludicrously inflated feature-film-rate expenses on the outfit, flowing trousers and top in a multicoloured Florentine print. I'd been younger then. I'd only worn it twice since. Polly had unerringly picked out my only expensive clothes. How is it people can do that? I can't, just as I can't tell great wine from drinkable stuff from the local offy.

Polly was giving little cries of distress. 'How could you leave it crumpled in a ball, Alex? You didn't WASH it, did you? Oh my God, it's raw silk.'

'Silk washes,' I said, teed off.

'Not when it's made up like this – look at the facings and the buttons. Run a bath, quick. We'll steam it first.'

'Can I use the bath to wash in as well, please, miss?'

'Drink it if you like.' She bustled about, organizing me. I didn't mind. I sat in the bath sipping the coffee Polly provided, with the sacred garments dangling from the shower rail. She genuflected to them every time she passed. 'What time is he picking you up?' she said, sorting through my make-up bag.

'Eight o'clock.'

'Only half an hour, help. Hurry up and get out of there. Your skin needs to cool down before I do your make-up.'

'And then I'll be transformed and Barty will fall at my feet, stunned at my newly revealed beauty? Come off it, Polly, face facts.'

'Why won't you ever give it a go? You've got to stop being so timid, Alex.'

'Timid? Me?'

'You're shy and retiring, underneath, and not as far underneath as you think. You pretend to be above looks and actually that's because you think you haven't got them, and it's not true. You've got good features, thick hair—'

'Mouse-coloured—'

'Not now. Your body is well-proportioned—'

'Too broad—'

'Strong. In proportion. You have good ankles, lovely skin, thick eyelashes—'

'Stubby—'

'Terrific green eyes, and you sparkle. Men look at you. You must have noticed.'

'That's a load of crap. Anyway, why should you care?'

'Because we're mates, that's why, and you listen to me drivelling on about Clive. I owe you a lot.' She did, of course, but I didn't know she knew it.

Barty came to fetch me in a taxi, presumably intending to sweeten a date with me by drinking himself stupid. He said I looked nice, and maybe I did, but people have to say that anyway when you've obviously tried. He was still in a dark suit but he'd changed his tie; it no longer said 'I belong'. It said 'I've plenty of money to waste on expensive ties'. He didn't look nearly as tired as he had that morning and I wondered if it hadn't been tiredness but depression. He always seems cheerful when I see him but his work must get him down, it's a perpetual struggle. About a quarter of the time his films don't get shown; his downstairs toilet is wallpapered with restraining injunctions and he spends whole days kicking his heels in court. Even if his work does get broadcast, the scandals he reveals cause only about a week's upheaval and then the water closes over them.

He took me to a really posh place, one which he clearly often used because the waiters knew him. Probably he took Annabel there. It was the kind of place where waiters threaten you with padded menus like deadly weapons and in which the price of the food is exceeded only by the pretensions of the customers. Barty fitted in. I didn't. He smiled at me reassuringly. 'Are you ready to order?'

'Order for me.' I wasn't being an unreconstructed Barbie doll, I just don't give a toss about food.

'Any particular preferences?'

'No. Just lots of it.'

He went into a huddle with the waiter, then the wine-waiter. I was getting the full treatment. When he'd finished ordering, he said, 'This is supposed to be a treat. Enjoy.'

'I know. Sorry, I'll lighten up.'

'Not on my account,' he said, and squeezed my hand. I snatched it away, discomfited. 'Behave as you please.'

I was compos enough not to say 'Gee, thanks', but only just. I did the next worst thing. 'How's Annabel?' I said.

'As well as can be expected,' he said, 'considering her natural disadvantages, as far as you're concerned. She's out with Charles.'

'Charles?'

'Or Harry or Marcus or Dominick. I don't umpire. She's efficient.'

'At work or with Harry or Marcus or Dominick?'

'Grow up, Alex.' He said it very gently as the waiter appeared with a microscopic variegated starter on a huge plate.

I owed it to Barty to get a grip. He was certainly being nice. He was probably making a move on me, that was the trouble, and I only have two behaviours for responding to that. Either I blush and run, crushing people's feelings as I go, or else I say, 'Do you want to fuck?' Polly tells me most men find the situation equally awkward and one should be kind to them. Polly does not feel as unattractive as I do, however. Nor does she fear the loss of a major source of income.

I tried deep relaxation breathing and waved a fork in the direction of my starter. 'I'm sorry, Barty,' I said. 'I must sign up for evening classes to make me more ept.'

'It'll make a change from the evening classes in target-practice,' he said seriously.

I misunderstood; I thought he meant it. 'Target-practice?' He'd probably forgotten. My last evening classes were in karate.

'Shooting yourself in the foot.' He was smiling. Eventually, I smiled back, then laughed. 'That's better,' he said. 'Sometimes you make me feel old.'

'Don't say "old". Say experienced. Mature. Suave.'

'The new after-shave for MEN. Eat up, there's four more courses.'

'How'd it go in court today?'

'Not bad. We won. I think the opposition will appeal it, but never mind.'

I couldn't think of anything to say. There was a pause. I ate a piece of bread roll; my chewing sounded loud in my own ears. 'Do you mind if I talk business?' I said.

'Not at all, during dinner. I don't want to have to take Rollo Sherwin to bed with us, though. How could I measure up? It'd be inhibiting.'

Smoothly done, Barty, I thought. 'We've no reason to suppose he was any good in bed,' I said airily, remembering that Polly had tried to lend me her high-cut black lace bed-me pants. We'd compromised on black camiknickers. 'Just that he had lots of practice.'

'True. Now eat your salmon and spinach mousse, it's feeling neglected, and if you leave it the chef will cry.'

By the end of the main course (a little more food, an even huger plate) and the first bottle of wine, Barty was up to date with Charlotte Mayfield, Patrick Revill and the state of play with Miss Potter. I had plenty to tell him and I spun it out. 'So you think you can get her to talk?' he said, pushing his plate aside, still half-full. Mine wasn't.

'If she's got anything to say.'

'Any idea why Charlotte got her knickers in a twist about Toad?'

'I'm not wasting time speculating. When Toad's friend gets back to me I'll know. It's nothing to do with the Sherwin murder, I'm sure of that.'

'Have you heard from Eddy Barstow yet?'

'He's only been working on it since yesterday evening.'

'I'll be happier when we have an angle.'

'So will I.'

We'd exhausted business. I drank more wine and tried not to show how desperate I was to get dinner over with and leave. By mistake, I caught sight of myself in a mirror on the opposite wall I'd been avoiding ever since we came in. I looked ridiculous, I thought, and jerked away.

'What's the matter, Alex?' said Barty gently. He was being kind to me, maybe because of me telling him about my mother that morning, maybe because he was making a pass, maybe both. He'd always been kind to me. I had to handle him right. 'Tell me what's the matter,' he said. 'The truth. I can take it.'

The truth would be easiest, gussied up a bit. I tried to explain. I was a freelance. He had provided just under half my income last year. Our relationship was great as it stood. Anything else might go sour. I might be a disappointment to him. I couldn't afford to be.

'For Christ's sake, Alex, you sound like the serving-wench in a melodrama. Things have changed. No big deal. Is money that important to you? There are other things, you know.'

'Not for me. I have nothing to fall back on, no capital, no relations, no trust funds, no qualifications, no expectations. There is no camp fire burning for me. I'm not One of Us. I'm one of Thatcher's children, and she's on her way out.'

'You're a very good researcher.'

'And when the recession bites deeper, what then? When more staffers are laid off, when the indies go to the wall, when interest rates hit twenty per cent, when I can't afford the mortgage on my flat and I can't shift it either, what then, Barty? I won't need a lover, I'll need an employer.' Damn it. I was crying. 'If you want sex, use Annabel or her sisters. Don't condescend to me. You don't understand the first thing about me. For God's sake, you bring me to a place like this for a treat. I hate every moment of it, with these sodding superior waiters looking at me and wondering what I'll get wrong—'

'Waiters don't wonder,' said Barty, 'except about the size of their tip, and possibly in this case how I got lucky with you, considering our relative pulling power—'

'And don't try to heal my wounds with cheap public-school flattery—'

'That wasn't what I had in mind. At all.'

I was past caution. 'Then you haven't *got* a mind, or you aren't using it. Just like all your programmes, useless. Romantic and useless. Who gives a toss if they're unkind to blacks in the Household Cavalry? Nothing's going to unseat the bosses in this country, certainly not your footling efforts, and come to that why should they care? It's a system that works, for them, so at least someone's happy. If you had a spit of sense you'd hang on to what you've got and not piss your money away. It's a hard world, Barty, face it. Who cares—'

He caught one of my gesturing hands and held it still. He's stronger than he looks, for all he's so skinny. I've seen him carry and operate a Steadicam for hours at a time, in Egyptian summer temperatures. 'It'll occur to you later that maybe saying all that wasn't the best way to make sure I keep hiring you.'

'And?' I said. He was right, of course. And I hadn't even had the sex, which of course I wanted. 'And?'

'And then you should remember what I'm about to tell you.'

'Which is?'

'What you say about me could well be true. And I know it. And I like you a lot. Eat your pudding.'

Chapter Eighteen

On the way upstairs, I banged on Polly's door. 'You're early,' she called after me, sounding shocked. 'Can I come up for coffee? Clive's gone to Amsterdam on a peace mission. He sent me guilt chocolates. Shall I bring them?'

'Bring them.'

'So how did it go?'

'Not great.' She had every right to ask but I didn't want to discuss Barty.

'Bit of a bugger?'

'Bit. Thanks for all your help, anyway.'

'You look terrific.'

'Hardly.'

'You should dress up more often.'

'Lay off, Polly, OK?'

'Whatever you say. Where did you eat? Is there anything good on telly? I'll make coffee.'

I stood at the window, looking out, thinking about Barty; what he would do, what I would do, what I wanted from him. He'd managed, just, to prevent our dinner becoming a debacle. If I'd co-operated, even a little, we might have reached the, presumably pleasant, intimacy that lovers glide into after rows. I'd never managed it, myself. It's something to do with bowing your head and being grateful. I am never grateful. I stopped being grateful a very long time ago, and I stopped pretending to be grateful, except for work, when I turned eighteen.

Polly brought the coffee and I stopped thinking about Barty. It was too painful. My relationships were always like this. Even if they began well they ended badly; more often, they began so badly they aborted on launch. The Jesuits were right. You had to get some things sorted young. By seven, it was too late to learn to ride, or ski, or trust people, or feel attractive.

Polly stayed two hours and talked for one hour and fifty-five minutes. For the other five minutes, I yesed and noed and reallyed and laughed. When she went I was sorry to see her go. Left alone, I adopted my strategy of last resort. I got into the bath with a Robert B. Parker novel; within reach, on the lavatory, a stack of four more. I'd read them all before, several times, but not for the last six months, and I couldn't actually recite the dialogue verbatim.

I read two before I accepted that though I was exhausted, I wasn't going to sleep, and that Spenser's high-minded New Manism reminded me of Barty. Probably, that night, any male character would.

I finally slept just after four; heavy sleep with ugly, muddled, unhappy dreams. Patrick Revill was in there somewhere, with Barty, Miss Potter, my mother and the cocker spaniel I'd owned. Briefly. In the real world, the sound of the phone only just managed to wake me. I picked it up; at the beginning all I could manage was 'What? Hello?' then the telephone noise resolved itself into a breathless, young, half-familiar voice. It was Lally.

'I'm sorry it took me so long to get back to you,' said Lally, 'and to ring you so early, but we've got to go to work, even though it's Saturday, because we've taken so much time off looking for Toad. It's Toad, you see, we want to talk to you about Toad, and we were trying to find Charles and he's in Australia, and we can't find the right sheep farm. He's moved, and it was difficult to ring people, because of the time difference and everything . . .' She rambled on as my mind cleared. With the clearing came a dreadful apprehension. I knew that I was worried about Toad. I had been, subconsciously, ever since my first meeting with Lally; much more so since seeing Charlotte. The worry had tried to force its way into the front of my mind, but each time I resisted it. Hidden, it had time to take a body and a form and now as I blinked at the alarm clock – it was past eight – scrabbled myself upright against the pillows and ruffled my hair, the worry squatted on my shoulder.

Something serious had happened to Toad, and I wanted to ignore it, because I was jealous of her. I was always jealous of people of her background, particularly of delicately nurtured young girls. I told myself I despised them, cosseted, arrogant and naïve as they were, but it wasn't true. I appeased my guilt by telling myself there was nothing I could have done, anyway, till I heard from Lally. In a sense, that was true. But I knew what I hadn't thought and what I hadn't done. I should, of course, have questioned Miss Potter much more closely about Toad, what she was like, how her relationship with her parents worked, whether she was the kind of girl who would just drop out of sight for a bit. I hadn't even asked for a photograph, which for me is always an important part of involving myself in a project. I had been much more interested in Barty's article and securing my money.

'So can we come and see you, now? What's your address?' Lally concluded. I gave her directions. She couldn't have been coming far; by the time I'd washed and dressed, the doorbell rang and I let them in.

I'd wondered about the other constituents of Lally's 'we'. It turned out to be one other person, in Lally's terms probably an Older Man in his early twenties. 'This is Toby,' said Lally. He was about six foot, thin, with a narrow intelligent face and brown hair in a currently fashionable cut, very close at the sides, longish on the top and gelled forward in locks over his forehead. He shook my hand courteously, apologized for the intrusion and accepted coffee and a seat on the sofa, talking all the time. 'Good place you have here. I'd like somewhere like this. OK, to business. I was rather worried, when Lally told me you were asking about Toad.

She says any information we give you will be confidential. Is that right?'

'Within reason. I'll pass any information on to Miss Potter, and she's only concerned with Toad's safety. Otherwise, I'm not interested in scandal or whatever. I'm not a journalist, you know.'

He didn't entirely believe me, I could see, but he decided to go on anyway. He knew he effectively had no choice, otherwise they wouldn't have come, and he wasn't a time-waster. I began to like him. 'So. Several of Toad's friends planned a Gap Year visit to India, Nepal and Tibet if possible, and China. At first Toad wanted to go with them and her parents were happy with that. Then her illness got worse.'

'Her illness?'

'Anorexia,' said Toby.

'You know,' Lally jumped in, 'where you starve yourself and think you're fat when you're not. It's very dangerous. Two other girls at school had it and they had to go to hospital and they weren't allowed to wash or brush their hair until they ate something which seemed cruel to me but even so they're not better yet—'

'I'm sure Alex knows about anorexia, Lally. Hush now,' said Toby, hugging her. 'Let *me* explain.' His mode was stern but kind; nobody his age could be as impressive as he thought he was, but he'd liked my flat and he kept to the point. A good man, I thought. 'Lally and I have been together a year now—' he blushed and dropped years off his apparent age – 'and because Toad and Lally were such good friends, I heard all about it.'

'It was terrible. Up to the end of the fifth year, Toad was such good fun. She was a bit overweight but she had a lovely face and she always looked good, but her mother nagged her about it and laughed at her. That was why she was called Toad, because her mother'd always said she was broader than she was tall. Then when we started our A Levels she went on a diet and at first it was fine, because she looked great and I encouraged her, and I feel awful about that because it was the absolutely wrong thing to do, but I didn't think of anorexia, because we were practically all on diets, except not me because I'm so lucky, I can eat and eat and I'm always like this. Toad said she was jealous of me and it wasn't fair and I thought she was joking, but I think she meant it. Then, this is the worst bit, I went off her because she went on and on about food and her mother and having to do as well in her A Levels as Charles—'

'He's her brother,' said Toby. 'He's a year older and the family favourite.'

'What's he like?' I asked.

Toby reflected. 'Bit of a dickhead,' he said finally.

'Toby! He's gorgeous-looking and he comes top in exams without doing any work and he passed his driving test high on coke!' protested Lally.

'That's my point,' said Toby patiently, and nodded, with genuine appreciation. 'Go on, Lally,' he prompted. 'Toad went on and on about food . . .'

'So I went off her rather though we were still good friends, of course, in fact I was still her best friend because the other girls had gone off her too. She kept losing weight in the second year sixth and I tried to stop her and she said she was eating but actually I think now she must have been throwing up what she ate, because last May, just before A Levels, it was really bad. She wouldn't come swimming and she wore long skirts and big long sweaters even though it was hot. One day I walked into her room when she was changing and I saw how thin she was, and I was really shocked, and I tried to make her weigh herself with no clothes on in front of me but she wouldn't. So I had to tell our housemistress. Toby made me, actually.'

'So the housemistress brought in the school doctor who brought in the headmistress who brought in the parents, and Toad took her A Levels in the San.'

'Sick bay. We call it sick bay.'

'Sure,' said Toby soothingly. 'It wasn't your fault. Don't blame yourself, Lal.'

'OK,' said Lally miserably, and laid her clicking braids on his shoulder.

'Then the end of term came,' he went on. 'She'd managed to sit her exams—'

'She got two As and a B,' said Lally proudly.

'And she'd even put on a bit of weight, because Matron had made her eat. Her mother came to take her home and look after her. Lally was worried by that because Toad doesn't get on well with her mother.'

'It's not right just to say she doesn't get on with her mother. She HATES her mother, absolutely LOATHES and DETESTS her. Her mother's barking.'

'Barking?' I knew the word, but I thought of it as Barty's own. I didn't want to remember Barty; his intrusion disconcerted me.

'Howling, woof-woof mad. Deranged. Off the wall, off her trolley.'

'Do you know that yourself, or is that what Toad told you?'

Lally hesitated. 'I don't know Mrs Mayfield well. I stayed at the house a lot when I was younger but we mostly saw au pairs and cleaners. She's very prejudiced, I think. She didn't like me being black.'

'Do you know that, or is it what Toad told you?' I persisted.

'I suppose . . .' began Lally reluctantly.

'When she talked about how mad her mother was, what kind of examples did she give you? What stories did she tell?'

Lally shrugged. 'They'd sound like nothing to you. It was partly Charles, her brother. Mrs Mayfield dotes on him. She'd ignore Toad completely and she was all over Charles, and when she did say anything to Toad it was always critical, how she must do better in her exams, how she should have boyfriends, how she should be thinner or prettier. That kind of thing. Toad didn't like to talk about it.'

She was right, it didn't sound much; just a run-of-the-mill, unsuccessful mother-child relationship.

'I got the impression the family picked on Toad,' said Toby. 'It's all third-hand, of course. Anyway, Lally rang her at home at the beginning of the holidays, but she was never allowed to speak to her. Someone always said Toad wasn't there, but they never said where she was.'

'I tried London, they have a flat in London, but they said she wasn't there either. So eventually I thought, maybe she was in hospital but they didn't want anyone to know. Then I went away to Thailand for six weeks, and when I came back I rang Toad in the country again, and Mrs Mayfield said she'd gone with the others to India. I didn't understand how she could have got that much better so quickly, because anorexics don't, but I suppose I wanted to believe it. Then I got the postcard.'

'When was this?'

'I lied about that, I'm afraid,' said Lally uncomfortably. 'Because I thought you were interfering, and it was none of your business. I said I got one last week, and I didn't. They both came in September, from India.'

'And were they from Toad?'

'Definitely. I know her writing. Here, I brought them.' She thrust them at me.

Hi! India is fantastic and tragic at the same time. The poverty is terrible but the people are brilliant, so kind and gentle. Lotsalove, Toad

Hi again. Wish you were here to see all the beauty, but there's so much hunger, I can hardly bear it. We're trying to get visas for Nepal, spend all day queuing. Lotsalove & hugs 'n things, Toad

'Um,' I said. 'Her mental state doesn't sound great.'

'Looking back it doesn't, but everybody says that about the poverty in India, don't they? And she was with some good people, I knew they'd look after her,' said Lally, 'I *knew* they would.'

'And did they?'

'That's the point,' said Toby. 'When Lally told me you'd seen her, I was worried, as I said, so she rang round, to get feedback from the trip.'

'From the parents and friends of the other people,' said Lally, 'to see if they mentioned Toad.'

'And they had,' said Toby. 'According to the others, Toad flew back to England from Delhi. In early October. They made her go because she was ill. Not too ill to travel, but too ill to go to Nepal.'

'And so I rang Mrs Mayfield last night,' said Lally. 'She hadn't heard anything about Toad coming back. She thought she was still in Nepal or China or somewhere.'

There was a silence. Lally waited to be reassured. Toby waited to have his suspicions confirmed.

'Oh,' I said flatly.

'Exactly,' said Toby. 'We kept trying to get hold of Charles. He's in Australia, I think Lally mentioned it. I thought he could do more than we could – or, forgive me, than you could – to get some sense out of Mrs Mayfield, make her go to the police or whatever. But we haven't managed to get him.'

'Thanks very much,' I said, pulling myself together. A combination of guilt about my earlier indifference to Toad and my trust in Toby's judgement were tugging me to share his apprehension, which was irrational, on the face of it. Now I knew Toad had anorexia, the obvious solution was that Charlotte, who would probably feel that an anorexic daughter wouldn't help her husband's career or her own reputation, had simply tucked the girl away in a private hospital under the supervision of a private doctor. 'I'll need the names, addresses and telephone numbers of the people you've spoken to who've heard from the other members of the party. The ones who have evidence that Toad came back,' I said.

'Here's a list I prepared earlier,' said Toby in an attempt at parody, but his heart wasn't in it. 'I put our last contact number for Charles on it, and my work and home numbers, in case I can help,' he added, and they left.

Chapter Nineteen

'Sod it,' I said to the empty flat. 'Sod it, sod it.' I had to give Miss Potter the information they'd just given me. It would then take time to find the girl, if her mother was determined to hide her: meanwhile Miss Potter's anxiety would certainly distract her from the Sherwin murder and I'd been just an inch away from pinning her down. In common decency, and I never try for the uncommon sort, I'd have to hang around helping her with the Toad question, working for nothing.

I wasn't going to bother to check with the people on Toby's list. His evidence was good enough for me. I rang Miss Potter to warn her I was coming, and then went round to Penelope's.

It was raining again, heavily. The short walk had soaked my jeans. I stood in Penelope's well-appointed hall shaking my leather biker's jacket, scattering droplets of water all over the gracious wallpaper and gracious carpet. Miss Potter didn't notice. She was listening to the news about Toad: she'd insisted I tell her straight away, soaking or not. When I'd finished she sat down abruptly on an upright chair, clutching her warm, all-enveloping blue wool dressing-gown about her. She must have been in bed when I rang: odd she hadn't dressed before I arrived. She must have been really ill. 'So you say Toad returned to England in early October? Oh my dear,' she said, 'poor Toad. How dreadful. How dreadful, to have my suspicions confirmed. What shall we do?'

I wanted to shout 'Bugger Toad.' I took a pull on myself. 'Come into the kitchen,' I coaxed. 'Let's have a cup of tea.'

She followed me into the kitchen, accepted the tea and sipped it. 'What shall we do?' she asked again.

I seemed to be appointed Nanny. 'You must ring Toad's father, tell him what you've heard, ask after her. If she really is missing, he'll have to report it to the police. It's much more likely, you know, that she's in hospital being treated for anorexia and Charlotte doesn't want to admit it.'

'Do you believe that?'

'Yes.'

'Perhaps it would make things clearer if I explained the sequence of events to you.'

I didn't know what events she meant, but I took out my notebook and pencil. 'Fire away.'

Five minutes later, I looked at the notes and saw her point.

Early June: Builders start work on Ashtons Hall, repairing roof and dry rot on top floor. Scaffolding erected.

Late June: Builders laid off for six weeks. Village gossip thinks it odd.

Late June: Laura gives Miss Potter two last-minute, free tickets for Mediterranean Culture Cruise, July-Aug. Miss Potter goes, taking friend.

Early Aug: Miss Potter returns, sees Toad who seems tense, unhappy. Promises postcards.

Mid-Aug: Laura dies, Charlotte inherits. Builders restart work.

Late Aug: Toad leaves for East, Charlotte gives Miss P. two months' notice to quit the lodge.

Very early Oct: Charlotte inspects the lodge, says Miss P. hasn't kept it in satisfactory condition, picks a fight with Miss P. – effectively throws her out. Orders removal van for two days later.

Early Oct: Miss P. goes. Builders laid off again.

Give Miss P. her due, she could keep to the point when she wanted to, and string facts together to tell a story. I looked at my notes again, to talk her through it and test her conclusions. 'You think Charlotte took Toad home from school at the end of June and kept her at Ashtons?'

'I know she did that. I saw Toad in August, remember. She said she'd been ill and her mother was looking after her. Most uncharacteristic of Charlotte, I thought at the time.'

'And you think the freebie trip Laura sent you on was to get you out of the way while Charlotte was dealing with Toad? Why would she need to?'

'Perhaps because of the harshness of her planned regime,' said Miss Potter quietly. Her understatement was menacing.

I tried to dismiss it. 'Come on, Miss P. She probably just made her repeat "Anorexia won't help Daddy's career" while eating country-house breakfasts four times a day.'

'Flippancy won't help. And I must say, Alex, I am becoming increasingly irritated by your affectation of class-consciousness. You cannot seriously believe that a young girl's background disqualifies her from simple human consideration. Why do you pretend you do?'

'Fair enough,' I said. It was. That was the nearest to an apology she'd get, and she knew it. If I had felt the justice of her reproach less, I might have acknowledged it more.

'Continue, please,' she said.

'And you think Charlotte asked Laura to get you out of the way? Were they close enough for that?'

'They were very similar. "Close" is too warm a word. They would act in concert when their interests coincided.'

'And you didn't suspect anything when Laura gave you the trip?'

'No. She claimed that an acquaintance of hers had won it in a draw for which she was not even aware she had entered. That happens increasingly, nowadays. The acquaintance had already made holiday arrangements and would not, in any case, have enjoyed the cultural aspects of the cruise.'

'And you think the builders were laid off to keep strangers out of the place?'

'Toad's room, once the night nursery, is on the top floor of Ashtons Hall.'

'So you think she was locked in her room?'

'Possibly. In any case, the builders would have been witnesses.'

'But there must have been other people about in a house like that. The cleaners, for instance.'

'We are dealing with a very large house. Once the builders started work on the top floor, the cleaning women were instructed to leave it. Kate, who helps – helped – me once a week, was also employed at the hall. She tends to gossip.'

'What about the husband? What about Ludovic Mayfield? Surely he must go to Ashtons sometimes? Don't he and Charlotte get on? Doesn't he care about his daughter?'

'He is conventionally fond of Toad, I believe, but no more. Toad frequently complained to me that her father was always too busy to visit her at school or attend school functions, whereas he often found time for Charles. Charles is the favoured child of both parents. As to the relationship between Charlotte and her husband, I would describe it as an alliance. They are both ambitious, with high hopes for his career. He works very hard and is seldom in the country, even at weekends. The family time at Ashtons has always been the Christmas and summer holidays. Mr Mayfield would certainly regard the care of Toad and decisions about her health as lying within Charlotte's province.'

I remembered Charlotte's answer to my question about her childhood and whether the Sherwins were a close family. 'Not particularly,' she'd said, or something like it. 'We didn't have to be. It's a big house.' It was still a big house and there was the flat in London too: plenty of long dining-tables for the Mayfields to sit around and semaphore courteous platitudes to each other.

I should have asked all these questions when I began the quest for Toad, of course I should. Guilt made me aggressive. 'And you've seen Toad a lot, this year?'

'Several times in the Christmas and Easter holidays. Once, as I told you, in August.'

'How come you noticed nothing about the anorexia?'

'I noticed she had lost weight, naturally, but she had plenty of weight to lose. I was more concerned with her tension and unhappiness. I have been retired some years, Alex. Anorexia was not so prevalent among the young in my time.'

'OK, Miss Potter. But whatever Charlotte's treatment was, Toad survived it. She was better enough to go to India.'

'And ill enough to be sent back. Since that time, I have not heard from her. If we suppose that Charlotte knew Toad was returning early, we must assume that she picked a fight with me – on *entirely* fabricated grounds – to remove me from the scene once more.'

'And laid off the builders. It makes sense, I suppose. Why did you agree to go so quickly? Why did you agree to leave the lodge at all? Surely if you'd got a decent solicitor he could have made a case for you as a sitting tenant, or something?'

'At first I had intended to employ a solicitor. But then the – discussion with Charlotte was so unpleasant, I knew I couldn't stay.'

'But you had rights.'

'Possibly. I would not enforce them. In any case, Penelope came to my rescue.'

'But only till after Christmas. Only temporarily.'

'Let us return to Toad.'

'OK. Well then. Worst possible scenario, she's at Ashtons Hall being looked after by her mother.'

'That is not possible.'

'Why?'

'I mentioned that my cleaning woman also cleaned at the hall? Her name is Kate. Two weeks ago, I spoke to her on the telephone. She told me that Charlotte was spending much of her time in London. The house has been, effectively, closed since mid-October.'

'But the builders haven't returned to work?'

'No.'

'Wrong time of year for outside work, of course.'

'Not all the work was outside. And the scaffolding remains idle, which I believe is expensive. Charlotte is never extravagant. Moreover, she undoubtedly footed the bill for my cruise. She must have had a very good reason.' She looked at me expectantly. 'We must act.'

'What must we do?' I was pleased. It was dealing time. I'd pursue whatever batty course of action she wanted, so long as she'd come clean with me.

'Charlotte is in London, you say?'

'She said she was coming up yesterday.'

'Then we must borrow Bartholomew's car and go to the hall.'

'To do what, exactly?'

'To investigate.'

'The hall?'

'Yes.'

'What for?'

'My peace of mind.'

We wouldn't find anything, of course, but it might be a quick way to stop her fretting. 'Will we have to break in?'

'No. I shall borrow Kate's keys.'

She hadn't thought it through. If we borrowed Kate's keys and things went wrong Kate would be in trouble. We'd probably have to make it look like a break-in anyhow. It didn't matter to me.

'Are you well enough?'

'I will have to be.'

'Right,' I said. 'I'm game. But you'll have to do something for me, in exchange.'

'Explain.'

'Stop messing me about. When I went down to the hall and saw Charlotte yesterday, I also saw Kate and your dog Joss, and I realized something.'

'What was that?'

'Hang on a minute. Don't you want to ask me about Joss?' I said.

'He is well?'

'Yes. He looked well and happy. Kate said to tell you she wasn't forgetting his arthritis pills.'

'I'm pleased to hear it. There isn't much more to be said about him, is there?' She looked at me quizzically. 'What is your point, Alex?'

'All those hours we talked, you never mentioned your dog.'

'I fail to understand you.'

'I failed to understand you,' I said, 'because you misled me. I knew you were upset and confused, I knew you were deliberately giving me the runaround. I thought it was because you were desperate for someone to talk to, for human contact. In fact you were pretending to be a little old lady all alone in the world while actually you're the Queen Mum of Warwickshire with strings of friends ready to crack a bottle of gin and hang on your lightest word.'

'That is a flagrant exaggeration, Alex, and a cheap and flippant dismissal of a great lady.' Glacial pause. 'I repeat, what is your point?'

'I think you've kept me on a string until I locate Toad. Now it's show and tell time: I want you to answer my questions. I don't care if you don't know beans about the Sherwin murder. I want you cleared out of the way so I can write my piece.'

'Very well. What do you want to know?'

'Not now. If you're determined on a spot of breaking and entering, let's get on with it,' I said. 'I'll nip round to Barty's and fix the car. You get dressed and ready to be honest with me on the drive down.'

She didn't like my tone, but she could lump it. She needed me, and it was well time she stopped treating me as a pupil and started seeing me as an equal. 'Very well,' she said. 'Kindly wash up the cups.'

Seeing that it was Saturday morning, I tried Barty's front door first. When there was no answer I tried the basement office, half-expecting no reply. He might have gone to the country too. I certainly didn't expect to find Annabel, but she answered the door. 'He's here,' she said, 'come through.'

After last night's dinner, I expected seeing Barty to be awkward, but then I always underestimate the upper-class capacity to ignore embarrassment. He greeted me smilingly, embraced me ritually, and told Annabel what a lovely evening we had had. I nearly scowled and snapped. I hate other people saving my face: it's my face, for god's sake, to lose if I want to. Annabel watched us with a proprietorial, bawdy expression like the Nurse in *Romeo and Juliet*.

Barty was prepared to lend us the car but he wasn't keen on the enterprise. 'Sounds like trouble,' he said. 'Let me come with you.'

'To look after me?' I snapped. Annabel stood behind him, nodding encouragingly and mouthing 'yes'.

'I might be able to keep Miss Potter in line,' he said, unconvincingly.

'No thanks,' I said. 'I can look after myself.' Annabel was shaking her head and shrugging in despair. 'Try keeping *her* in line,' I said, indicating Annabel. Barty turned round, by which time, of course, she was straight-faced. I took the keys and left Annabel to sort it out.

Chapter Twenty

Miss Potter was waiting to leave. She was sitting on the hall chair clutching her shopping basket. She was wearing trousers, a sweater, serious walker's shoes and a green Barbour. 'My gardening trousers,' she explained. 'In case we have to move quickly.'

'Ah,' I said, trying not to smile. 'Have you had any breakfast?'

'A cup of tea.'

'When did you last eat?'

'Really, Alex, does it matter?'

'OK. Can I use the phone for a local call?'

'Of course,' she said. 'I will make a note of it for Penelope. Use the study.'

I sat down behind the desk in the study and reached for the phone, then paused. Miss Potter had been working there: she had a small leather zip-up writing case with little pockets for stamps and a matching address book. The writing paper was white Basildon Bond. She even used the piece of paper with printed lines as a guide for her shaky but deliberate hand. I read the unfinished letter on the pad, addressed to the head of a North Kensington comprehensive. *Dear Madam, I would like to apply for the post of History teacher advertised in the 'Times Educational Supplement'* . . .

The application was ridiculous, of course. She was much too old to go back to work and she wouldn't last three periods in a London school. I reflected on her foolish rectitude in using her own notepaper when the study desk was full of Penelope's expensive white Conqueror, much of it not headed, then picked up the phone and dialled Polly. Luckily, she was in, and game to prepare an extensive but ungreasy breakfast in my flat. I wanted Miss Potter in good nick for the expedition.

I glanced at her letter of application as I left the study. Was she serious?

'Come into the kitchen,' she called. I did. 'Would you like a cup of coffee before we go? There you are.' She placed a large, thick mug on the counter and filled it up to the brim.

'A mug!' I said.

'I bought it for you. Yesterday.'

She had noticed I drank coffee in large quantities, and that I was irritated by the little cups. She had spent at least two pounds on the mug: two pounds she didn't have. I refused to be touched, but there was no harm in being polite. 'Thank you,' I said, and gulped the coffee down. Fortunately, I can drink almost any amount at almost any temperature.

'I expect you saw the letter I was writing. It's quite absurd for me to expect employment, of course. I know that. I found it comforting, last night, for a short time. Don't worry about me, Alex.'

'Thanks very much for the mug,' I said. 'It's kind of you. Shall we go? I have to drop in at home first.'

'Very well.' She took the mug from me, washed and dried it, and put it by the kettle. 'Ready for our return,' she said, like a talisman.

As soon as we were in the car, I started on her. I wouldn't mention, yet, that I'd spoken to Rosalind, but I wanted to give her something to think about. 'I saw Revill again yesterday. He confirmed the affair with Rosalind.' There was a silence so prolonged I thought she hadn't heard. 'He also said Rollo was threatening to divorce Laura.' She said nothing. She didn't even put me right on the Sherwins' style and title. 'Miss Potter? Did you hear me?'

'Yes, indeed. You said Mr Revill confirmed that he had an affair with Rosalind.' She was slurring her words like a punchy boxer or a drunk. 'I don't think . . .' she tailed off.

I'd leave it to simmer, I thought, and told her we were going to my place to have breakfast. She didn't argue. Then I nattered on about Polly, since it was small-talk time, and when we got there she pulled herself together enough to appear a pleasant, if slightly distracted guest. You couldn't fault her self-control, or her stamina. She picked at scrambled eggs and mushrooms, nibbled at toast, and chatted about Polly's accountancy training and her family. I learnt more about Polly's family in half an hour than in all the five years I've known her. She turned out to have a large, close family which she'd hardly mentioned to me. Perhaps because she knew it would upset me. I've underestimated Polly.

Breakfast was over and Polly was making 'I'll let you get on' noises when Miss Potter said, 'Don't leave just yet, my dear. There is a difficulty I'm puzzling over and I'd like to hear your view, as well as that of Alex.'

Polly looked flattered and excited. She loves considering 'what-ifs' and 'what-shoulds'. I was trying to call the shots, but beyond a conviction that we'd be talking about Rosalind I didn't even get close. 'You will have to use your imagination. We are considering a young girl, but not a young girl of today. A strictly brought up young girl some thirty years ago.'

'How old?' asked Polly.

Seventeen, I thought, but let Miss Potter say it. 'She is funda-mentally good, with sound principles, but lonely, fatherless, and plucked out of the environment she knows,' she went on. 'A pas-sionate and impulsive girl. You would agree that such a girl might well enter into a liaison with an older man?'

'Sure,' said Polly. 'Of course.'

'Alex?'

'You know what I think, Miss P.'

'Neither of you would condemn her for that?'

'No way,' said Polly.

'No,' I said, thinking of Patrick and how sorry I felt for the long-ago Rosalind stuck with that big girl's blouse. So far, I couldn't see Miss Potter's difficulty, though I could see a conflict of standards.

'The difficulty that presents itself – My problem –' she ground to a halt and rubbed her knuckles as if they hurt. 'In circumstances such as I have described, can you imagine the girl involving herself with two?'

'*Two* older men?' I said, before I could stop myself. Who on earth could she mean? I ran through the cast of characters in my head.

'No,' said Polly. 'Absolutely not.'

When she heard this, Miss Potter turned green and clasped her hands to her mouth. 'Please excuse me,' she managed, and made a dash for the bathroom, closing the door behind her. It's a small flat. We could hear the retching noises. Waste of Polly's breakfast. Miss Potter is strong on privacy so I put Ella on the tape machine, loud. Ella loud could probably come off best against a San Francisco earthquake.

'Ooops,' said Polly. 'I've said the wrong thing. What's the matter with her, Alex? How could it be so important? And do you think I'm right? Older man, father figure, you don't have two of them at a time. You might have a young guy on the side. What d'you think?'

'I think you're right.' I couldn't see the implications. I was sorting through everything I knew as quickly as I could but I still couldn't get it.

'I'd better go,' said Polly, collecting her things. 'I've got to meet some people at Camden Lock for lunch. I was going to cycle over but the rain isn't going to stop, is it, and there's no point taking the bike in this. Say goodbye to Miss Potter for me, will you? She's great. I hope her problem sorts itself out.'

I said yes, of course I would, thanks very much, see you later, before I'd really heard her words, the way you do. She'd gone before I heard them. Then, as Ella launched into a new number, I clicked. I heard 'cycle', and bit by bit, the Sherwin murder fell into place, and as it fell I watched it crack Miss Potter's life into the sharp pointed shards Ella wasn't letting me hear Miss P. try to vomit into my lavatory.

Chapter Twenty-One

Miss Potter couldn't face me. She wouldn't meet my eyes after she emerged, shaking and weak, from my bathroom. She refused offers of tea, dry toast, a glass of water. She sat down at the kitchen table and waited for me to speak.

I prepared to wait her out. Ella was still singing, this time about Paris. I turned her down, then sat opposite the hunched and shaking Miss P. at the table. She had her back to the project board. Behind her, another Miss Potter smiled at me, separated from her present self by thirty years and a shotgun blast. Barty would be pleased: we had an angle.

I sat nursing my coffee mug, looking at the sepia faces. I had hardly even considered Miss Potter as murderer, because of the lodge question. I still had to sort that out: I made a note.

Looking back, I also hadn't seriously considered Miss Potter because I hadn't seen a motive. Now I could guess at a motive, I still couldn't think of her as a murderer. She had shot him, but she wasn't a murderer. The word had implications that didn't apply to her. She had been catastrophically mistaken. She had come back early from church the day of Patrick Revill's guest performance, on her bicycle, perhaps with the children. She had caught a glimpse of Patrick in Rollo's clothes, in Rollo's bed, with Rosalind, and a few days later, she had killed the wrong man. To protect, or avenge, Rosalind.

I didn't know the details. I couldn't imagine, for instance, why she hadn't simply taxed Rosalind with it. An affair with Patrick Revill would have been mildly shocking, but surely Rosalind would have 'fessed up, if only to stop Miss P. doing her nut about incest.

Failing Rosalind, of course Rollo would have denied it, and of course she wouldn't have believed him.

I tried to think my way into Miss P.'s head. Disappointed by Rosalind's behaviour, certainly: appalled, betrayed by Rollo's, certainly. *Noblesse not obliging*. But shooting him? She must have done, though, otherwise she wouldn't be so devastated by her mistake over Revill. If there hadn't been major consequences, it would merely have been a slightly bizarre misunderstanding. She'd claimed to have important information and by god she had. No wonder she was writing her memoirs; no wonder also she wouldn't publish before she died. She'd been stringing Barty along, and me too. Manipulative old banana. Poor old banana. She must be feeling like hell now her suspicions were confirmed. 'I killed my employer to protect my pupil' had a ring to it. 'I killed my employer because I got the wrong end of the stick' – it made even me wriggle with embarrassment, and it wasn't my faux pas.

I don't like waiting, but I can. I trained for it in a fairly hard school. I kept still and concentrated on the music. Ten tracks later Ella had joined Ray Charles: they both agreed it was cold outside. I wondered if my chosen tape had any significance. It was a compilation Barty had made for me. One drunken evening last year, in a second-rate hotel in Blackpool – it was only the two of us crewing a doco shoot of his, Barty directing, interviewing, lighting and camera, me on sound and everything else (don't tell the union: we were doing two and a half people's jobs each, and I'm not ticketed for sound) – I'd annoyed him by not picking up any of his music references. Next day he'd put together a golden oldies tape for me. This was it. When I played it, of course, it reminded me of Barty. Presumably I'd put it on because I wanted to think about him.

Miss Potter still hadn't spoken. She looked better, though, and she was beginning to tap her fingers on the table. 'Had we better be going?' she said.

'Not for a minute or two.'

'Why?'

'I want information. I want to talk about the murder. I know you did it.'

'How – can you know that?'

'I worked it out.'

She sighed, a deep sigh that went all the way down her gardening trousers to her sturdy walking-shoes.

'I suppose there is no point in denial.'

'None at all. I'd like to hear the details, though, and I'd like to see your memoirs. Let's go back to your place and pick them up.'

'I brought them with me,' she said. 'In my shopping basket. Ready to give you in case we find Toad. But it seems they are based on a misapprehension.'

'Most memoirs are based on several. Can I have them, please?'

She bent to the shopping basket, steadying herself with her other hand on the table, and passed me the manuscript. 'I do not understand how you can be so calm. Knowing what you know about me. Are you not afraid?'

'Why should I be? I interviewed a man once who'd killed about two hundred people, maybe more.'

'A mass murderer?'

'A retired major from Cheltenham who had a good war.'

'The cases are not the same.'

'They are, in one important respect. I had no reason to suppose he'd be any more likely to kill me than my plumber. Rather less, considering the rows we've had. Look, Miss P, you can't keep not talking to people. Have you ever told anyone about what actually happened?' She shook her head. She was rubbing the knuckles of one hand with the fingers of the other. 'I'm curious, I want to know exactly why you did it.'

'And what will you do then?'

'I don't know yet.'

'Will you tell Bartholomew?'

'Probably.'

'Will you tell the police?'

'I don't know.'

'You should. There is no statute of limitations on murder. If you do not inform the police you will make yourself an accessory after the fact.' I shrugged. 'Do not take the matter so lightly, Alex.

The laws exist to protect our civilization.' Then she saw the absurdity of her attitude, and smiled, weakly. We sat in silence for a bit. The tape had stopped. I listened to the fridge hum. Eventually she tapped her manuscript. 'Read the last chapter,' she said.

The chief topic in the household, that November, was the Hunt Ball. Lord Sherwin had decided not only that the ball should be held at Ashtons Hall with Laura as the hostess, but also that she should play a full part in the preparations. This she would not do, and indeed so little part did she play in the running of the household in the normal way that it was hardly to be expected that she could. I concluded this from my own observations, supported by the comments of Mrs Crisp. You may feel Mrs Crisp was not an unbiased commentator; I too did not place unqualified reliance on her self-aggrandizing tongue, but in most matters I found her to have a sound, if mean-spirited, grasp of reality. Fortunately for the West Warwickshire Hunt, towards the end of October Lady Paxton, Stephanie's mother, assumed responsibility for the arrangements.

Lady Sherwin had declared herself ill in early autumn, very shortly after the announcement of Lord Sherwin's decision about the ball. Dr Bloom was in constant attendance. He, apparently, accepted her as the sweet, frail and put-upon creature that she took care always, in his presence, to be. It puzzled me somewhat that he should be so deceived; in other matters he was shrewd and sometimes even cynical. That he was deceived was always likely and became certain when he married her.

Lord Sherwin did not accept his wife's illness and constantly renewed his verbal assaults on her. His voice was at all times resonant and carrying and, when raised, was audible well outside the room in which he was speaking. I tried to keep the children in ignorance of the disagreements between their parents, in vain. At this stage my sympathies lay with Lord Sherwin. Despite the laxity of his moral views, I believed him to be a very good-natured, affectionate, straightforward man.

Unhappily, my opinion of Lord Sherwin was suddenly and radically altered by the events of a Sunday morning, early in November. He was supposedly away, visiting friends. Rosalind refused to attend church that day, on the pretext that she had homework to do. I merely thought that she was sulking, as she had been so frequently of late. Lady Sherwin had recovered sufficiently to spend the weekend with Lady Paxton. Colonel Farrell, an irregular churchgoer, had agreed to drive Candida to church on this occasion while, as usual, Charlotte, Penelope and Helena rode their bicycles with me in attendance. By now they had come to enjoy the ride, as I had always done. It was a clear, mild day for the time of year.

Before the sermon Penelope became ill. I took her outside and established that the illness was not serious, merely one of her recurrent headaches. She declared her intention of cycling home. Leaving Colonel Farrell to bring the others in the car, I accompanied her, and we had a pleasant ride back to the Hall. Once there, she declared herself recovered. I believed her headaches to be largely psychosomatic, caused by the tension in the household, but as a precautionary measure we went upstairs to take her temperature. As we passed Lady Sherwin's bedroom I heard a noise, and moved closer. The door to the bedroom was very slightly ajar. Forewarned by the nature of the noises, I instructed Penelope to precede me to the schoolroom and myself went to investigate.

I approached very quietly and looked through the partly opened door. An extraordinary sight met my eyes. On the bed was a man, fully clothed in Highland dress, engaging in sexual activity with a naked girl. One glance was enough to establish that the girl was Rosalind.

The shock to me was considerable. I withdrew to my bedroom to recover my composure and decide on a course of action. That Rosalind should so forget herself as to behave in this fashion on her aunt's bed was bad enough.

I stopped reading there. I had questions to ask. 'You immediately assumed it was Rollo?' I said.

'I had no idea, then. My first impression was—'

'Go on.'

'I knew, of course, it couldn't be true.'

'What couldn't?'

'My first impression was that it was Lord Erroll. The man reminded me of Lord Erroll.' Miss P. looked abashed. 'I realize it must seem absurd.'

'No, it doesn't,' I said. I'd done it myself often enough, recognized past lovers in a turn of the head or a gesture. Wishful thinking.

Miss Potter coughed. 'And before we proceed, Alex, I must confess that I misled you about Lord Erroll.'

'He didn't have good knees?'

She quelled me with a schoolroom glare. It restored her vigour. 'I misled you about our assignation in the billiard-room.'

'You turned up and he didn't?'

'Is it so easy to guess?'

'It's so often the way of it. He was probably delayed. Maybe something came up. Anyway, why did you eventually decide the man on the bed was Rollo?'

'I realized it must have been. Lord Erroll was long dead. I do not believe in ghosts. In that bed, and in those clothes, the man must have been Lord Sherwin. He had a Scottish title, you know. I asked Penelope if her father ever wore the kilt and she told me he did, for traditional Scottish occasions.' Including, presumably, the traditional Scottish practice of tossing the niece. Miss P. could see I was unconvinced. 'There was no one else it could have been,' she said. 'I didn't want to believe it, of him, or of her.'

'Which annoyed you more?' I said.

'*Annoyed?* What a strange word to use.'

'That's what you sounded, just now.'

'I deny that, absolutely. I was – outraged.'

'Jealous?' I was goading her deliberately, and she half-knew it, but she couldn't restrain herself.

'JEALOUS?' she said, in the nearest thing to a shout I'd ever heard from her. 'WHY WOULD I BE JEALOUS?'

'Of Rosalind. She was yours, wasn't she, you'd brought her up, you felt you had to break off your relationship with her because of Laura's bitchy letter, you'd had to watch her being unhappy without helping, you'd already lost her and this meant you'd lost her finally, to a man.'

'You are quite wrong,' she said. The emotional temperature had dropped sharply. 'Quite, quite wrong, although curiously you have made the same mistake that Rosalind did. That was the conclusion she came to, or claimed she had come to, when I remonstrated with her.'

'What did she say?'

'It was a most disturbing confrontation.' She folded her lips and gazed at me. I gazed back. 'Do you want me to tell you about it?'

'Of course.'

'Then let us set off for Warwickshire. I will answer all your questions, Alex, I give you my word. Please. Let us go and look for Toad.'

'Are you up to it?'

'I will have to be. I do not believe I am really ill.'

You could have fooled me. She staggered out to the car like someone hamming it up at audition for a really ill part. She sat in silence while I fastened my own seatbelt, then hers, switched on my tape recorder and started the car. Then she sighed, and began.

Chapter Twenty-Two

'Right,' she said. Then she stopped.

'Rosalind,' I prompted. 'When you spoke to Rosalind. About the after-church episode.'

She took a deep breath. 'Yes. On the days following that Sunday, I was appalled to observe that Rosalind seemed in altogether excellent spirits. She had been depressed, on her return from Wales: now, suddenly, she was in what I used to call, in happier days, her Tigger mood.'

'Bouncing, glorious Tigger?'

'Exactly.' No wonder, I thought: Rosalind'd got her own back on Patrick. I sent her, thirty years on, belated sisterly approval.

Miss Potter went on. 'She came to the schoolroom for tea, two days later. The preparations for the ball had afforded the Crisps an excuse to discontinue drawing-room tea altogether. Colonel Farrell was reduced to begging a cup of tea from the kitchen.' She saw my impatience, and approached the point. 'Rosalind came to the schoolroom and joked with the younger girls. They were just finishing their afternoon task, copying Churchill's speeches.'

'In the entirety?'

'Selected passages. Much-needed handwriting practice, and an excellent example of English prose. Charlotte always objected. It was a sign of her deplorable cast of mind. "I hate copying stupid speeches," she used to say. "Mummy says all that Battle of Britain stuff was just propaganda, to get those poor little train-spotters in the Raff to fly to a certain death" – or words to that effect.' She stopped again, her face softening as she remembered. 'Rosalind was – very happy, that day, at first. Penelope asked if there would be ices, at the ball. Rosalind replied that there would certainly be ices, chocolate, vanilla, strawberry, and the ball would be such fun that Penelope would enjoy it even if there were fishpaste ices. We were eating fishpaste sandwiches, at the time.'

I pulled in to the kerb. 'I'm not going on till you get to the point, Miss P.'

'Very well. But, please, hurry.' I started the car. 'Rosalind was in the schoolroom, as I told you. I asked her to remain behind after tea and sent the younger girls downstairs with the trays. I then told her that I had seen her, on Sunday, in Lady Sherwin's bedroom. She looked – devastated.' Embarrassed, humiliated, I guessed. 'She said nothing. I asked her how she could, what had possessed her. I said – I'd believed in her. Her response was some childish remark such as "it's not that bad, it was a mistake". A mistake! I asked her to consider what Lady Sherwin would feel if she found out. She said she didn't think Lady Sherwin would care, she said she, Rosalind, wasn't going to have a baby, she said it didn't matter, I was the only person who knew.'

Miss Potter was breathing deeply. I left her in her silence for as long as I could bear to. 'And then you said . . . ?'

'And then I asked her about her partner. I used the word "partner". I could not bear to name Lord Sherwin. She said, "He won't talk about it. He's a coward, scared of his own shadow."'

'And you still thought she was talking about Rollo?'

'What else was I to think?' she said helplessly. 'I was – insulted. I reproached Rosalind. I said that I was disappointed in her, that I had thought her a young girl of principle. I had spent so long with her, Alex, and tried to give her so much. She was, in a way, my life's work. She attempted to excuse herself, and explain. Like a child caught in a minor peccadillo. She kept saying, "pax". Pax, as if she had stolen apples! She wanted to explain, she said. As if anything she said could explain what she'd done! I continued to—' she stopped.

'You went on telling her off, shouting at her – you were angry—'

'And then she said, "You're just jealous. You don't want me to grow up. You want to keep me for yourself. You're a jealous old maid." She was going to leave. She tried to get up. I pushed her back in the chair, and she said, "Don't touch me. Get your stinking hands off me, you old – lesbian."'

Silence.

'And you said . . . ?' I prompted.

'I could say nothing. What was there to say? If that was what she thought . . .'

'It wasn't what she believed,' I said, wondering if that was true. 'It was probably the worst insult she could think of. She must have been feeling guilty and upset. It would've made her aggressive; it does me.'

'I've noticed,' she said tartly. 'I found the accusation particularly difficult to shrug off, Alex. I had believed that Rosalind, at least, understood the nature of my feelings for her. I wished her only the best. I was not possessive; my attempts to disassociate myself from her when we first returned to England were at least partly motivated by my reluctance to separate her from her own people. We were separated by – a great rift valley. She had to rejoin her family, I thought. It was only after some time at Ashtons Hall that I realized there was no "family" for her to rejoin – only individuals, unhappy, impotent or selfish individuals.'

'Lots of families are like that.'

'Indeed. Drive faster, Alex, please.'

We were just past Oxford: at the rate we were moving, we would reach Ashtons in about forty minutes. I needed longer. When we got there, we just might find hard information about Toad, and I was afraid that when we did, Miss Potter would shut down. No more reminiscence, no more confession, nothing. I tried to frighten her by letting the BMW go. My ploy failed. She was a speed nut. When we topped a hundred and ten she gave an exhilarated little giggle. I imagined her cheeks were touched with pink, too, but I wasn't about to take my eyes off the motorway to look.

My nerve went first. 'That's it,' I said, slackening my pressure on the accelerator till we were crawling along at eighty. 'Let's get back to you and Rosalind. You were disturbed by your fight?'

'Of course. I have already told you that it was a most upsetting confrontation,' said Miss Potter, 'and I now see, fraught with misunderstanding. I didn't name Lord Sherwin, I couldn't, and I assumed, of course, that Rosalind knew who we were talking about.'

'As she assumed you did. If you weren't jealous of Rosalind, why were you so upset?'

'Surely it's obvious?'

'I'd like you to tell me.'

'It had to do with my feelings for Lord Sherwin.' She started fiddling with the clasp on her handbag. She was stuck. I prodded her on.

'Did you fancy him?'

'I have never grasped the subtleties of contemporary slang.'

'It isn't very contemporary and it's certainly not subtle. It means desire, find attractive, like the look of, shave your underarms and hold in your stomach for. Come on, Miss P., you've got so far, you might as well tell me the rest.'

'Are you not shocked, Alex?'

'What by?'

She waved her hand in an uncharacteristically helpless gesture. 'I'm not sure. I find you very disconcerting.'

'I'm sorry, Miss P.' I was, sort of. She'd produced her big secret: the least she could expect was shock. I'd been all shocked out long ago, but that wasn't her fault. I dredged round for a reaction. 'I'm sorry,' I said.

'Sorry for me?'

'It must be embarrassing for you. Killing Rollo for something he hadn't done. I hate that feeling, when you've cocked up in a major way and you blush all over when you realize it. What you need is perspective.'

'Do you think you can provide that?'

'Almost any sentient human being who wasn't involved could. Nothing easier to sort than other people's problems, right?

You've spent your life doing it. Tell me about you and Lord Sherwin.'

'I nearly loved him. He was a most attractive man. One evening we were alone together and he flirted with me. He made it clear that an affair between us was possible.'

'An affair?'

'Perhaps that is a little grandiose. It might be more accurate to borrow an expression from our American cousins and say "a roll in the hay".' She stopped abruptly. 'But I have already told you that. Had you forgotten?'

I hadn't, but I wouldn't have minded her running it by me again. She'd probably tell me a lot more the second time, and now I wanted every detail, every tiny little human snippet for my money-coining, luscious, sex-and-snobbery piece.

'You turned him down?' I prompted.

'That evening, yes. Later, I gave the matter much thought. I was, after all, nearly thirty-eight, without sexual experience, very soon to be a confirmed spinster, the most inconsiderable of God's creatures. I began to feel that I did not want to die without ever knowing – without ever having – And yet, he was a married man. Even had he not been, I never held the view that sex was no more than fun. Fornication is sinful.'

'But?'

'But most of my life had been so dull. Surely, I thought, no one should reach forty without having done ANYTHING?'

'You had done things.'

'What, exactly?'

'You'd done your duty. You'd looked after Rosalind. You'd done what you were brought up to do.'

'The Nuremberg defence. Not, in my case, for acts of mindless brutality, but for acts of mindless respectability. You must remember I am an Anglican. I believe in the duty of the individual to follow her conscience.'

I'm not great on Anglican theology; she'd lost me. 'And your conscience dictated a roll in the hay with Rollo?'

'Not necessarily that. Action, my own action, of some kind.

That's what I meant about not following maps. At the time, I saw the scope for action as limited, effectively, to sexual action. I must have been deranged. A hormonal disturbance, possibly.'

'You mustn't say that. The feminists wouldn't like it.'

'The feminist movement does not command my allegiance. I cannot subscribe to a system of thought which functions mainly by ignoring inconvenient but self-evident realities. No, Alex. My behaviour could more usefully be analysed by the disciples of Freud. I was in my late thirties, marriage seemed very unlikely, and if it came, it would not, I felt, have been with anyone as – as – *experienced* as I guessed Lord Sherwin to be.'

'You thought he'd be a fantastic screw.'

She laughed. 'Now you are teasing me, but yes, I suppose that is what I thought.'

'He might have been awful.'

'You must also remember that I had little choice. I was not exactly besieged with offers. I considered very carefully. Looking back, I suppose I was also influenced by the interest that he had shown in me. Not romantic interest, you understand. Simple human interest.'

'Like what?'

'He asked me to tell him the story of my life. Of course, he did not mean that literally. I imagine he expected to hear a considerably abridged version. Nevertheless, he had spoken to me as if I was a human being, with experiences and feelings.' She looked at me, sharply. 'What are you forbearing to say, Alex?'

'Nothing.'

'I was deluding myself, of course. It didn't seem delusion at the time. I felt Lady Sherwin need not be a factor. She had refused Lord Sherwin his marital rights since the birth of Candida eight years before.'

'How did you know that?'

'My dear Alex, everyone at Ashtons Hall, including the outdoor servants, knew it. Lord Sherwin's voice—'

'Was resonant and carrying. I remember. What did you decide?'

'I decided to – see if the offer was still open. My decision was precipitated by my experiences during a visit to an old schoolfriend, Caroline, and her family. She had been a good friend for many years. It had been Caroline's aunt I had stayed with during my first fateful visit to Kenya, and it was through Caroline's aunt that I obtained my first employment in Kenya. Caroline and I had corresponded faithfully over the years, and met whenever she visited her aunt. Naturally she had pressed me to stay when I returned to England. I was reluctant, partly because, as she had a husband, three children and a small house in Orpington, I knew hospitality would not be easy.'

'But you went.'

'Yes. Early in November, I went. Caroline was kindness itself and her family made me very welcome, but I was uncomfortable. It was all so – domestic. They had family jokes. I was expected to admire the children.'

'And you didn't?'

'Uncharitable as it must sound, I didn't. They were, I thought, ill-disciplined, ill-educated and unintelligent. They found me petty and foolish; they imitated my manner of speech. I am sure they meant it kindly, but it was a busman's holiday. By then I was less than fond of young people, whom I viewed as work. The ten-year-old girl, Leila, was learning the piano, much against her will. The supervision of her practice sessions fell to me. I have never much admired the little music book of Anna Magdalena Bach, but in justice to the composer I must suppose that Anna Magdalena had at least some talent for the instrument. Caroline herself – I may have been over-sensitive, but she seemed to condescend to me, as if my own lack of children barred me from full membership in the human race. I returned from Orpington determined to take my chances with Lord Sherwin.'

She looked at me, appealingly.

'It seems fair enough to me,' I said. It did. I didn't add that it also seemed sure to end in tears, because it so emphatically had, and the superiority of hindsight is an occupational hazard I try to avoid.

'You are, of course, of a different generation, with a much more liberal attitude to sex.'

'It used to be. It's all gone difficult again now.'

'Why is that?'

'Aids and condoms. The end of the one-night stand, mid-eighties some time.'

'Would you say that was generally true?' Miss P. was noticeably calmer. Nothing seemed to suppress her desire for information. If she'd been born forty years later, she'd have made a good researcher. Or a good almost anything, come to that.

'Depends how cautious you are, but for many people, yes, I think so. Have you ever seen the James Bond films?'

'Those made during the nineteen-seventies. When I was a house-mistress it was sometimes part of my duties to escort the girls to the cinema. At one school particularly the headmistress indulged the girls excessively, I thought, in such matters as parties and treats, to compensate for the inadequacies of the provision in other areas, such as qualified teachers, facilities and hygienic accommodation.'

'James Bond is a good social indicator. Recently he only beds one girl a film.'

'I can imagine that that would make substantial inroads into the plots, as I remember them. Thank you, Alex, but we have had enough distracting conversation, I think. Shall we move on?'

'OK. Where shall we move to?' No answer. 'Go on about Rollo,' I nudged. She didn't hesitate.

'I was in a difficult position. How was I to – offer myself to Lord Sherwin? I could not go to my employer's bedroom, uninvited, and I suspected that he would find any stratagem of mine as transparent as I found the stratagems of my pupils. I watched and waited. Latish one evening, I went to the library, ostensibly in search of a book. I passed his study door, which was ajar. He called me in and offered me a drink, which I accepted. He admired my blouse. I told him it had an antique lace trim. He said as long as it wasn't trimming an antique, he didn't give a damn.' She looked at me anxiously. 'What are you thinking, Alex?'

I was thinking that Rollo's techniques should have been remaindered before the First World War. Perhaps it was the way he told them.

She went on, without being pressed. She liked talking about Rollo. 'We sat down. He made a jocular reference to his daughters, something like "How are things in the nursery? Rabbits nibbling their school-work, are they?" Then he asked me why I had come. I said I had been thinking over what he had said the last time we met. He evidently did not remember what he had said: he may not even have remembered the occasion. I realized then, forcibly, how insignificant I was in his eyes.' She paused, hurt and perhaps insulted by the memory. Had she killed him partly because she was slighted? 'He made me feel foolish,' she said. 'He asked me why I was there. I told him I had come to the library for a book, but he laughed. He said that I had come specifically in pursuit of him. I denied it, but he was right, of course. He even described what I had done. He said, "You waited till Crisp locked up and Farrell and Rosalind went to bed, then you brushed your hair, and pinched your cheeks and put on your best blouse and a bit of lipstick, and came to find me." I could hardly deny it. I blushed. I have always had an unfortunate tendency to blush.'

'I've noticed.'

'Then he said, "Come over here." He extended his hands to me, palm up. He said I had beautiful hands. Then he kissed my fingers, lightly.'

There, Miss Potter stuck. 'He kissed your fingers? Then what?' I prompted. Silence. 'You obviously remember it very clearly. Did you write about it in your memoirs? Can I read it?'

'No. No. I omitted any mention of a relationship between us. My memoirs are not – always absolutely frank. I was humiliated, I think.'

'Humiliated because you went to bed with him?'

'No. Humiliated because I didn't.'

That did surprise me. Rollo was evidently a successful operator. He had a reputation to soften her up, he took enough trouble to pay her flattering attention, and she'd already committed herself in her own mind. A persistent garden gnome could have had her, surely? 'What happened? Why did you wimp out?'

'I didn't. I felt like it, of course. I was thoroughly self-conscious and close to panic, but his kisses were very calming.'

'Calming?'

'To my fears. He seemed to know what he was doing. No, it was Lord Sherwin's decision not to . . .'

'Why?'

'My dear, I wish I knew. I've considered it, often. Immediately after that night, until I thought I saw him in bed with Rosalind, my mind was filled with it, and I never could decide.'

'What actually happened?'

'We kissed a little. Then he said, "You're a serious Mouse, aren't you? Better get off upstairs before you turn into a pumpkin."'

'Those were his exact words?'

'Yes. I wrote them in my diary, immediately. They were obscure to me then, and have remained so.'

'What tone of voice did he use? Apart from resonant?'

'Gentle. Amused. Rather tender. I found it very affecting. Alex, I wish I understood his motives. Especially now I know that he was not in fact involved with Rosalind. I was so mistaken in him, for so long.'

'And you killed him.'

She bowed her head. I passed her a Kleenex. She dabbed her eyes and blew her nose. I fished in my pocket and gave her a barley sugar.

'Bay of Biscay time,' I said.

Chapter Twenty-Three

After two barley sugars and five more Kleenex, Miss P. was back on line. 'D'you want a break?' I asked. I wasn't sure how much she could manage at a time. The stimulation of talking about Rollo had ebbed: she looked every day of her age and very tired. We were already past Banbury. I'd left the motorway too soon and slowed down to forty, but even if we crawled we'd soon be there and I wanted to hear her out before I had to start picking locks. Besides, breaking and entering is best done under cover of darkness and it was only about half-past two. Even in Warwickshire, the November sun couldn't set before half-past three. 'Would you like a cup of tea?'

'Thank you, my dear, but no. We must press on.'

I drove more and more slowly, in silence apart from the swish of the windscreen wipers. They were very up-market wipers: I enjoyed the choice of five settings. Miss P. was too preoccupied to notice that we were being overtaken by a determined cyclist. 'I must admit it seems as if you were right, to a certain extent,' she said.

'What about?'

'It does help to talk about what happened.'

'Shining light into dark places brings the spiders down to size,' I said, trying to sound as if that was always a good thing. I didn't know how she would feel when she was left with tiny, withered spiders, rather than a tragic secret.

'Let us continue,' said Miss Potter decisively. 'I'd like to hear your views,' she said. 'Why do you think Lord Sherwin sent me away?'

'All kinds of possibilities. Do you want best scenario or worst scenario?'

'Worst scenario.'

'You were a lousy kisser.'

'That was what I feared. Not exactly in those terms, but along those lines. I simply wasn't attractive enough.'

'I was joking,' I said.

Her look was half-reproachful, half-impatient. 'This is important to me, Alex.'

I wasn't going to let her get away with it. 'It is and it isn't, Miss P. For one thing, it's done and over long ago. For another, we're never going to know what Rollo meant or intended. You didn't know at the time and you're the only witness we've got, and a very interested witness. Yes, I can think of reasons Rollo sent you away with a pat on the head. He was meeting someone else and needed to get rid of you. He didn't feel like sex. You bored him. He'd taken a vow of celibacy that morning. He was too drunk to get it up. He had the clap. He didn't want to take the risk of you coming over all infatuated and making trouble. He knew you didn't really want to do it even though you thought you did. He knew you'd regret it in the morning. He didn't want to take advantage of you. He had your best interests at heart. I don't know which it was.'

'Is it possible he had my best interests at heart?'

'Of course.'

'That is what I hoped.' She was looking at me, anxiously. I'd battered her enough, and who knew? It could have been magnanimity, Rollo the gentleman and aristocrat.

'You were there. If that's what you think, that's probably what it was.'

'At the time, I was bewildered. Very relieved; I had been wrong, I knew it, even to consider such a thing. I was grateful for his thoughtfulness. That was my eventual reaction. But at first I felt cheated, belittled, and when I saw Rosalind with him I felt angry and sick. Not because of Rosalind. Because of him. He hadn't wanted me and he did want her, and she was just a child.'

'Was that why you shot him?'

'I don't know. I've never known, quite.'

'Tell me about it. Describe the evening, if you can remember it.'

'If I can remember!'

Silence. Come on, come on, I urged. The recorder was still running. I wanted a confession. A confession, on tape. I still couldn't quite believe my luck. There had to be money in this. 'Stephanie said Lord Sherwin was annoyed with his wife, that evening?'

That topic was safe enough: she plunged in. 'He was. I overheard them quarrelling in her bedroom. She was refusing to attend the ball. He insisted that she get dressed. He repeated his demand for a divorce. He said that if she refused to dress, he'd carry her downstairs as she was.' Miss Potter's cheeks glowed at the memory: she evidently found his machismo appealing.

'And so she did dress?'

'Naturally. In less than twenty minutes she was downstairs, playing hostess, being charming to the Master and his wife. If anything, her performance was overdone.'

Silence.

'The little girls?' I prompted, to ease her back in.

'Penelope was very excited. All the children were excited and happy, getting dressed. They had new dresses. Charlotte was teasing Penelope: she threw her new white socks on top of the cupboard. Candida, the youngest, couldn't manage the buttons on her new black patent leather shoes. Penelope fetched a button hook, to help her.'

'And then at the ball itself,' I nudged.

'Penelope danced with Candida, before the guests arrived. Charlotte approached Rollo, I imagine to ask him to dance with her, but he avoided her and came towards me. Charlotte was his least favourite child. I ignored him. I was helping the barmen to wipe and set out the champagne glasses. I was wearing my dark blue taffeta, and white gloves. I had freed my fingers from the gloves, and folded them back at the wrist.'

There was, for the first time, a glibness in Miss P.'s voice. She was hiding something. But I couldn't afford to stop her, and

I hoped it was something unimportant. Perhaps she'd agreed to dance with Rollo after all, incestuous villain though he was, and left the barmen to it.

She went on. 'Rosalind was looking very beautiful: she was wearing her mother's pearls, and the sight of her, coming down the stairs, made Colonel Farrell cry. Then they danced together, and the other guests began to arrive. The ball appeared to go well. I received two invitations to dance: under normal circumstances, I would have accepted, but I was too – preoccupied with what I believed to be the relationship between Lord Sherwin and Rosalind. They danced together, several times. Looking back, I can see she was relieved to escape from Patrick Revill, who monopolized her. At the time, I could not understand what he was doing there at all. Colonel Farrell hovered while Rosalind danced with the actor. He was sensitive, in some ways. I suppose he was trying to pluck up the courage to cut in, but of course Lord Sherwin, once he saw Rosalind's plight, acted decisively and effectively. When Lord Sherwin and Rosalind danced, she was happy.'

And you watched, spitting nails, I thought, jealous of them both, excluded by them both, angry beyond words at Rosalind's behaviour.

Nothing would stop Miss Potter now. 'As the evening wore on I had to force myself to carry out my duties, to supervise the children and see them to bed after supper. Charlotte didn't want to leave the ball; I saw her, an hour or so later, in her night-things, watching through the banisters from the first floor landing. I dealt with her summarily and dragged her back to bed. I nearly dislocated her arm. She had the sense to say nothing. When I returned to the party, Lord Sherwin was nowhere to be seen. Rosalind was dancing with a young man I didn't know. She was flirting. I could not believe that, bearing such a burden of guilt, she could be so indifferent. Had I taught her nothing, in all those years?'

'Where was Rollo?'

'I went to look for him. I am not sure why. He wasn't on the dance floor, or on the terrace with the small group watching a foolish, drunken guest shooting rabbits, nor in the dining-room amid the remains of supper. He was not in his study. I went into his study for a moment, and remembered the last occasion I had been there.'

'When he kissed your fingers and sent you to bed?'

'Exactly. The band was playing a gallop. I could hear the music, and the guests' barbaric whoops and shrieks. I was bitterly angry. I despised them, Alex. I thought, they are nothing. Why have I served them for so long? Then I heard raised voices from the gun-room, next door. One of them was Rollo's.'

Miss Potter stopped talking, suddenly, as if she was choking on the words. It was the first time I had ever heard her call him Rollo. Intimacy was allowable between murderess and soon-to-be victim, perhaps. 'What did you hear?' I said. 'Who was in there?'

'The gun-room door was shut. I listened to them quarrelling. Rollo and Laura. She sounded – vicious. "Don't think you'll get away with this and live happy ever after with your latest floosie," she said. "I'll take you for every penny, see if I don't, and your precious house."'

'Are you sure that's what she said?'

'I have an excellent memory. It was a significant occasion, for me. I am nearly sure.'

'What did he say?'

'"If I was rid of you, it'd be cheap at the price, believe me. But the lawyers say there's no chance of that."' Miss Potter was speaking slowly, stickily, as if she didn't want to form the words.

'Go on,' I said.

'I heard a scuffle, as if – as if they were pushing at each other. Then Rollo said, "Don't be so stupid, Laura. Put that down. You know it's not loaded." I realized they were talking about a gun, and I heard the click, click, snap, of the loading process. Then Laura said, "It is now. Don't you dare come near me or I'll blow your head off, Rollo, see if I don't. I'm upset. You've upset me," in her usual querulous tone, as if that was the ultimate sin. I assume, to her, it was. "You've upset me, Rollo,"' mimicked Miss Potter, in a sickening croon. '"You've never loved me. Never. You don't know what love is. You think it's rolling round in a sweaty bed with a cheap little tart."'

She ground to a halt once more.

'And then?'

'And then I heard a shotgun blast. It took me some moments to understand that the noise came from outside, from the terrace. It was mingled with the maddening, insistent thump of the band. It made me jump. Then Rollo spoke again. "Put that bloody thing down," he said. "Keep away from me," said Laura. I heard a slap, and a scream. Then the door opened. I retreated to the study with undignified haste, and waited until Laura's sobs receded down the corridor and up the back stairs.'

Pause. I cleared my throat, but she went on without a prompt.

'When the sobs had gone, I couldn't resist going to Rollo.'

'And?'

'I told him I had overheard.'

'What did he say?'

'He seemed shaken, but he made a visible effort to appear unconcerned. "Hello, Miss Mouse," he said. He had called me that before, when we were alone.'

'It sounds an affectionate name.'

'Patronizing, Alex, not affectionate. He called his daughters "rabbits", and that was not affectionate either. It was patronizing and dismissive. I may not have been – important, or beautiful, or considerable in his eyes, but at least I was a human being. I said, "Don't call me that. My name, as you know very well, is Sarah." I was – very angry with him.'

By now I was driving so slowly that I could afford to watch her. I'd have preferred to stop, but was afraid to break her concentration. She was flushed, excited. She was enjoying the memory – or, depressing thought, the fantasy. I didn't know how much to believe.

'He seemed to me arrogant and – rather thrilling. I thought – how spoilt he was, how careless, how like Rosalind. "I despise you all," I said. It was not entirely true. "Why?" he said. "How can you ask that?" I said. I confronted him with it. "I must tell you, Lord Sherwin, I saw you on Sunday." "Saw me where?" he said. I thought he was affecting innocence. I thought he was dismissing me. "On your wife's bed. With Rosalind," I said. I could hardly form the words, and he just laughed. "Christ Almighty. Everyone's gone mad. Get back to the rabbits, Miss Mouse," he said, and moved towards me, perhaps to go past me to the door. I seized the gun from the chair where Laura had left it, and stopped him. "I demand an explanation," I said.'

She paused, breathing deeply. 'I now see that he could not have understood me. At the time, I felt goaded by his barefaced denial of his – misbehaviour. "Demand away," he said. "I don't know what the bloody hell you're getting at, and I need a drink. Give me that gun, it's loaded." I stood my ground. "I know," I said. "I've done some shooting in Kenya. I will not stand by and allow you to degrade Rosalind." He laughed again. "Get out of my way. You're talking rubbish," he said, moving towards me. "Out of my way, Miss Thing." It was – the last straw. "My name is Sarah," I said. I was so angry, so angry, Alex.'

'Of course. Of course,' I said. 'And then?'

'I—' she gestured, vaguely, with trembling hands. 'There was blood and brains, spattered on the walls, on the sofa, on the carpet. He was obviously dead. I stood for a moment. I don't know what I thought, or if I thought. Then I left the room, closing the door behind me, and made my way to the terrace.'

Miss Potter was crying. I pulled over into a layby, grabbed more Kleenex and wiped the tears from her cheeks as they fell. 'There, there,' I said. She didn't move to push me away.

'He was all in pieces, Alex. He was so handsome. He was – blown apart.'

'I know he was handsome. I saw the photographs. Hush, Miss P.'

'The blood was everywhere. It didn't show against his coat. He was in hunting pink, with hunt buttons. I think I – I think I loved him.'

'No wonder. Anyone would. Hush now.' I hugged her. I could feel her bones under the flesh. She had very delicate bones. I felt like a hippo comforting a quail.

'He hadn't even done what I thought he'd done. He wasn't *guilty*. He wasn't guilty.'

'It was bad luck. He was furious with Laura, he would have listened otherwise.'

'He always just – brushed me aside, as if I didn't exist. He never remembered my name.'

'He didn't know what you thought. He couldn't read your mind. It was a misunderstanding, that's all. Here, blow.' I held the Kleenex to her nose and patted her on the back. 'Blow your nose, Miss P.'

'I was of no account, to them. He didn't even know my name. He didn't see me.'

Gradually, she calmed down, blew her nose, and gave me a watery blue-eyed smile. 'I haven't been sleeping, since you first suggested Rosalind's – involvement with Mr Revill. It was worse than the night after – after the ball. At least, then, I believed that Rollo was guilty, of corrupting Rosalind, of terrible arrogance, thinking he could do what he liked, with her and with me.'

'What did you do next?'

'I waited for the police. The servants didn't find him until the next morning, but I thought, when they did, they'd come to arrest me.'

'Why didn't you tell them you'd done it? What about a citizen's duty?'

'They never asked me if I knew the identity of the murderer. If they had asked me specifically, I would have told them. They kept asking me where I'd been, what I'd done, and I gave them an edited version. I was invisible to them, too.'

'It has its advantages.'

'I suppose I was lucky.'

'What did you feel?'

'My dear, do you really want to know? You've been most kind to listen, but your interest is in facts, is it not?'

'I'm interested in you.'

'Why?'

'Don't fish for compliments. Just tell me. What did you feel?'

'I was too shocked to feel at all, for weeks. I did the best I could for the children. I kept away from Rosalind. My clearest memory is of Lady Sherwin. I don't think she felt a moment's grief for her husband.'

'Who did she think had killed him?'

'She was scarcely interested. She was a selfish woman with a commonplace mind. To her, I was merely the children's priggish governess, too insignificant to pull the trigger of a gun she had loaded. Besides, the death of her husband was a great relief to her. If a tramp could have been apprehended she would have been delighted, but she was chiefly concerned that the police did not discover that she and Lord Sherwin had been arguing, that night. I think she felt that, if I cared to tell the police that I had over-heard an argument between them, and moreover an argument that involved the shotgun, they would believe it had culminated in his death. They already suspected her.'

'You told her you'd overheard?'

'Yes.'

'And that's how you got the cottage? She was still frightened, all those years after?'

'Yes. She would have lost her inheritance, you see. That was her chief anxiety.'

'She might have been hanged.'

'Most unlikely.'

'So you blackmailed her?'

Miss Potter pursed her lips, considering the word. 'Yes,' she said.

'Didn't the police get anything out of you?'

'The officer conducting the investigation was a very stupid man. Self-righteous and rude. I did not feel encouraged to co-operate. I have always tried to do my job, whatever it might be, to the best of my ability. I saw no reason to do his. Above all, I didn't want them to find out about Rosalind. I did not want her involved, in any way. However appalling her behaviour had been, the responsibility was overwhelmingly Lord Sherwin's. She was a young girl. Her life could have been ruined. The publicity was, in any case, intolerable. We were besieged. Reporters hid in every hedge.'

'It'd have been much worse now.'

'It was quite bad enough then.'

'And you didn't tell Rosalind?'

'What I knew? Certainly not.'

'In case she told the police?'

'No. I was prepared to take my punishment. I was not prepared for her to feel herself responsible for my guilt and my feelings. It would have been an unendurable burden. It was a strange time, Alex. Sometimes the shock lifted for hours at a time and then I felt furious and betrayed and deeply sorry, all at once.'

'And jealous?'

'I think, now, I must have done. That is not how I characterized it at the time. I could not understand how I had been so mistaken in her, and how my tutelage had so failed her. It seemed to make a nonsense of my life. Whole days went past in which I worked and spoke and ate, but of which I could remember nothing. I kept the children occupied but I had little to give. Penelope felt the lack, I know. She was hardest hit by her father's death. I also, looking back, failed Colonel Farrell. But I did my best. I prayed and waited.'

'What were you waiting for, exactly?'

'To make amends in any way I could. Particularly to the little girls, who had not only lost a father but who had been left in the sole care of Lady Sherwin. Their father's death had left their situation changed, irretrievably, for the worse. I tried to convince myself, at the time, that Lord Sherwin's behaviour towards Rosalind might eventually have extended itself to his daughters, but I did not, even then, believe it. How could I have been so stupid, Alex? Looking back, it's absolutely clear to me. Lord Sherwin was not at all the incestuous type. But I had seen them, I had seen them, and I could not erase the image from my mind. Not just my mind; it pervaded my body and being.'

We sat in silence for a while. Then she sighed deeply. 'Drive on, Alex,' she said. 'I've kept my side of the bargain, have I not? You have your story. Now, please, resume your search for Toad.'

I handed over more Kleenex and restarted the car.

Chapter Twenty-Four

The cleaning woman, Kate, was out when we arrived, bless her. The council house was closed and silent. I pressed the doorbell for an unreasonably long time, pleased by the echoing of the impotent chimes. With any luck I'd have another half-hour or so alone with Miss Potter, I dashed through the rain back to the car, composing my face to disappointment.

'Oh dear,' she said blankly. The predictable setback seemed to have filleted her. She looked very old. 'Alex, I . . .' she trailed away, started again. 'I must . . .'

'Never mind,' I said, 'she'll be here soon, surely. We can ask the neighbours.' The houses on both sides were obviously occupied.

'Under normal circumstances she would be here by now.'

'She will be.'

'Perhaps we should go straight to the hall and break in,' she said. 'Surely that is not beyond your powers, Alex?'

It probably wasn't, not with scaffolding up. People were getting much more sophisticated about burglar alarm systems and security locks, but my bet was that Charlotte was meaner than she was paranoid. Ludovic Mayfield might have persuaded her to fortify the place, though, and in any case I didn't want to do anything until I'd squeezed Miss Potter dry and it was dark. 'Let's hang on for a few minutes,' I said. 'Tell me some more, Miss P. Tell me what it was like after the murder.'

'Must I? I would like to rest.'

'Soon. When Kate comes back . . .'

'And if she doesn't?'

'Then I'll break in to look for Toad, but not till it's dark.'

She could see the sense of that. She watched me weakly while I changed the tape in my recorder. 'Don't you ever tire?' she asked, rather wistfully.

'Of course. But I'm quite a bit younger than you, and I've got a job to do.' I felt half-bad, forcing her on, but not enough to forgo the story. It was the best chance I'd ever had and it wasn't my fault she'd got herself into such a mess.

'I was – as vigorous as you, once.'

Give the woman credit, I'd listened to hours of self-revelation and read two volumes of memoirs, and it was the first time I'd ever known her self-pitying. She must be on her knees, I thought. Or else she was up to something, trying to avoid going on with her story.

'After the murder . . .' I said.

She sighed. 'Very well. Penelope had nightmares. Charlotte had shown her the murder photograph: she told Penelope that Rollo was being eaten by worms. She kept chanting "Daddy's in his coffin, Weetabix for Worms", and wriggling her fingers. The young can be very cruel . . . Rosalind and I tried to reassure Penelope with assurances of an after-life. Charlotte insisted there was no life after death. Penelope often went to Rosalind's bed in the middle of the night. Rosalind comforted her with stories of her life in Kenya. Laura lay on the sofa. She decided the children must go to boarding-school. I prepared their uniform trunks. Rosalind was to go to London with the Paxtons.'

She ground to a halt, looked at me appealingly, saw I was expecting more and went on. 'Colonel Farrell was very shaken by Rollo's death. Partly from genuine feeling, partly because he was anxious about his future, with good reason. Laura was not especially fond of him: the chances were she would have asked him to leave, and he had nowhere to go, and no resources. Rosalind suggested to him that she should buy a flat in London for them to set up house together.'

'Sounds like a great idea,' I said. I'd never taken to Farrell, but he was a simple old fool, and by all accounts fond of Rosalind. 'What went wrong?'

'He asked my advice. He asked if it would be best for Rosalind. He valued my judgement. I advised him, strongly, against it. I told him that Rosalind had recently shown me that she was by no means a good girl, and that she needed a very firm hand. I said that he would be the worst possible person to have charge of her. He was very disappointed, but he took my advice and refused Rosalind's offer. He was innocent, foolish and biddable.'

'You didn't really fail him,' I said bracingly. 'As far as you knew, Rosalind did need a very firm hand, and she was probably better off with the Paxtons. Farrell died of a heart attack soon after, didn't he? So it didn't make much difference. He died before he and Rosalind would have set up house together.'

'He died holding a shotgun. He intended to kill himself. He left a note confessing to the murder of Lord Sherwin.'

'Why?'

'I imagine, because he wanted to protect Rosalind, whom he thought was involved. I must have given him that impression. Rosalind found him and came to me. We removed the gun, and the suicide note. In the event, he had died of natural causes, probably of fear. He had a very timid nature.'

'Poor old boy,' I said.

'I found him exasperatingly dim-witted,' she said. 'I blame myself. I did not pay attention.' She lay back in the seat and closed her eyes and I looked at her closely. She still looked old, but less frail: the colour was back in her cheeks. Barty was right, she was unimaginably tough. She might even weather this.

Well, Barty and I had an angle. I had enough for my piece, even if she clammed up on me tomorrow. She'd kept her side of the bargain: now I had to keep mine. 'OK, Miss P.,' I said. 'Let's go and get some tea. You must eat something or you really will be ill. Where's the nearest tea place?'

'Stratford, at this time of year,' she said. 'But—'

'Trust me,' I said, and started the car. As I drove, something nagged at me, something wrong about Kate's house. It was dark, locked up, silent. Why shouldn't it be? There was a reason: some-where kicking around in the back of my mind was a reason. I switched my attention away from it. I'd remember if I didn't try.

After three rounds of dry toast, she looked stronger still. She glanced around the tourist-trap tea shop with its ridiculously small, over-flounced tables littered with grubby stand-up triangles of cardboard advertising the special *As You Like It* all-inclusive snack lunch, dabbed her mouth with a napkin, took a deep breath. 'Alex, would you clear up a small point for me? Your name. What is your real name? You cannot have imagined I would believe your fabrication.'

'My mother meant to call me Alice.'

'A perfectly acceptable name with both royal and literary asso-ciations. Why did you choose Alex?'

'The registrar did. My mother had a mental illness, Miss P.'

'Post-natal depression?'

'In a manner of speaking. It came on after she was born and it's lasted fifty years, give or take the odd remission.' If she was making small-talk, she was obviously well enough to go on. 'Miss Potter, when you originally agreed to help Barty, what did you intend to do? What was going on in your mind? You couldn't have published your memoirs, could you?'

'I was behaving stupidly. I was angry with Charlotte. She was extraordinarily unpleasant to me, Alex.'

'When she picked the fight to get you out?'

'Yes. She accused me of – she said—'

'Spit it out. It's better said.'

'She said – I had deviant sexual tendencies.'

Chalk it up to me, I didn't laugh. I didn't even smile. My Catholic foster-mother (the obsessive cleaner) would have said I added a jewel to my heavenly crown. 'What's that to do with your suitability as a tenant?' I asked, mildly, defusingly.

She looked puzzled.

'I expect Laura gave her the idea. She had a lot of success up-setting you, back then, suggesting unnatural intimacy, didn't she?

Forget it. You don't value Charlotte's opinion about anything else, do you? Well then. The woman's a bitch.'

'Which one?'

'Both, but one's a dead bitch, thank God. Go on, explain. When I first met you, what did you have in mind to reveal about the murder? I know you wanted to finagle me into finding Toad, but apart from that, what were your intentions?'

'I think I intended to expose Lord Sherwin's behaviour with Rosalind; perhaps even to accuse Laura. Charlotte would have found the resultant publicity most irksome.'

'Particularly if she wants to be Mrs Prime Minister.'

Miss Potter was taken aback. 'Are you speaking in general terms of her ambition, or is that a possibility?'

'Some people seem to think Ludo's in the running for leadership of the party, yes.'

'But it is dreadful! Dreadful! Charlotte Sherwin in Downing Street!'

'I don't think it's very likely,' I said. I wanted to get back to the point. 'You couldn't have accused Laura falsely, surely? You couldn't have told a direct lie?'

She smiled at me. 'Perhaps you are right. I must confess, however, I did consider it, albeit not for long. Latterly I have been inclined to simple confession.'

'Because it's every citizen's duty to co-operate with the police?'

'No. The inefficiency of the police investigation was a great sadness to me. Prior to Lord Sherwin's death I had always had a profound respect for the English police. Regrettably, I must say that I was motivated solely by a desire to annoy Charlotte. She has inflated notions of her own importance. She behaved as if I was of no account. I was also tempted by an even more unworthy motive, Alex.'

'Which was?'

'I wanted to talk about Rollo. I have spoken to no one about the matter for thirty-two years. I never called him Rollo. I wanted to say his name.'

'I wish I'd met him.'

'He would not, I fear, have seemed remarkable to you.'

She blew her nose on a small, embroidered cotton handkerchief. I'd run out of Kleenex. There was nothing to be said.

I poured her another cup of tea and waited. Eventually I said, 'Did you have any doubt about the relationship between Rollo and Rosalind?'

'No. What I wanted to obtain from Rosalind was permission to make it public. I knew you would speak to her, and that you are persuasive and shrewd. If she discussed the matter with you, that would have been enough.'

'She's a grown woman. You haven't seen her for years. After all this time, what she wanted still mattered to you?'

'Is it so strange?' Miss Potter looked determined and almost defiant. 'I had failed in my duty towards Rosalind, not entirely through my own fault, admittedly. I had not taken proper care of her. If Laura had not frightened and annoyed me, and failed in her own duty, the child would have had appropriate protection and guidance.'

'Plus, you care what she thinks because you love her.' I didn't think Miss P. would like the word. Laura had poisoned it all those years ago. It seemed to me Laura had had a nice line in poison, all round.

'I don't think, exactly – she was my responsibility—'

'You loved her.'

'Very well. If you insist. I loved her.'

'And you loved Rollo?'

Miss P. went pink. 'I *fancied* Rollo.'

'And you threw your knickers onstage.'

'Ah, yes,' said Miss P, with a bright blue-eyed smile. 'Unfortunately Rollo threw them back.'

After that, I couldn't delay the Toad project any longer. Back in the BMW, I drove the dreary, featureless, country road towards Kate's and the Sherwins' village. By now it was well and truly dark: still raining. Miss Potter sat beside me, more jumpy every mile, until she finally said, 'I have deceived you, Alex.'

'What now? Don't tell me. Let me guess. You killed Lord Lucan's nanny.'

She sighed. 'I suppose, given time, I could become accustomed to your flippancy. What I want to say, is that I deceived you about Kate. She and her family are away for the weekend, staying with her mother.'

Then, of course, I remembered. The silence of Kate's house. No dog: no loyal Joss, guarding the house while the family were out. No old dog left indoors on a wet cold day to snooze in front of the fire while the family went shopping. I should have worked it out. I was too busy thinking about Miss Potter's wonderful, money-spinning revelations about the Sherwin murder – (hint of incest, lust, romance, suppressed spinster, English high life: surely a mini-series? with Meryl Streep or Julia Roberts as the young Miss Potter, hauntingly, bankably, inexplicably American?) – to use my wits.

I swallowed. 'And you knew that all along? You never intended to borrow Kate's keys?'

'She might have got into serious trouble.'

'What about me?'

'You are audacious, resourceful and self-employed. I cannot imagine that Charlotte Mayfield's displeasure will significantly affect your career.'

'Ludovic Mayfield could.'

'I do not imagine that Mr Mayfield would welcome any disclosure or allegation I might make, whether concerning his mother-in-law's murderous attack on her husband, or his wife's treatment of their afflicted daughter.'

'Blackmail,' I said once more.

This time she didn't pause to consider. 'Yes,' she said.

I was still puzzled. 'If you knew Kate was away, why on earth were you so shattered when we got there and she was out?'

'Guilt,' said Miss Potter. When I turned to look at her, she was smiling.

What could I do? She'd manipulated me again. 'I wasn't taken in by your touching little present,' I said.

'The coffee mug? What can you mean?'

I now remembered something else. That letter of application, the heroic, pathetically deluded letter of application that had so touched me, though I'd tried not to admit it to myself at the time – it hadn't been dated. Miss Potter would ALWAYS date a letter. Unless, that is, she had written it as a device to create precisely the effect it had, and left it waiting for me in the study, waiting on the off-chance that one day I'd go in.

I didn't want her to think she'd got away with it. 'Or the letter of application you left for me to read. I didn't feel in the least sorry for you.'

'Yes, you did,' she said simply. 'And now we're going straight to Ashtons Hall.'

'Oh no we're not. *I'm* going to Ashtons Hall. *You're* going to the vicar's.'

'The vicar's?'

'I'm not religious myself, but don't vicars supply tea and succour on demand? Isn't that item number one on the job description? But if you're not keen, it doesn't have to be the vicar. Any friend's place. Anywhere I can leave you safe and warm while I scramble round on scaffolding peering in through windows and scoping the place out. I'll be able to look in through the windows, you know. I'll soon see if Toad's there, which I'm sure she isn't.'

'I'm not sure you fully understand, Alex. Looking through windows isn't enough. You are searching for – you may be searching for – a body, or signs of Toad's recent presence. That is why I am coming with you, to help. I know the house. We can ignore the ground and first floors, I should think, since the cleaners have been allowed to work there. We must direct our attention to the top floor, especially the old nursery wing.'

I did drop her at the vicar's. She was still protesting, but in practice she had accepted that if she insisted on joining me, I wouldn't go. A middle-aged woman – wife? housekeeper? – answered the rectory door. I waited in the car at the foot of the drive until Miss

Potter went inside and the door closed behind her, then set off on my mission.

The reader may have guessed that I wanted to go alone not merely, or even chiefly, to protect Miss Potter. Without her at my elbow, I could get away with doing much less. I wasn't looking for a body. I was still convinced Toad was tucked away in a hospital somewhere. I meant to give the place a once-over, maybe go up the scaffolding and look in, then take Miss Potter back to London. We could always tackle Charlotte head-on about Toad's whereabouts.

The rain was steady. Not great drops, but insistent, dense, soaking rain. I hesitated just before turning in through the gates to the drive. If I had taken the enterprise seriously I'd have parked up the road and walked. But it was wet and I was excited, and the drive was inordinately long, so I drove up to the house. I didn't even turn off Barty's multi-adjustable headlights with their power-ful, efficient, Teutonic beam.

It served me right. The ancient, heritage oaks screened the house from me until the last curve of the potholed drive. By then I was only fifty yards away and it was too late to cut the lights and kill the engine when I saw, with a shock out of all proportion to the circumstances, that Charlotte Sherwin Mayfield was standing in the porch, waiting for me.

Chapter Twenty-Five

She couldn't have been waiting for me, of course. She didn't know I was coming. She must have heard the car. Or perhaps she had been at a window and seen the headlights through the trees. Or perhaps she was waiting for someone else. I parked the car as far away from the door as I could, to give myself time to prepare a story, and sat for a moment in the driving seat for deep relaxation breathing.

I was annoyed with myself for being so rattled. She was alone, as far as I could see. Only one car was parked by the door, a blue Volvo estate, the classic wife's car. She was only a woman, for God's sake. I outweighed her and possibly outbrained her and I'd learnt to take care of myself in situations she would probably find unimaginable. More important still, I wasn't easily embarrassed by someone I disliked. For women like her, embarrassment was the weapon of choice.

I decided on my story, adjusted my expression to an aggravating, confident liar's smile, and strode across to the doorway. 'Good afternoon, Mrs Mayfield,' I said. 'I'm looking for Miss Potter. She isn't here, by any chance?' I reached the door and made to keep walking in, through her. She hesitated until I thought I actually would have to push her aside, then stepped back at the last second to follow me in. Round One to me.

'Miss Potter?' she said. 'Why should she be here?'

I watched her eyes. They swivelled till she was looking up the stairs: up the stairs towards the old schoolroom, Toad's room, the place she most feared Miss Potter would be. Only people very practised in deception can control the direction of their eyes. Charlotte, the ice queen, could manage the voice and the expression and even the hands, which were still hanging, relaxed, by her side, but she hadn't managed the eyes. She hadn't had my advantages. Round Two to me.

I kept talking, in a Polly mode. I wanted to avoid confrontation if I could: fewer bones broken, that way. The less I forced Charlotte into a corner, the easier I made it for her to admit the truth, however glossied up she chose to make it, the more useful it would be for Toad. If the girl really was upstairs (could she be? the house was still freezing cold, unheated), the sooner she was in an ambulance and off to a private clinic, the better. 'Miss Potter was worried about your daughter, Toad, isn't it? Charming nickname. Miss Potter knew that she was here and that she was ill: she wanted to see her. I drove her down to visit Kate and her dog, and she's slipped away, and I wondered if she might be here because I need to get back to London. You know what old people are like when they get ideas into their heads. Miss Potter's wonderful, of course. She has a terrific sense of responsibility. I said that *you'd* be looking after your daughter, naturally, such a tragedy, anorexia, I blame the media. It's all the pictures of thin models and the emphasis on bodies, little girls don't have a childhood any more, do they? And naturally you wouldn't want the poor girl to be bothered by the newspapers, and they might be interested, with Mr Mayfield being so important. I absolutely see your difficulty. I wouldn't have come here and bothered you, but you know what Miss Potter's like when she gets an idea into her head, and the old are so unreasonable, aren't they?'

Her eyes were now fixed on mine: she was thinking. The front doors were still open, both the heavy wooden outer door and the pair of glass porch doors. Rain drifted in, carried on the erratic wind which lifted the thin hall carpet under my sodden boots and her narrow and elegant (Italian?) leather loafers. I rattled on. 'I'll close these, shall I? You don't want wet floors. Lovely wood, this floor. Oak, is it? I do admire your house. Wonderful workmanship, in the old days, they really were craftsmen, weren't they? England led the world.'

'England still leads the world,' said Charlotte. 'Miss – er—' She groped for my name, once too insignificant to remember, now a potential weapon in her manipulative armoury.

'Tanner,' I said. 'Alex Tanner. Please call me Alex. So Miss Potter isn't here, then? Perhaps we should look.' I moved towards the stairs.

She blocked me, with a quick movement. Disconcertingly quick. I was certainly stronger than she was, but her physical reaction time left me planted.

'Miss Tanner, of course, how silly of me to forget. I've a lot on my mind just now. I'm glad you've come. I think we should talk. Perhaps I can get you a cup of tea? Or a drink?' Arm curved, she swept me towards a green baize door. 'Let's just nip along to the kitchen, shall we?'

Her attempts to ingratiate herself were alarming. I wasn't going to walk ahead of her. I needed to watch her. When she was behind me the hackles rose on my neck. 'Coffee would be lovely,' I said. 'Do lead the way, it's such a big house. I'm not used to big houses. You can't exactly get lost in my London flat.' I'm not usually disloyal to my flat, but she'd be less volatile if she felt superior.

'London is so expensive,' she said smugly, and let me drop back. I followed her neatly dressed, narrow figure along a gloomy passage. Her blonde hair glimmered in the shadows. She was in green, today. Dark green skirt, lighter green cashmere sweater, white blouse showing at the neck, green tights, black shoes.

The kitchen was enormous and wretchedly designed. She switched on some lights, but the four distant corners were still shadowed as she sat me down at the central massive, rectangular, scrubbed wood table and set out on the cross-floor hikes necessary to assemble two cups of coffee. 'I'm rather glad you've come,' she said. 'I've been thinking. I was wondering whether I should really help you and Bartholomew O'Neill with your article. Now, I've made up my mind. I will help. I'll tell you all I know about my father's tragic death.'

That was a slap in the face. I had all I wanted on her father's tragic death from Miss Potter: up until the moment when I saw Charlotte waiting for me in the doorway, I'd been writing the piece in my head.

The worst of it, though, was that her offer to help signalled, louder than anything else could, how much she had to hide about Toad. Her natural instinct, as far as I was concerned, was to assist me down a bottomless crevasse, not to give me coffee and information. I was alarmed, for Toad. I was frightened.

I don't like fear. I feel it very seldom. I was born with plenty of physical courage: no merit, just luck. I've never had to use it, much. My Cretan VC told me that courage is a capital asset and even the bravest person eventually runs out, if they have to suffer enough. I hadn't had that kind of suffering. I had plenty of resources to face this selfish, pretentious, icy, slender woman in her ridiculous dark green velvet Alice band.

But I was afraid. I was afraid to see what she had done to her daughter. I hate deliberate cruelty. Mistakes and madness, I understand. There's a human warmth about those, even if you end up like a geriatric Ophelia, incontinent in mud-coloured garments.

Afraid or not, training tells. I gave an appreciative nod, then another for good measure, then a grateful smile. 'That would be wonderful,' I said. I hadn't brought my tape recorder from the car, of course, because I hadn't thought I'd need it, so I tugged my damp notebook from my biker's jacket, which I hadn't been invited to remove. 'Thank you so much.'

She brought the coffee and sat down opposite me, five feet away. 'And if I help you, what will you do for me?' She gave me a ghastly smile. She meant it to be charming, conspiratorial. She knew her usual superior teeth-flash wouldn't do; she wasn't stupid. But her facial muscles couldn't cope with the task. She hadn't had to be charming enough, often enough. The appropriate muscles had spent forty-odd years doing nearly sod-all and now the best they could manage was a rictus.

I smiled warmly, responsively, a 'gee-thanks' smile. 'I'm not sure . . .'

'You must understand, Alex, that poor Toad is very ill. She's being supervised by a wonderful doctor. From Harley Street. He treats all the best people. I'm following his advice. Anorexia is a dreadful thing. I know so little about it, I'm merely following doctor's orders. It isn't easy for me. I'd do anything for Toad. Anything. I'm keeping her here, with nurses round the clock. Have you any idea how difficult it is getting nurses to stay at a place like this, in the country? I've had to import a housekeeper for them. Nurses demand that regular meals are prepared for them. They insist. You'd think they could boil an egg.'

Unreasonable nurses, I thought, wanting to eat. What are the lower classes coming to? But I didn't waste much time considering them, since they and the housekeeper were fictional. She was selling me a bill of goods and I'd pretend to buy it. 'I see,' I said. 'Gosh, how difficult for you. I am so sorry.'

'It is a baffling disease,' she said, looking not so much baffled as remotely, coolly furious. 'Toad was a very ordinary little girl, a bit podgy, rather clinging, but quite normal. Very fond of her father. You'd think she'd understand the damage it could do to his career, and to her own health . . . I'm only asking her to eat. You'd think that would be easy enough, wouldn't you? Just a small thing. But she absolutely refuses . . . So you see, we're managing as best we can, but it would be tragic for Toad if the news got out. That is why I said she was still on her Gap Year trip. You know how despicable the tabloids can be. They make money out of human misery. So if you could persuade Miss Potter that I'm acting for the best – and if I can tell you what you want to know about Daddy's death—'

The offer hung in the air between us. I rose to it like an innocent trout. 'Oh, yes, Mrs Mayfield.'

'I think we understand each other, don't we, Alex?'

'Oh, yes.'

'Very well. My father's death was a tragic accident. I know all about it: I was listening outside the door. You know what children are. I'd been sent to bed with the others but I came down in my pyjamas. I didn't want to miss the party.'

Crowded, that night, outside the gun-room, I thought, waiting for her fiction. It would be believable, concise, and leave the family squeaky-clean.

'My father and mother had a row. He told her he wanted a divorce. My father hit my mother and she picked up a gun, to defend herself. She was distraught. She knew nothing about guns. My father tried to take the gun away from her, and it went off. A terrible, terrible accident.'

I wrote in my notebook, *accident scribble scribble keep her happy*.

'My mother was delicate, I told you that I think, and I imagine she was too nervous, too upset, to tell the police. We never discussed it, of course. She didn't know I knew.'

'Can you remember any details, Mrs Mayfield?'

'Details?' She was impatient, but she controlled it. Condescension, she understood. Throw the Rottweiler chunks of meat, make a contribution to the policemen's widows and orphans' fund, kiss the electors' babies, judge the flower show. She was estimating how much she'd have to give me. 'What they said, for instance?'

'Excellent.' I sat, pencil poised, as if I really wanted to hear.

'My father said, "You've never loved me," and something about making a new life in Kenya and leaving the rabbits behind. He meant us, the children. Then I could hear my mother loading the gun. She was very angry. She spoke crudely, for her. She said something like, "You think love is rolling around on a bed with a sweaty little tart".'

I felt as if I'd been sandbagged. Charlotte *had* been there. She was reporting the same scene Miss Potter had described. Unless Charlotte had heard her mother say that on another occasion. Perhaps it was merely part of the day-to-day matrimonial exchanges *chez* Sherwin, which were overheard because Rollo's voice was resonant and carrying. But Laura's wasn't. By all accounts Laura's voice was ever soft, gentle and poisonous. And Laura never argued. Laura sobbed instead.

My mind scrabbled for a foothold, my hand scrawled *damn damn damn*.

'What happened next?'

'A shotgun went off. Not in the gun-room, outside.' It was the same scene. Maybe Laura had told her? Not likely. Laura wouldn't confide, not even in her daughter, not about this. It didn't reflect well on her.

So where had Charlotte been? The gun-room had no windows. More than one person couldn't have listened at the door, not without knowing they had company. Either Miss Potter was lying, or Charlotte was. And if they – whichever one it was – was lying about this, then they were likely to be lying about other things.

When Miss Potter told me her story, I'd believed it, including her claim to have murdered Rollo. But what if – what if Charlotte had been in the room, somewhere, under the sofa, behind a chair, a little girl sneaking down, prying, the same little girl who'd crept into the murder room and stolen a photograph of her shattered father, a souvenir, perhaps, because she'd heard her father dismiss her once again as a rabbit, heard her father say he'd leave her, and seized the gun and blown his head off for not acknowledging that Charlotte Sherwin was the most important person in Ashtons Hall, Warwickshire, England, Europe, the World, the Galaxy, the Universe? I could see it. God, I could see it. And I could also see Miss Potter claiming to have shot her beloved Rollo because she had lived so long and done so little.

Charlotte was watching me. I wrote, busily, in my notebook. *Let me out let me out let me out.* I should ask some questions, pretend to be interested, but I wanted to get away, to get back to Miss Potter, to return with the police and a doctor. Miss P. would know the local GP. She probably took bowls of broth to his poorer patients. 'Mrs Mayfield – how amazing. Thank you so much. Perhaps we could talk further in London, when I've had time to tell Barty about this. He'll want to speak to you himself.'

'That would be best,' she said. 'I'm rather surprised he didn't come to see me in the first place.' She was relieved; relaxed, I thought. Then, like a snake darting, her hand snatched my notebook and she read what I'd written.

Our eyes met. 'Oh dear,' she said.

Round Three to her, I thought, and went for the door, my boots slipping on the quarry tiles. She had to run round the table, but god she was quick. I was through the door ahead of her, slammed it, pulled a chest across it to delay her and made for the hall, the front door. I'd left the keys in the BMW. It would start. It always started. Out, and away.

My sweaty hands were fumbling at the handle to the glass doors when I heard the feeble cry.

'Help me please help me I want to have a bath . . .'

I looked up. At the bend of the stairs, clinging to the banisters, was – a naked figure. Filthy, with matted hair. A naked skeleton. No, of course not a skeleton. An emaciated girl. Toad.

'I want to have a bath please,' said the skeleton, in a skeleton's voice, reedy, bodiless.

What choice did I have? 'Gordon Bennett,' I said, ridiculously, and made for the stairs, scrunching up the carpet in my desperation. If I could get her to the car—

By the time I reached her Charlotte was in the hall, between us and the door. She was carrying something but I didn't, immediately, register what. I picked up the girl – she was bones, bones – and kept running, up. I knew you shouldn't run up. Big mistake, to run up. But there had to be back stairs, didn't there? I tried to remember the floor plan of the house – Charlotte was behind me – the girl was squeaking. 'Mummy's coming Mummy's coming Mummy's coming . . .'

I knew sodding Mummy was coming. I could hear her Italian-shod feet nimbly outpacing my Doc Martens. If it hadn't been for the girl I'd have turned and socked Mummy one in the jaw right after I kicked her kneecaps in, but the girl was terrified. She was so thin I was amazed she still lived. The added shock might kill her, if this didn't. I went for the schoolroom. I could remember the schoolroom. Miss Potter'd talked about it enough. It was Toad's room, now, and if Mummy had kept her prisoner there, I hoped for a key in the door. Lock ourselves in, go down the scaffolding. 'It's OK,' I gasped to the trembling thing in my arms. 'It's OK.'

Schoolroom door. No key. Charlotte must have it. Window. Schoolroom window. Bars.

I put the girl down, pushed her behind me, turned to face Charlotte. As I turned, she hit me with the barrel of a shotgun.

Chapter Twenty-Six

When I woke up my head felt as if the BMW had driven over it. I was still dopey and slow. It took me a while to realize that I couldn't lift my arm to look at my watch, not because I was paralysed but because my wrist was handcuffed to a brass bedstead. It took me longer still to work out that the persistent whining noise wasn't a result of my head injury. It was a semi-human voice. Toad.

'. . . and she just doesn't understand how fat I am and how horrible it is to be so fat and she put masses of mirrors in here and I can't bear to look at them so I broke them and she took them away but it's the best thing for me I know it is and she's got my best interests at heart and I've got to pull myself together and I do try but it's so cold and I haven't earned any clothes yet and I can't wash and there's no lavatory and it's the system that I have to earn my privileges and it's what the best doctors say to do in Harley Street and it's the only hope of a cure and then I'll have lovely clothes and someone nice will want to marry me and Charles will be best man and they won't laugh at me because I'm fat I wish Lally was here I've written to Lally and she hasn't written back and she's supposed to be my best friend but Mummy says you can't trust blacks but Lally's not black I mean she is but not inside if you see what I mean and her father's a tribal chief or he was and they're like kings aren't they so it's not the same except she hasn't written back so maybe it is the same and I'm so cold are you awake yet I do hope you are I've been so lonely and I can't do things much any more and I haven't cleaned my teeth properly for weeks and I rub them with my fingers but it isn't the same thing and I *have* been eating I *have* but Mummy says not enough . . .'

'Toad,' I said. 'Toad.'

'Ummm? Yes?' She turned to me with bright inquiry, a smile which was all discoloured teeth and huge, sunken eyes. She was so thin I could see the shape of her teeth when her mouth was closed. 'Have we met?' she asked brightly. 'I'm sorry I don't remember I'm forgetting things a lot recently my watch battery went and I'm not even sure what day it is . . .'

'I'm Alex,' I said. 'Alex Tanner. We haven't met. I'm a friend of Miss Potter's.'

'Are you really?' For the first time, she sounded normal. 'Oh, good. Is Miss Potter coming? Everything's all right when Miss Potter's there, don't you find?'

'Yes,' I said. By now I was conscious enough to take in my surroundings, to weigh up the good news and the bad news.

The bad news was that I was handcuffed to a huge bedstead evidently constructed in the heyday of British craftsmanship. The handcuffs, too, were well made. The room reminded me of home, and my mother, before the social workers came. It was freezing cold, damp, indescribably dirty, with faeces piled in a corner, a tangle of filthy blankets, and a decomposing dog.

The good news was that Toad and I were alone.

'Is the door locked?' I asked.

She nodded, a death's-head. A perky death's-head. If only she'd stop being so bloody sparky. 'Oh yes. Mummy always keeps it locked to protect me you see it's part of the treatment but when she heard the car I suppose it was you arriving she went downstairs without locking it and I thought oh good I'll get out because I really want to get out of this room but then when I did I didn't really want to and now I'm back I'm rather relieved specially since you're here . . . have you ever been to India? I was there this summer and it was so beautiful but there were so many people and lots of them were living on the streets and some of them were dying there and they didn't have any money at all and I suppose they don't have overdrafts there I'm not sure they even have banks because if you have no money in this country I mean really no money you can always get an overdraft but in India you beg in the streets instead that's why it's called an underdeveloped country I suppose . . . so I was really quite glad to come back because it made me cry and the food from street stalls upset my stomach as well so the others were right I should have come back but I did want to go to Nepal because Miss Potter always told me it was beautiful and high and pure and clear and not dirty because India was very dirty and I wanted to see somewhere clean and I was going to send her a postcard . . .'

'You must be cold, Toad,' I said, to stop the voice. 'Why don't you cover yourself in a blanket?' I couldn't bear to look at her.

'Oh no, I can't do that, the blankets are dirty.'

So was she. Filthy. I remembered how it felt. Odd, really. Until my first foster-mother taught me hygiene, I hadn't minded being dirty. It had been cosy, comfortable, familiar. I remembered my mother taking me to church on Christmas Eve when I was four. I'd liked the Nativity scene, all the animals and the holy family in the stable together. I hadn't noticed other church-goers moving away from us, as, looking back, they must have done, to avoid the smell. We must have smelt. I liked our smell.

Toad would mind, though. 'We'll get you to a hot bath soon. Miss Potter and me,' I said. 'Meanwhile, Miss Potter would want you to wrap yourself in a blanket.'

'Would she? Are you sure?'

'Quite sure,' I said, and she obediently huddled herself into a blanket. It had always worked with my mother, too. She did whatever I said Clark Gable would have wanted.

While she was wrapping up I did a time check. Damn. I hadn't been unconscious long. It was six o'clock: only an hour had passed since I left Miss Potter. She wouldn't have started worrying about me yet, wouldn't have raised the alarm. I liked those words, *raised the alarm*, with their comforting vision of fat policemen on bicycles saying 'now then now then what's all this'. Then I remembered. She'd hesitate to call policemen, fat or thin. I was supposed to be breaking and entering. She'd do something, certainly; but how long would she wait?

I wrestled with the handcuffs. No chance of slipping my wrist out: I have sturdy bones. Charlotte had fastened my right wrist, so even if I'd had something to pick the lock with, I probably couldn't manage. I'm hopeless with my left hand.

I didn't know what Charlotte intended, but it wouldn't be pleasant. I'd been in trouble when she'd taken my notebook, in worse trouble once I'd seen Toad, but the real decider had been Charlotte's attack on me. Now she'd knocked me out and cuffed me up, she'd gone beyond explanation, excuse and the protection of privilege. Unless, of course, she cleaned up Toad's room, then called the police and claimed she thought I was an intruder. She might risk that. It would be my word against hers . . .

Then I realized. That plan would work even better if I was dead. Alone with her tragically ill daughter, she hears an intruder, runs to the gun-room, then blam! exit Alex.

Not if I could help it. I'd despised her to start with and our relationship had gone downhill from there. I wasn't going to give her the satisfaction of killing me. Apart from anything else, where would that leave Toad, the witness?

The room. I must check the room, for possible exits, for weapons. It was about fourteen feet by twelve, with a high ceiling and a fitted, beige carpet. In one long wall, the door to the corridor outside. Opposite it, barred sash window, large for a third floor window, the sill three feet from the floor. On one of the shorter walls was an empty fireplace, surrounded by built-in cupboards, floor to ceiling. The top of the cupboards opened separately, presumably for long-term storage. Against the other shorter wall, my bedstead. No mattress. Each side of the door, two sturdy chests of drawers. In the middle of the floor, the pile of stinking blankets. On the right of the window, a radiator. Tied to it, the body of a dog. Beyond the dog, in the corner, Toad's waste pile: probably the dog's too. Toad had done what she could, to clear up. Beside that, a reeking bucket.

Between the dog and the blankets, Toad.

Nothing else. No supply of drinking water: Charlotte must have brought it in by the cupful. No washbasin, no food, no other objects at all. She'd been here over a month. She hadn't managed to earn many privileges.

My head hurt and I felt sick, but it was only like a medium-awful hangover. I tried to stand up. I was cuffed about two feet from the floor: I could stand if I bent over. The bed was on rusty castors. I could tug it about the room, very slowly. I tried moving towards the door, hoping to hide behind it and ambush Charlotte when she came in, but the chests of drawers were too heavy to shift and I couldn't get the bed close enough. Wherever I put myself, I was in plain view.

I tugged the bed towards the window. That was better. I could just see out. Darkness. Rain. Scaffolding. Scaffolding, easy to climb down. Not so easy to get through the bars. Not even Toad could: her head was too big.

She was talking. 'And I thought I'd go to see Daddy when I got back to England they said I wasn't well enough to go on to Nepal but I was actually but they didn't realize and they made me come back and I went to see Daddy in London and get him to tell them I was well enough to go to Nepal but Daddy didn't look at me even . . .'

'Toad? Hey, Toad?'

'I saw what he was looking at I could see he was looking at a photograph of Charles if I get as slim as Charles Daddy will look at me then I know he will I know he will I know he will I thought he would when I got my results two As and a B but Charles got three As I expect that's why Daddy didn't look at me and he said Mummy knew best and Mummy would look after me and she has she has looked after me it's the treatment you see it's what the best doctors do in Harley Street but Mummy and I have never got on really because I'm so difficult I suppose but I didn't want to be difficult I wanted to be a good girl I wanted to be a really good girl and slim and pretty so she would love me I wanted her to love me . . .'

'Toad! Miss Potter would like you to talk to me.'

'Yes, Alex?' Radiant smile, head cocked on one side.

'That dog over there—' I pointed with my free hand at the stinking, oozing mass.

'That's Tigger,' she said buoyantly. 'My dog Tigger.'

'That *was* your dog Tigger.'

'I know. He's dead.'

'What happened to him?'

'It's part of the treatment you see Mummy tied him up there and said she wouldn't feed him or take him for walks till I ate something and I tried I tried I tried but I'm so fat she wanted to make me fat she said I hadn't eaten and I had and he stopped breathing he was quite old anyway I think perhaps he had a heart attack he whimpered then he stopped whimpering I don't remember when it was but after a bit I took his blankets because I didn't think he'd mind Mummy'd left him blankets because she said it wasn't fair for him to be sold but I didn't have any and I didn't think he'd mind but actually he was dead and so I took them but they're very dirty and they smelt of dog but then dog blankets do . . .'

It was then, I think, that I began to hate Charlotte Mayfield. I don't usually waste time hating people, it eats you up and doesn't hurt them, but I'd make an exception for rotten, sadistic, self-satisfied Charlotte.

I squatted by the window and thought. The best revenge is victory. What did I know, what could I use, what should I do?

Escape. I couldn't. Bars. Handcuffs. Bed. Anyway, try the bars. They looked solid, but the place had dry rot. I gripped the bars with my left hand, braced my legs against the wall, and pulled. They moved. I pulled again. They shifted further. Pull pull pull. My head throbbed. The bars came away in a rush of rotten wood and plaster. So far so good. I wedged the bars back up as best I could. They'd only deceive a very casual glance, but that might be all Charlotte would give them. If – when – she came back, I might have a second's advantage if she thought I was still unconscious.

No bars now. Toad could get out, she could climb down the scaffolding and away. I looked at her and dismissed the thought. She was naked and frail, almost certainly too frail to manage the climb. If she did reach the ground safely she was so out of it she'd probably come straight back into the house, and even if she didn't she'd have to walk nearly a mile in the freezing rain to get help, and warmth.

I was still cuffed to the bed. I pushed it back to its original position, fished out my penknife and opened two blades with my teeth. The larger, a weapon of last resort. The smaller, a potential picklock. Then I set to work on the lock with my clumsy left hand.

I kept trying long after I knew I couldn't do it. Toad had stopped talking. She was curled up in a foetal huddle, fleshless thumb between bloodless lips. She was asleep, or unconscious. I heaped more blankets over her and flexed my legs to keep the circulation going. My jeans were still damp and I hunched my shoulders inside my blessedly thick leather jacket. Lord, it was cold.

I tried to think about the Sherwin murder, to decide whether I believed Miss Potter. I'd been so sure I'd got my angle: a new candidate for murderer, a candidate who wanted to talk about it: the best of all sources. But Charlotte had been there. If she knew Miss Potter had done it, why hadn't she said?

I can usually rely on work as a distraction. However bad things are, I can concentrate on work.

This time, I couldn't. My whole body was listening for Charlotte's footsteps. I was listening so hard, at first I didn't believe my senses when I heard them.

I closed my eyes and played dead. The key scratched in the lock: I could hear the door open. 'Toad!' said Charlotte. 'Wake up, Toad! Time for a bath!' She sounded – normal. A normal mother, talking to a young child, holding a shotgun casually under her arm.

'Hello Mummy hello Mummy hello Mummy . . .'

'Come along. It's time for your bath now. Is Alex awake?'

'A bath a bath have I earned it oh thank you Mummy . . .'

'Is Alex awake?' asked Charlotte again, a steelier note in her voice.

'Who's Alex, Mummy?'

'This is Alex, here,' said Charlotte. 'Has she been awake?'

'Oh yes she's been awake and she wanted to know about Tigger she's a friend of Miss Potter's she told me Miss Potter wanted me to put this blanket on . . .'

'I'm sure Miss Potter wants a great many things she isn't going to get,' said Charlotte. 'Do stop pretending to be unconscious, Alex. You're not very good at it.'

'I think your daughter is very ill, Mrs Mayfield,' I said, left hand gripping my penknife tightly in case she came close enough to stab. She was standing about four feet beyond my longest reach, and she was pointing the shotgun at me. 'Shouldn't you call an ambulance? Now?'

'I don't want to go to hospital I'm not ill I don't want to go to hospital and the tabloid press will get hold of it you know what the tabloids are like it'll damage Daddy's career Daddy's career is poised to take off he could be Prime Minister and then Mummy would be the Prime Minister's wife and Charles would be the Prime Minister's son and I'd be the Prime Minister's daughter and I wouldn't be so fat and we'd live in Downing Street actually I don't want to live in Downing Street I want to stay at home I want to be here I'm going to decorate my room this room could be lovely when the treatment works and I earn some privileges I can have new curtains the windows face south-east . . .'

'You shouldn't have come here,' said Charlotte to me, silencing Toad with a glare. 'You see what I have to put up with. Toad is not well. She's better here, with me. She's not responsible for her actions.'

'She should be in hospital,' I said. 'She's very ill.'

'It's her own fault,' explained Charlotte reasonably, patiently. 'I gave her every chance. All she has to do is to eat. That's not much to ask.'

'It's an *illness*,' I said. 'You're right, she doesn't know what she's doing.' I knew I couldn't make the woman understand, but I had to try. My own dealings with her would end, one way or the other, very soon, and either I'd be back to my own life or I'd be dead. But Toad might recover, and then she'd still have her mother to cope with. 'Look, Mrs Mayfield, it happens to plenty of girls, even from the best families, and their mothers are the worst people to handle it. There's too much passion involved, too many hopes and expectations, too much guilt. She needs a doctor.'

'Guilt?' said Charlotte wonderingly. 'There's no guilt. She's my child and I know what's best for her. Don't you dare give me that half-baked psychology, you little bastard from the slums with a common accent and a tin-pot career in the *meejer*, ruining my floors with your ridiculous boots. I'm a successful mother and a successful wife.'

Toad nodded smiling agreement. I wasn't sure which aspect of her mother's tirade she found persuasive, but Charlotte was certainly carrying fifty per cent of her audience. 'Charles is the success, I suppose,' I said, hoping to divide mother and daughter, give Toad some fighting spirit. She must have plenty, somewhere: anorexics are stubborn as hell. You'd have to be, to starve yourself to death.

'Charles is everything Ludovic and I ever hoped for,' said Charlotte, readjusting the shotgun, I hoped merely because it was heavy. 'Come along, Toad, bath-time. You've earned a bath.'

Toad was puzzled. 'No I haven't actually you said I'd have to eat for three days before I had a bath I don't think I've done that I've rather lost track of when I did eat but it's just as well because you want to make me fat and I mustn't get fat because the tabloids can be so cruel and they'd print fat photographs of me . . .'

What? Was she rambling, or was she echoing what Charlotte had said to her? Even Charlotte couldn't have been so vicious as to suggest to Toad that she was overweight, surely? But I'd got the impression up to now that she was merely a parrot. 'Toad!' I snapped. 'Toad! Miss Potter wants you to answer my questions!'

'OK,' said Toad, smiling obligingly.

'Why do you think the tabloid press will print fat photographs of you? You're slim.'

'I've always been fat Mummy told me that's what they did in the newspapers like the Duchess of York they took fat photographs of her well they'd do the same for me because if you have my metabolism Mummy said you always have to watch what you eat . . .'

I met Charlotte's eyes. She wasn't stupid. She knew that I knew what she'd done. Some treatment.

'So I don't think I've earned a bath and we must keep to the rules otherwise I won't get better oh listen there's Tigger barking that's Tigger I can hear Tigger it's definitely Tigger oh good . . .'

'Don't be ridiculous,' snapped Charlotte, glancing despite herself at the remains of the late Tigger.

It wasn't Tigger, of course, and it wasn't coming from inside the room, but a dog was barking. Outside.

'That's Joss,' I said, to rattle her. 'That's Miss Potter's spaniel, Joss. I'd know that bark anywhere.'

'I'll see to you in a moment,' she said. Lightly, gleefully. 'Wait here.'

She locked the door behind her, and took the key. It seemed to me the room temperature soared.

'Are you sure it's Joss I can't really tell barks apart can you? You must be a really doggy person . . .' warbled sanguine, batty, dying Toad. 'Gosh you were right he must have come with Miss Potter there's Miss Potter hello Miss Potter . . .'

'Do belt up, Toad,' I said. *She* was beginning to rattle *me*.

'Hello, Toad,' said a muffled but unmistakable voice. 'Could one of you open the window and let me in?'

Chapter Twenty-Seven

I *just* couldn't reach the window catch. The window was set in a deep embrasure and I couldn't stretch far enough. The tips of the fingers of my left hand groped the air an inch or two shy of it.

'Come along, Toad,' said Miss Potter briskly, through the glass. She tapped the window sharply to attract Toad's attention. 'Come along now. I'm becoming extremely wet, out here, and I have had an arduous climb.'

I shuffled the bed back, out of the way. Toad obediently addressed the catch. For a dreadful moment I thought she wouldn't have the strength to release it, but Miss Potter helped her by taking the weight of the upper window. Then, wincing slightly (pain from her arthritic hands?) she slid the window up far enough to wedge her fingers beneath it, and seconds later, awkwardly but quickly, she was inside the room.

'I'm sorry I'm sorry I'm sorry I'm sorry,' said Toad, 'I'm so glad you're here Miss Potter but I'm sorry my room's such a mess but it's the treatment you see . . .'

'Quiet, Toad. Everything will be all right now. Just be quiet while Alex and I have a talk. Cover yourself up, my child. It's very cold.'

'Alex said you'd want me to put on a blanket and I did I did but then I stood up and it fell off . . .'

'Toad, if I want you to speak again I shall say so,' said Miss Potter firmly, and Toad sank down on to a pile of blankets and squirrelled herself into it.

Outside, the dog was still barking. Presumably Charlotte

hadn't found it yet. If she was looking for it, not coming straight back.

'I can't undo the handcuffs,' I said. 'You'll have to handle Charlotte on your own. Unless you've brought the SAS.'

'The vicar is downstairs. It is his dog you hear. I wedged my silver brooch, open, inside the unfortunate creature's collar with the pin pressing into its neck, to create a diversion. I – I haven't called the police. A mistake.'

She wasted no more time on apology, if that was apology. She stood, soaked, Barboured trousered, to me enormously comforting, surveying the wreckage of her schoolroom and the results of Toad's treatment. Several strands of white hair had escaped from her bun and were plastered to her cheek, she was breathing heavily, but otherwise she seemed composed and competent.

In her presence, my confusion over the Sherwin murder was resolved. I believed Miss Potter. If she said she'd killed Rollo, it was true. I left the question of Charlotte's presence to think about later. If there was a later.

'Take Toad,' I said. 'Send the vicar back for me. I can look after myself.'

'How did Charlotte manage to overpower you?'

'Sorry. My mistake. She hit me with a shotgun.'

'It would be unwise to leave you, I think.' Pause. 'Toad, have you cleared the old schoolroom equipment from the upper cupboards?'

'No, Miss Potter,' said Toad brightly. 'No, I haven't. I've been busy.' Then she met Miss Potter's eye and hung her head. 'Actually, I kept them on purpose. I wanted to keep them. They reminded me of you, and Aunt Penelope.'

'That's good,' said Miss Potter. 'Alex, move the bed under the cupboard near the window, if you can. Quickly.'

I obeyed the order, puzzled. Did she envisage stunning Chalotte with a globe, or choking her with chalk? My efforts with the bed disturbed Tigger, and the stench increased. Miss Potter paid no attention. 'That'll do,' she said, and scrambled up, first on the bed, then on the bedhead, where she balanced precariously and groped inside the cupboard, emerging with a small wooden box which she passed to me. It rattled.

'Handcuff key,' she said. 'If those are the handcuffs from the dressing-up trunk. The label should be readily identifiable.' Then she returned to her excavations of the cupboard.

Bark, bark, from outside. The dog sounded frantic, now. Was Charlotte still down there?

I put the box on the floor and opened it. Several labelled keys: sure enough, one said HANDCUFFS. The box was sandalwood. The old, faint, sweet smell (Kenya?) lifted my spirits as my trembling left hand worked at the key.

'Those aren't the handcuffs from the dressing-up trunk,' said Toad, blithely, crushingly. 'Those are Charles's handcuffs. He stole them from a policeman in Windsor. For a dare.'

The accounts I'd heard of Charles had not endeared him to me. He had never been my favourite person. Now, I heartily agreed with Lally's friend Toby. Charles was a dickhead.

It was worse, now, to be cuffed, because I'd been so sure I'd soon be free, we'd all be free, of this room and that woman. I kept going with the key anyway, but it didn't fit. Things didn't look good. Unless the vicar was an ex-rugby player and his dog a pit bull terrier. Bark bark bark.

'Tell me about the vicar and his dog,' I said.

'Kipper is a mongrel.'

'Large? Fierce?'

'A dachshund/spaniel cross.'

'And the vicar?'

'Mr Routledge had the call late in life. He was previously an administrative grade civil servant in the Ministry of Agriculture, Fisheries and Food.'

'Ah,' I said. 'What are you looking for?' I was partly talking to shut out the barking. If it rasped my nerves, it would be worse for Charlotte, I hoped.

'The twelve-bore,' said Miss Potter.

'What?'

'The shotgun. I told you, Colonel Farrell intended to commit suicide with a shotgun. Rosalind and I purloined it, but we could not return it to the gun-room, so I concealed it here. With a box of cartridges. Ah!'

She passed me the gun; she brought the cartridges with her as she climbed, carefully, down to the floor.

'Will it still work?' I asked, stunned, stroking the barrel lovingly.

'It was clean and oiled when it was hidden. I made sure of that, naturally. It is a valuable gun. Besides, the threat alone may be sufficient. Give me the gun and replace the bed, Alex. Quickly. I need a clear line of fire from the window to the door.'

I obeyed. In this mood, Miss Potter commanded respect. She broke the gun, with difficulty (would her hands hold up?) and loaded.

'How much help can we expect from the vicar?' I asked.

'He is a witness. I did not attempt to explain the circumstances. It would have taken too long to convince him. Besides, I wasn't sure what we would find.'

'Do you think Charlotte will give up, now the vicar's here?' I knew the answer myself, but I wanted to be wrong.

'No,' she said. 'I'm going outside the window, now. Do not worry, Alex. She may surrender to a threat of force.'

And Toad may recover and lead a normal life, and we may see the resurgence of the British manufacturing industry, and sanctions may work on Saddam Hussein, I thought, watching her heave herself laboriously through the window.

Toad started to wail. 'Don't leave me don't leave me don't leave me it's all right when you're here . . .'

I understood her feelings.

The barking had stopped. Irrationally, I knew that meant Chalotte would come back.

I was frightened. I could taste the fear. The taste was familiar: like loneliness and anger. Stomach acid, I supposed.

'Mummy said I could have a bath I want a bath I want a bath . . .'

Miss Potter was outside the window, the gun propped on the

sill, her body half-protected by the wall. She must be crouching. Could she do it? Would her body hold out? She was way too old to scramble up scaffolding in the rain. Would her fingers be strong enough to pull the trigger? The gun would be stiff.

I huddled my body into as small a space as I could, and settled down to my least favourite occupation: waiting.

I didn't have to wait long. Charlotte came back, confident and happy, the gun held loosely in her arms. She stood in the doorway.

'You've opened the window, Alex.'

'*I* opened the window,' said Miss Potter, from her hide. 'Good evening, Charlotte. Put that gun down please, or I will shoot.'

'You ridiculous old woman,' said Charlotte blankly. 'What do you think you are doing? Where did you get that gun? I never invited you to my house. Leave at once.'

'Where is Mr Routledge?' Miss Potter's tone was conversational, so normal Charlotte was led to answer normally.

'Seeing to his wretched dog. Then he's going to look at the boiler. It's broken down, you know.'

'No it hasn't no it hasn't you told me you'd turned it off until I ate something that's what she told me Miss Potter honestly I don't think it's broken at all . . .'

There was spite in Toad's voice. Miss Potter's presence gave her the strength to oppose Charlotte. I remembered Lally's remark, 'She *hates* her mother.' Perhaps Miss Potter could use her, but I couldn't see how.

Miss P. went on. 'Most inconvenient, having to leave the house unheated. There may be serious consequences for the furniture . . . Mr Routledge is extremely good with his hands, of course. Put the gun down, Charlotte. We'll help you lay fires in the downstairs rooms. At least we can save the Chippendale chairs and the Regency dining table.'

'If the furniture is damaged it'll be entirely Toad's fault,' said Charlotte. 'She has no sense of responsibility.'

'I've got a sense of responsibility I really have I'm really trying

I know I owe it to Daddy and Mummy and Charles and Tigger and Miss Potter . . .'

We all ignored Toad.

Since I gathered Miss Potter's policy was to keep Charlotte talking, I wanted to give her a hand, but apart from a passing tribute to the lasting qualities of the Sherwin-owned iron beds, I was all out of observations on country-house maintenance. 'Mrs Mayfield was outside the gun-room when her father was shot,' I said. 'She told me her mother did it.' As a change of subject, I thought the lack of elegant neatness was more than compensated for by intrinsic interest.

'*Outside* the gun-room! Indeed!' said Miss Potter. 'You always were a liar, Charlotte.'

'Fat lot you knew about me,' said Charlotte, twelve again. 'Actually I wasn't outside, I was under the sofa. I didn't want to stay in bed. I didn't see why I should be left out; everyone else was having fun. Rosalind was dancing with Daddy, and he hadn't danced with me. I went to the gun-room to try some whisky. I didn't like it. Then Daddy came in, and I hid under the sofa.'

'And you actually heard your mother shoot your father?' I asked. Miss Potter was listening with an air of courteous inquiry. The longer Charlotte talked, the better chance we had, I hoped, and I liked the idea of child Charlotte under the murder sofa – a good touch for my piece, though I couldn't understand why, if she really had been there, she didn't tax Miss Potter with what she must know she had done. Unless she couldn't hear everything, and missed her mother's departure and Miss Potter's arrival. Keep her talking, keep her talking. 'But you never told anyone?'

'It was my secret,' said Charlotte smugly. 'I like secrets. And Daddy deserved it. He was going to leave us. We'd have lost the house.'

'Mummy's Daddy is dead,' confided Toad proudly. 'He was shot ages ago before I was born . . .'

The stench was worse, I registered suddenly. Waves of ex-Tigger were wafting from the radiator. Which must therefore be warming up – yes, I could just feel the edge going from the icy damp of the room. The vicar must have turned on the boiler. He'd be looking for Charlotte and Miss Potter soon, surely. Miss Potter and I opened our mouths to speak at the same time. I expect she was trying to keep the conversation going; I certainly was. Chalotte overrode us both. 'That's enough talking. Stand up, Toad. Come over here.' Toad, obediently, smilingly, stood up and crossed towards her mother. Miss Potter no longer had a clear line of fire. Toad was directly between Charlotte and the window.

'Terrific bed,' I said, rattling my handcuffs. 'Mrs Mayfield – I do think this is a terrific bed. Brass, is it? Victorian? Is it Victorian, Toad? There's some writing on it, just here. Come and look, Toad, tell me what it says, it might be the maker's name, it might be valuable, come and read it to me, Toad, come now.'

Toad turned towards me, still obedient, still smiling. Charlotte lashed out with her left hand and slapped her daughter across the face. 'Stand still,' she hissed. Toad, standing still, smiling, began to cry. Tears slid down what was left of her cheeks, and dropped from her chin to her chest, where only nipples marked where breasts should be.

'Charlotte, do put the gun down,' said Miss Potter. 'You have nothing to gain by harming us. We can find proper care for Toad and she'll recover. Think, Charlotte. You can set it right.'

'I'm giving her the care she deserves,' said Charlotte. Her voice was no longer icy, it was thick with anger. 'You stupid, stupid woman,' she said. 'Self-righteous. Just a little governess. You've never been important to us. You thought you were, but you're not. My father never even knew you existed.'

'It's time for some home truths, Mrs Mayfield,' I said. It was a gamble. She was already angry: if I could make her angrier, she might lose her co-ordination. She might even go for me, and give Miss Potter a chance for a shot, or to order Toad away while she was out of her mother's reach. Playground insults were called for. 'Your son Charles is a dickhead,' I said. 'He's a queer. He's in Australia shagging the sheep. Barty told me, all London is laughing at him. Lally Lambert kicked him out of bed.'

'No, Alex!' said Miss Potter.

Charlotte darted towards me and swung the gun like a club. I ducked my head, swung my legs. The gun hit my shin and I heard it break. My shin: not, unfortunately, the gun. I didn't feel any pain. I was too angry. I kicked at her but she was away, out of my reach but not yet shielded by Toad. 'Go for it, Miss Potter!' I called. Then Charlotte was back, swinging the gun. Crack! – there went my thigh. 'Oh shit!' I howled. The pain hadn't hit yet. That's almost the worst moment, waiting for it.

'Can I have my bath now Mummy please Mummy can I have my bath?'

Toad was swaying. Charlotte stood behind her, close. Toad was taller than her mother, though much, much thinner. Miss Potter no longer had a clear shot. Shotguns scattered, anyway, didn't they? She'd be bound to hit Toad. No way Miss Potter would fire now, I thought, resigned. I tried to stand up, go for Charlotte, bed and all, but I couldn't. My right leg wouldn't hold me. I could feel the grinding of the broken bone as the breaks worsened.

Charlotte's gun was pointed at me. I crawled towards her, tugging the bed. I wasn't going to die cowering. I really didn't like Charlotte Mayfield. 'Get down, Toad. Now. DOWN! NOW!' called Miss Potter. I heard the gun, knew I would die, remembered you didn't hear the shot that killed you, and looked up. Toad was on her hands and knees, facing me. The tears still dripped from her chin, straight to the floor – the red floor. I looked up further. The pale cream wall behind where Charlotte had been was spattered with red and grey and pink. The floor was – the floor was how you would expect. Near me were Charlotte's Italian shoes, and her legs, and – I didn't look. I'd look in a moment.

'Something's the matter with Mummy,' said Toad. 'I don't think she's well I think she's dead can I have my bath now please Miss Potter?'

'Yes. In a moment. Hush, Toad.'

I felt sick. I didn't try to bite it back: I let it gush. I didn't think, considering the state of the schoolroom, that a little vomit would hurt. Then Miss Potter was beside me, holding my head, wiping my mouth.

'My poor child,' she said.

'You might have killed Toad,' I said. I couldn't believe it. If I hadn't been so shocked, I wouldn't have said such a tactless thing, I hope. 'It was a terrible risk. Why? Why did you nearly kill Toad?'

'Triage, my dear,' said Miss Potter. 'You should approve, surely? Besides, I knew she would obey. She has been brought up to obey.'

'Delicately nurtured,' I said, and began to laugh.

'Not nurtured at all,' Miss Potter said coolly. 'Flippancy I can, reluctantly, accept, Alex. Please spare me hysteria.'

'My leg has been broken in two places,' I observed, 'but at least she missed my kneecap.'

'I will procure you medical assistance. The pain must be acute,' said Miss Potter scrambling to her feet.

'Have a bath,' said Toad cheerfully.

A stocky elderly man puffed in, looked round, and clutched the door-jamb for support. 'Good heavens,' said the vicar.

Chapter Twenty-Eight

The rest of that night was a shambles, as far as I was concerned. Right after the vicar came in, I passed out. I woke up in an ambulance and stayed awake long enough to say, 'I'm not unconscious.' Then I passed out again.

Doctors, nurses, and grimy draughty corridors came and went like a television set on the blink. At one point they gave me something local for the pain and reset my leg, plastered it, and shuffled me along another corridor to an orthopaedic ward where they strung me up to a complicated system of weights and pulleys.

I didn't try to stay awake. Alone, bookless, in pain and immobile in a country hospital, sleep was my drug of choice. I had plenty to think about tomorrow, but right now I'd sleep.

The day after, I was woken at seven by a tired Irish nurse with milky tea. She told me that I had concussion and that my leg was a real mess. I supposed trying to stand on it hadn't helped. Charlotte Mayfield must have been a tennis player: she had an effective smash. The nurse also gave me Miss Potter's shopping basket. When I looked inside, there were her memoirs and my tape recorder, which she must have rescued from the BMW. 'Miss Potter brought this along early this morning,' she said. 'She asked me to be sure you were conscious when I gave it to you, and to send you her regards.'

The only person in England still sending regards, I thought. She and my major in Cheltenham. He'd asked me to send his regards to my next interviewee, a crony of his from the Cretan resistance, a murderous brigand who had found his niche murdering Germans.

'You know Miss Potter?'

'She helps with the coffee shop. She's the Secretary of the Friends of the Hospital.' I might have known.

I asked after Toad, realizing as I asked that I couldn't remember her real name. I made do with 'Ludovic Mayfield's daughter'. Oh, yes, of course, Ludovic Mayfield's daughter, poor little thing, she only weighed just over four stone, did I know? And she had pneumonia. Could I see her? Oh, no, she'd gone in an ambulance straight to a clinic in London.

'On Sunday?' I said. 'Nobody goes to London on Sunday.' The nurse gave me her best I'm-trained-to-deal-with-concussion smile. She told me it would be at least a month before I could go home and the hospital book trolley came round once a week. On Saturdays.

At least I had some insurance: being self-employed, you have to, so the mortgage would be paid as long as the doctors signed me off work. I didn't know how long it would be before I could earn again. There wasn't any work about, and I could hardly drum any up: not much demand for researchers in Richard III orthopaedic ward, and a long queue for the telephone trolley, when it functioned.

The highlight of the next few hours was a blanket bath. Then the visitors started.

The CID stayed only an hour but they had some grip on the facts. They'd already seen Miss Potter. The superintendent looked like a prize bull and spoke little; what he did say was drawled in a broad country accent, Warwickshire, I supposed. His inspector was small and educated, for a policeman.

The inspector conducted the interview. I told the truth, but only in answer to his questions. I didn't volunteer anything. Eventually he closed his notebook and said that the whole thing could have been avoided if the doctors and social workers had been called early enough in Miss Mayfield's illness, and that it had been very unfortunate that Miss Potter had resorted to force instead of going through the proper channels. He said that Mrs Mayfield was a devoted mother and might have been suffering from the menopause, and that a mother's protective love for her child was a wonderful thing, but it could go too far. It sounded as if he'd read a combined social sciences course and had a healthy respect for public relations.

'Did you see the schoolroom? The place where the girl was kept?' I asked.

'Yes, indeed,' he said.

'And the dog?' I pursued.

'Certainly,' he said, puzzled. 'The Public Health people went in today to set it to rights.'

I looked at the superintendent. 'Do you think the Public Health people can set it to rights?'

'Ah, well,' he said in his Warwickshire drawl. 'I'm old-fashioned. I'm not much for the Social Services, but I do believe in good and evil.'

The inspector frowned and the superintendent smiled at him. 'I've known Mrs Mayfield a long time, since she was a child. My two younger sisters were mad on ponies. Riding morn, noon and night. Gymkhanas and Pony Club. She was the worst loser I ever saw. Couldn't stand to be beaten, even in the egg and spoon race.'

The inspector shifted uncomfortably and cleared his throat.

'Ah, well,' said the superintendent again. 'Seeing as the Social Services weren't alerted to Mrs Mayfield's difficulties before tragic circumstances drove her to cause multiple fractures of your leg, Miss Tanner, and you'll be stuck in hospital for a while, I think we can make do with your statement, for the inquest. It'll be written up and sent along for signature.'

The inspector looked so unhappy I threw him a crumb. 'She must have been unbalanced,' I said.

'Quite,' he agreed. They left.

*

Next came Routledge, the vicar, who proved to be a practical Christian. He didn't mention God once and he went straight home to fetch me an orange-box full of books. They were all cosy English detective stories, but I was grateful anyway. The nurses weren't. They rearranged my cluttered bedside locker and said, 'Surely you won't need *all these books?*' I only had thirty.

In the afternoon, Barty came. In a suit and a guilty expression. He was obviously trying not to say 'You cocked up' and 'I told you so' and 'I should have come with you'. It was a sticky visit. I looked terrible, even worse than usual. I was in a yellow hospital gown. Yellow is not my colour. The best thing to be said about me and yellow is that it tones with my teeth. I think I was being prickly, and I complained about bloody Warwickshire until I drove him away.

I didn't tell him about Miss Potter killing Rollo. I was tired and the effort would have been too much. Besides, I had to sort it all out in my mind, listen to the tapes through again, take notes and put it in order. I did ask him to ring Polly and get her to bring down her laptop and my notes and tapes on the Sherwin case. He dragged his heels on that, said we'd have to discuss it. What was to discuss? He couldn't renege on the deal now, surely.

In the afternoon, an hour before my next painkiller was due, I started to cry. Not sobs: leaky, dribbling tears, as if the washers in my eyes needed replacing. I had concussion, of course, and my leg hurt. Badly. Plus I suppose I was in shock. When I closed my eyes the tears didn't stop and I saw pictures, like a slide carousel jerking in my head. It went on without my pressing the button, an automatic lurch from frame to frame. Toad's room. Charlotte Mayfield's chilly and chilling face. And the dog Tigger.

My mother bought me a dog for my fifth birthday, a cocker spaniel. She tied it to the radiator in our flat. It strangled itself, somehow, very quickly. She didn't think it was dead, and at that time I'd still believed what she told me. We both wondered why it wouldn't eat. After a while I knew it was dead. I didn't like the smell, much, but I watched it change. Nothing much changed, in the flat with my mother.

My mother's flat and Toad's room had some terrible point of contact. Not just the dirt and the smell, but the corruption. It wasn't my mother's fault: it had been Charlotte Mayfield's. She'd chosen to exert her will where will was irrelevant. So nothing changed and Toad decayed, just because Charlotte wanted something.

My eyes were still leaking: this time, I knew, for Toad – for the time I had wasted not looking for her, for my stupid mistake in going up to help her instead of driving away, and for the years of misery she had endured not being all her parents had ever dreamed of. Charlotte Sherwin the child had bought made ponies. Much better if Charlotte Sherwin the woman could have bought made daughters, all set to trot round the ring wearing rosettes.

In the evening, Miss Potter came. Her hands were swollen and obviously sore, but otherwise she looked astonishingly well, pink, handsome and strong. Shooting people agreed with her. Barty was right, she was unimaginably tough. I knew I should apologize to her for the cock-up I'd made and try to thank her. She'd saved me: she'd nearly killed her precious Toad. I knew she'd regret it. She'd probably regretted it the moment she'd done it. Triage wasn't her philosophy, it was mine, and besides, from her point of view, she'd chosen the wrong casualty to save. I couldn't find the words.

I asked after Toad. 'My dear,' she said, and I could guess the rest from her tone, but I let her say it, 'Toad died this afternoon. I was with her. Her heart gave out.'

'I'm so sorry,' I said. I was. Sorry that Toad had died, and very sorry that I hadn't done a better job for Miss Potter, although she hadn't helped me much, come to think of it.

'It was probably for the best,' she said briskly. 'We will talk about it when you are stronger . . .'

She'd brought me a toothbrush, toothpaste, face-flannel, soap, a voluminous white cotton nightdress, and (for *hospital?*) several pairs of M&S white cotton pants, still in their wrappers. She noticed my bewilderment. 'It can be so – ungainly, being in traction,' she explained delicately. She'd also brought grapes (in November?), lavender-water, and *War and Peace*. I'd read it but I didn't say so. I prefer Dostoievsky. I didn't say that either. Let her think I was illiterate, I didn't care. We talked about her health, my health, and the National Health. She was the only one in good shape.

As she was leaving, something struck me. 'Hey, Miss Potter – you must have come directly from the clinic in London to see me. How did you get here?'

'Bartholomew was kind enough to lend me his car.'

'The BMW? You drove the BMW? Yourself?'

'Indeed. And I must say, Alex, rather more speedily than you drove substantially the same journey yesterday. In fact I must suppose you hold the all-comers' record for the slowest time over the distance.'

'But you can't drive! You know nothing about cars!'

'Why should you think that? I have driven regularly, without incident, since 1938. Moreover, in those early days one did not merely drive, one had to have a more than superficial understanding of mechanics. Barty's engine needs tuning.'

'But you *told* me you knew nothing about cars!'

'No. You thought so, and I did not correct your assumption.'

When she left, I was alone. The woman in the next bed listened to *The Archers*, and when I said I didn't, she told me what had been happening in Ambridge for the last thirty years. Her words washed over me. I was trying to think, but my head was fuzzy. Concussion and pills, I suppose. There were connections I had to make, information which could be linked, which should be linked, but I couldn't do it. I leaked tears instead.

Next day, nobody came, not even the police, and that lasted

thirty years too. I hate bedpans. I faced the prospect of a month of them, then considered the likely alternative: death, and a month, an eternity, of nothing at all. It didn't make the bedpans seem better but it put a big ROAD CLOSED sign across the self-pity option.

Polly could have come, at least, I thought crossly. I wanted to work on the Sherwin murder piece, but I still couldn't concentrate. I also had a deep reluctance even to think about what would happen to Miss Potter if I published. I had an obligation to her, now. But she couldn't expect me to forgo my chance, could she?

Instead, I read four of the vicar's books, very slowly. The first author was a fascist, the second a snob, the third an enthusiastic gardener proud of her descriptions – *the body lay, pallid face upturned to the silvered moonlight, half-obscuring a well-established border of lupins, rich hollyhocks, perennial poppies and vibrant delphiniums* – the fourth . . . I didn't let myself categorize the fourth. I just tried to read him.

I cried myself to sleep, that night, too. I expect it was shock.

The day after was different.

The nurses were furious. They wouldn't speak to me, though they gave me an abrasive blanket-bath. Two hours later my weights and pulleys were dismantled and I was bundled on to a stretcher, wheeled to a private ambulance and mantled again. Now I knew why the nurses were annoyed. Anything private annoyed them, for ordinary people. It was different if you were Ludovic Mayfield's daughter, of course. I must still have been concussed because though I didn't know where I was going, I didn't ask any questions. I didn't care, as long as I was moving.

The ambulance stopped outside Barty's house, he opened the door, and the attendants carried me up the steps to the back room on the ground floor. The last time I'd seen it, it had been a library. Now the walls were still lined with books, but the library table and most of the chairs had gone, and there was a hospital bed, a system of orthopaedic pulleys, a big bedside table with a telephone, and two nurses. They moved me on to the bed and trussed me up. I looked round for Barty but he'd vanished: gone back to work, I supposed, disappointed. I'd changed into Miss P.'s white nightdress and I was looking distinctly better than the last time we'd met. I also wanted him to explain what I was doing there.

The nurses left the room before I got round to asking them to pass me a book: my doggy bag of hospital comforts seemed to have gone missing in the move. Then Polly came in, carrying her laptop and a holdall with the notes and tapes from home. She kissed me. She always kisses people.

'Brilliant, brilliant, you've arrived! I didn't visit you yesterday because we were trying to fix this up. We knew you'd have preferred your flat but the ceiling wasn't high enough and there really wasn't room for the nurses, and Barty hoped you'd like it here, and we knew you'd hate the hospital, and you *are* in a library, Barty says there are five thousand books, that'll take you a week or two . . .'

'Hang on, Polly, who's paying for the nurses? I can't possibly afford this—'

'Barty is, at the moment, but he has plans . . .'

'What plans?'

'Barty'll tell you later. How're you feeling? Is it agony? You're looking good . . .'

She kept on talking, but I didn't listen. I felt too uncomfortable. I'm always uncomfortable when people are kind to me, and I didn't like the position I was in, moved around without warning, a guest in someone else's house. If I was honest, though, of course I preferred it to the hospital. I'd hated the hospital.

'Hey, Polly,' I interrupted her, 'what's that?' I pointed to a double white line of camera tape on the floor across the doorway, like a barrier.

'That was Barty's idea. That marks your territory from his. This room is an independent sovereign state, he said. No one comes in unless you invite them.' He came up from the office at lunchtime and I invited him in. He was wearing his usual casual uniform, dark brown corduroy trousers, Canadian lumberjack shirt and old blue sweater. He was very familiar and very welcome. If I had to be anywhere except home, then I'd have chosen Barty's. He never makes conversation and he never asks if you *really mean* what you say. Why would you say it, if you didn't mean it?

I'd already decided I didn't want to discuss the Sherwin piece until I'd spoken to Miss Potter again, and he seemed happy to leave it. I thanked him for his arrangements: a bit charmlessly, I could hear myself, but I did my best. I *was* grateful. He'd been very thoughtful. He'd even got British Telecom to transfer my home number to the telephone by my bed.

He was cautious about explaining his plan about paying the nurses I needed. I think he thought I'd bite his head off for interfering, but I felt too weak for head-biting and liked his plan, which was to get Ludovic Mayfield to compensate me for loss of earnings and cover my medical expenses in return for not selling my account of Charlotte's last hours to the newspapers. Even more cautiously, he suggested that he negotiate the deal with Mayfield.

'OK,' I said. 'I'll leave it to you.'

'I don't think I heard that,' he said, grinning. 'D'you want to run it by me again?'

He wanted jam on it. I wouldn't say it twice. I saw a ghostly Annabel nodding and smiling approval, as it was. I shifted irritably: my leg hurt, my feelings were confused and my head felt as if it was stuffed with Spanish moss. I was glad when he left soon after.

Chapter Twenty-Nine

Next day, Wednesday, was better still. I felt unexpectedly at home, partly because Barty had brought in a radio and a television, and piled books around me. The nurses were OK, too, both black, one tall and plump, one short and wiry. The short one was stronger. Neither of them told me I drank too much coffee or complained about making it, both of them were deft with bedpans.

The evening before, Barty'd done a good deal with Mayfield. So good, I wouldn't be surprised if Annabel helped. Mayfield's paying for my nurses, for my loss of earnings, and for my silence. Fine by me. I've got far more out of the deal than a per diem plus even my most imaginative expenses.

By the next day I was still only about seventy-five per cent clear-thinking but I was well enough not to dodge the Miss Potter issue any longer. It was decision-time. Did I write and publish the piece, and land Miss Potter in it right up to her silvery bun, or did I file it under Altruistic Interment?

I couldn't understand my own hesitation. She was over seventy, after all, and had had plenty of life. At least some of it was of her own choosing. She'd had seven glorious years in Kenya, and not all the rest of the time had been bad. She'd certainly been Queen Bee down in Warwickshire, an indefatigably worthy, much admired member of the community. Not a barrel of laughs for most of us, but her line. If she was convicted she'd have plenty of scope for good works in prison, for heaven's sake.

I could make pots and pots of money, I knew I could, if I played the story right. She wouldn't lie and deny it, and she hadn't told me in confidence. Besides, I had her confession on tape.

On the other hand, she had saved my life.

That was her business, her decision, I told myself. I never asked her to.

She was due to visit me at eleven. At about ten to, my phone rang, again. It had been busy; a surprising number of my friends and acquaintances had heard about my injuries (Polly?) and called to ask after me. This time, it was Ready Eddy.

'How come you never called me back on the Sherwin murder?' he said.

'Sorry. I'll explain some time,' I said. 'Something else came up.'

'So d'you want the information, or not?'

I tried to sound interested. 'Yes, please, Eddy.'

'No hard evidence. But I had a drink with Ronnie Macleod. He's long retired, but he was the D/S on the case.' He paused, a dramatic, stringing-it-out pause.

'Yes?'

'You should have got back to me. I wanted to warn you to keep that source of yours, the Potter person, well away from shot-guns. Macleod reckoned she did for Rollo Sherwin, or that if she didn't, she knew perfectly well who had.'

I couldn't summon up any excitement, though Eddy deserved plenty. 'Why didn't he say so at the time?'

'He tried to. His guv'nor wouldn't wear it, he was convinced it was the wife. It's solid information, Alex, Macleod was a good copper. Trust your Uncle Eddy.'

I thanked him, though I was a little annoyed that my discovery had been pre-empted by D/S Macleod, agreed I owed him several, though we didn't specify what, and rang off just as the short wiry nurse opened the door to Miss Potter.

I still hadn't decided what to do. I thought that seeing her might help. She looked terrific: neatly dressed as ever, healthy, upright, pink-cheeked. She was carrying the mug she'd bought for me as part of her manipulation campaign, and more grapes. I'd left the last lot in hospital, for the nurses.

Oh, well. Oh, well. She was a sporting old trout, and I owed her one.

We spoke at the same time.

'I've decided not to publish,' I said.

'I have misled you, Alex,' she said.

We both stopped. Then the remaining twenty-five per cent of my brain came back and I made the link that had eluded me the last time I'd seen her.

I had two scenes in my head, both with Miss Potter.

The first was in the Stratford hospital. She is standing by my bed, on the point of departure, smiling as she talks about cars. I say, 'You *told* me you knew nothing about cars,' and she says, 'No. You thought so, and I did not correct your assumption.'

The second was in the BMW on the motorway, with me crawling along in the slow lane praying not to be spotted as a drunk by the motorway police. A distraught Miss Potter has just declared her feelings for Rollo. 'I loved him,' she says. 'And you killed him?' I say. And she bows her head, a tragic mute. A silver-headed, sanctimonious, treacherous old trout, lying by her silence.

She was a *literal* truthteller. She could lie me into the minor leagues by omission, by implication, by suggestion, but she *told* the literal truth. And she never actually *told* me that she'd killed Rollo. It was a relief to have my brain back. I re-ran her description of his death, and she'd never stated that she was the murderer. I'd thought so, and she hadn't corrected my assumption.

Charlotte Sherwin had done it. Of course. Charlotte had done it, because she was selfish and cold and dead common. Charlotte had done it for all the reasons I'd imagined as I sat across the kitchen table from her in that chilly and dreadful house, because she wouldn't let Daddy leave Mummy and sue the sofa from beneath her. He probably couldn't have taken the house, but Charlotte would have believed her father when she heard him tell her mother, furiously, resonantly, that he would throw them all out.

It has taken me much longer to explain this than to think it.

'You thought Rosalind had done it,' I said. 'You confronted

Rollo, just as you described, but you didn't shoot him. You couldn't. Maps. You had to follow your maps, and your map said duty and self-control and responsibility and thou shall not kill. But why did you think it was Rosalind?'

'I am glad to find you recovering from the concussion,' she said. 'May I sit down?'

'Please.'

'It is as you suppose. I left Rollo alive, and closed the door behind me. Then I heard him speaking, again. "Hello," he said. "What are you doing here?"' She paused. 'I could not, of course, continue to eavesdrop.'

'Why not? You'd eavesdropped up a storm just before.'

'I owed no loyalty to Lady Sherwin. Her treatment of others was never such as to earn my consideration. I need only remind you of her declared views on the brave pilots who fought and died for us in the Battle of Britain. But Rosalind was a different matter. So I continued to walk away. I had reached the hall by the time the gun went off, so by the time I returned to the scene, the door was open and the room was empty. Apart, of course, from the body of Lord Sherwin.'

'But why did you think it was *Rosalind* he was speaking to when it must have been Charlotte?'

'His relationship with Rosalind was in the forefront of my mind. I knew his interlocutor must have been hidden under the sofa, and I thought that it was a – youthful, loverlike prank.' How she must have hated that thought, at the time, since she was neither youthful nor his lover. 'But finally,' she went on, 'it was Lord Sherwin's tone of voice. It was – indulgent, affectionate. The tone he had used to me on the two occasions when . . .'

'When he treated you as a lover?' I phrased the comment deliberately.

'You are giving me the best butter, Alex,' she said, but I could see the thought pleased her.

'And I suppose he used the same indulgent, affectionate tone to animals and children?' So did Barty. He also, sometimes, used it to me.

'Exactly. Even to Charlotte, whom it would not be unfair to say he disliked. I did not think of Charlotte at the time, but I now see how foolish I have been.'

'So you covered for Rosalind.'

'Yes. I thought the guilt must be chiefly his, and she had been almost a daughter to me. You can imagine my distress when my recent dealings with Charlotte, and my observation of her treatment of Toad, led me to suspect that my assumption was wrong. I had behaved deplorably, throughout.'

She looked at me, almost in appeal.

Time she stopped wallowing. 'Not throughout,' I said briskly. 'Only once a week and twice on Sundays. It didn't matter to Rollo.'

'No. It did matter to Toad.'

There was nothing to be said, so neither of us said it.

After a while she cleared her throat. 'Now you can explain why you had decided not to exploit what you must have thought to be a highly lucrative discovery.'

'I owed you one,' I said. 'Let's leave it there, OK?' The whole thing made me uncomfortable. '*You* tell *me* why you spun that elaborate fantasy about Rollo's death.'

'I told you the truth,' she said. 'I described the events, and my feelings. I had never spoken about that time. I could never talk about – Rollo.'

'He sounds extraordinary,' I said. I lied.

Chapter Thirty

I'd signed my statement, when the Warwickshire police sent it, but actually the inquest was adjourned. The whole thing was being kept as quiet as the combined efforts of the police, the coroner, Ludovic Mayfield, and Conservative Central Office could manage. That still wasn't very quiet, and Mayfield's chance for the leadership had gone. For days after, Toad's plump teenage face stared up at me from the newspapers: for nights after, her Belsen face haunted my sleep.

How could I have been so stupid? I'd sympathized with lonely Rosalind and lonely Miss Potter but I'd assumed that Toad was all right, just because she was posh and had parents. Even with all the evidence piling up round me – Barty's sadistic father, the Sherwin children rattling, ignored, around their loveless house, what I knew of the entirely unmaternal Charlotte – I'd preferred to cling to my cosy preconceptions. I'd cornered the market in outsiders: only people I approved of were allowed to be misfits.

I despise smugness and prejudice, and I'd been blinded by both.

I told Barty all I knew about Rollo's murder, and that I was killing the piece. 'You don't want to write it, with Charlotte as killer?' he asked. 'Considering you can't libel the dead?'

'Miss Potter isn't dead. She'd look a prat, and she doesn't deserve to.' Then I realized he was having me on. 'You wouldn't let me, anyway,' I said. 'Just forget it. I've been paid.'

'I'm interested that Miss Potter's feelings matter to you.'

I wasn't going to go into it. I didn't think I'd see much of her in the future. Our relationship was over. Although she was visiting me every day at present, Mayfield was giving her back the lodge at a low rent until she died: soon she'd be off, back to the country, where she belonged.

The verdict at the inquest on Toad was Death by Misadventure. Then she was cremated, ten days after Bloody Saturday. I'd have liked to have gone to the funeral, but I was still attached to pulleys and likely to remain so for at least two more weeks. By then I was feeling much better and very restless. I rang around for work: nothing till the New Year.

I sorted out my Sherwin notes, reminded myself to tell Ready Eddy next time I spoke to him that his good copper, D/S Macleod, had been half wrong about Miss Potter, and chucked the lot. I wasn't even going to file them.

I also had a pile of clippings I'd been collecting since Charlotte's death. As I chucked those, one caught my eye. Quotes from Ludovic Mayfield: 'I had no idea my daughter had returned from India . . . my wife was devoted to the children . . . I can only assume that she thought Toad would be happier at home. I never dreamt that Toad was so ill, or my wife so desperate.'

I hadn't taken that in, before. I pulled the other clippings out of the bin-liner and went through them. There it was again, and again, and again. 'I had no idea my daughter had returned from India . . .'

He was lying. Toad's high-pitched voiceless babble was as clear in my mind now as it had been when I first heard it: 'They made me come back and I went to see Daddy in London . . . but Daddy didn't look at me even . . . he was looking at a photograph of Charles.' He had known, all right, and he hadn't cared. 'He said Mummy knew best and Mummy would look after me . . .'

In 1958, Laura had loaded the gun and Charlotte had fired it. In 1990, too, help for her enterprise had been close at hand. Mayfield had known, but he had shut his eyes. So, in a much smaller way, had Miss Potter. So had I.

It didn't help to think about it.

PAN
HERITAGE
CLASSICS

Bringing wonderful classic books to a new audience.

MURDER AT
THE OLD VICARAGE
A CHRISTMAS MYSTERY

JILL MCGOWN

THE HILLS
IS LONELY

LILLIAN BECKWITH

THE GROVE
OF EAGLES
A NOVEL OF ELIZABETHAN ENGLAND

WINSTON GRAHAM

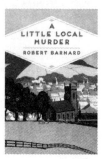

A
LITTLE LOCAL
MURDER

ROBERT BARNARD

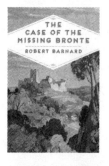

THE
CASE OF THE
MISSING BRONTE

ROBERT BARNARD

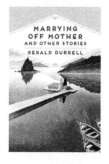

MARRYING
OFF MOTHER
AND OTHER STORIES

GERALD DURRELL

THE
ENCHANTED
PLACES

CHRISTOPHER
MILNE

MURDER IN
ADVENT

DAVID WILLIAMS

DR FINLAY'S
CASEBOOK

A J CRONIN